Lara's Secret

Ray C Doyle

DreamEngine Publishing

This edition published in 2022
by DreamEngine Publishing

ISBN 978-1-915212-04-7

Email: publishing@dreamengine.co.uk
Website: DreamEngine.co.uk
Social Media: @DreamEngineuk

Twitter: rayraycdoyle
Facebook: RAYCDOYLE
Website: https://raycdoyle.com/.

In Loving Memory of
Irene Kimmel 2022

ACKNOWLEDGEMENTS

A special thank you to David Baboulene and Edward J. Marsh of DreamEngine publishing, whose fantastic team have realised an ambition come true for me; my first publishing contract after thirty-two years of keeping faith and hope alive.

Much love to my sister, fellow artist Susan Thorne, and Kimber Coleman; their support has never wavered.

Thanks to Ant Gavin Smits, whose advice and great friendship I value and applaud.

Thanks to Suraya Dewing for her guidance and a ten-year friendship. It has been a privilege to work with her. And to all my colleagues at Story Mint NZ, who mean a lot to me.

A big thank you to Mat Clarke and colleagues at World Writers Collective AUS. It's a beautiful experience belonging to groups of really talented writers whose comradery and knowledge have helped me.

Special thanks to close friends Anton Johnson and Bob Wheatley Snr from Essex-UK. Jeffrey Clark from Louisianna and Bill and Rosanne Newton from Washington-USA. From Cyprus, Andreas Lambrou and Andrew Prime.

CHAPTER ONE

MOONLIGHT STREAMED THROUGH a hole in the torn, dirty curtains and glinted off the oiled barrel of the old Bren gun propped against the wall. Andreas Hrisacopolis sat on the edge of the bed, looking at it for several minutes. With hands on knees, his long fingers gripped and ungripped in time to a list of keywords recited over and over through his mind. The plan for the night's operation lay ingrained in his memory, yet he still woke from troubled sleep. He yawned and bent to pick up his socks lying on a newspaper. A picture of a smiling President Nixon appeared next to a story about Watergate in the latest *The Times of Cyprus*, dated February 1974. Andreas backheeled it under the bed.

He rose and pulled on a pair of faded green cords and a T-shirt. Sitting back on the bed, he pushed his feet into a pair of heavy boots. After tying the laces, he turned to Lara and traced his fingers across her body before gently resting a hand on her stomach. Lara stirred from sleep at his touch, her fingers searching out his hand. Half hidden beneath long dark hair, her face looked up at him, hazel eyes searching his as he bent to kiss her. He brushed the hair from her face and let the strands slide through his fingers as they kissed.

She touched his lips with one finger. "I'm afraid, Andreas. Do you have to go?"

"Yes. I always come back, though." He gently ran his forefinger down her cheek and half smiled. "My men are waiting."

Lara propped herself up on one elbow. "But Andreas ..."

"Lara, please." He put his arms around her and held her close.

Greek men were shedding their blood, fighting for sovereignty over Cyprus in a battle to the bitter end. General Grivas was dead, but his vision still fired national pride in the hearts and minds of his followers.

Andreas breathed deeply. "When this is over, we'll be together, I promise."

She kissed him passionately.

There was a light tap at the door. A gruff voice spoke one word. "Ready."

Lara grabbed Andreas's hand as he turned to leave but said nothing. A squeaking floorboard broke the silence, and she let his fingers slip through hers.

He picked up the machine gun and opened the door. He held a finger to his lips without looking back as Alexander started to speak. "Outside," he whispered.

There was a dull thud as the door closed behind them. They walked to the wooden entrance, ducking their heads as they stepped under the low beam and out into the humid night air. Heavy boots crunched on the gravel as they strode to where two bicycles lay on the ground behind a small thicket.

"You are taking a great risk being here," said Alexander, lifting a haversack onto his shoulders. "There are rumours amongst the men. They say your affair is a bad omen for our cause."

Picking a bike up, Andreas turned to face the big man. "I'm marrying her."

Alexander stopped. "No." He shook his head. "You can't."

Andreas raised a hand. "Shush. Keep your voice down."

Andreas wondered if the men would stay loyal as he mounted the bike. His father was another hurdle to worry about. A letter telling his father about his love for Lara and their marriage plans before the baby was born left the island the previous day on a fishing boat out of Kyrenia. Lara, he wrote, was going to Gozo in the meantime to stay with friends and hoped his father would send money for her upkeep. She could not remain in Cyprus. Her family would disown her, and Lara had agreed to go. He grabbed a strap on Alexander's haversack. "Come on."

Alexander pulled a beret down over his mass of tangled red hair before mounting his bicycle. He gripped the handlebars, lifted the front wheel, swung the bike around before slamming it to the ground, scattering gravel everywhere.

Andreas sat with one foot on a pedal. "Alex, enough, or we'll be late." He pushed off, peddling hard.

Cursing, Alexander followed the disappearing figure along a narrow winding track. He raised himself off the seat as his bicycle rattled down the steep, uneven ground, jarring his legs and feet.

Clenching his fingers around the vibrating handlebar, he ducked under branches and brushed past tall undergrowth and prickly hawthorns that snagged at his trousers. Avoiding small boulders and old stumps of Aleppo pine that protruded from both sides, he sped downward through flashes of moonlight and menacing shadows as the moon appeared between craggy outcrops of towering rock. A small lizard scurried in and out of shadows cast by the bony fingers of a eucalyptus tree as both men rode by and then disappeared into a black recess of rock.

A few minutes later, the track ended. A narrow path wound its way down between boulders, ever steeper as it neared a small cove and freshwater spring outlet. They hurried on, hiding their bicycles in a wide crevice between two large boulders, carefully keeping their footing on the loose shale. Nearing the cove, Alexander stopped to rest against a boulder, breathing heavily.

"We can't stop. There's still a fair way to go," said Andreas, looking back.

The big man took a deep breath. "I know," he gasped. His feet slipped on some loose stones.

Both men ducked as a swarm of bats flew from an overhanging tree. They started walking again.

"If there's a patrol in this area, they might have heard the bats and investigate," said Andreas, shifting the Bren from one shoulder. He was worried and looked up at the full moon as they made their way down to the cove. A gentle breeze blew inland, moving tall strands of grass back and forth at the base of the cliffs. At the north end of the cove, a path would be their exit route, much steeper than the one they had descended to the south. Above them rose a sheer cliff over one hundred feet high topped by thick undergrowth and hawthorns. Andreas looked at their surroundings as they approached the opening onto the beach.

He stopped at the entrance. Taking a goatskin purse from his pocket, he handed it to Alexander. "I know you disapprove, Alex, but I want you to do this for me if things go wrong."

"This is madness, Andreas. You're asking too much."

Andreas drew close. "I have no one else to ask, and she has no one. Make sure she gets my father's letter if… I know he will approve."

Several figures emerged from behind a group of large boulders at the base of the cliffs skirting the beach. Alexander stuffed the purse inside his jacket and whispered hoarsely, "We'll talk about this later."

Andreas gave the big man a light punch in the chest. "Thanks, now get the torches ready. I want this operation over and off the beach."

The men joined them and exchanged greetings with nods. Mostly unshaven, they dressed in torn, dirty clothing. They fought a guerrilla war against the British Army for several months, hiding in the Troodos Mountains. Villages in the area had been afraid to give shelter or food for fear of reprisals. Some men squatted, laying rifles and machine guns across their laps.

Andreas looked at Alexander. "Okay, let everyone have a torch and get them positioned up the beach."

The men took torches from Alexander's backpack and walked off along the beach. Every few yards, one of them stopped to take up his position, crouching, waiting for Andreas's signal.

Andreas looked at his watch. The fishing boat carrying the new men was out by the point. They had to be off the beach as quickly as possible and taken to a hidden truck on the Dyo Potamoi road for a trip inland to safety. Before that, a three-mile walk took the men near the British army firing range. With patrols everywhere, they had to stay vigilant. The recent shooting deaths of two young, off duty officers in a Famagusta nightclub put the army on high alert, renewing their efforts to search out Eoka - the National Organisation of Cypriot Struggle.

Looking out to sea, Andreas silently cursed the moon. Athens only informed him of the new shipment after it left the mainland. The risk of bringing men in under a full moon made everyone jumpy. They needed to be off the beach as soon as possible. It was now too late to turn back. He strained to see a flashing lamp out to the bay's northwest. He waited for a second flash to be sure he had seen the signal when it came. He pointed his flashlight up the beach and flicked the switch. Immediately, five lights flashed five times out to sea. A red light answered them and blinked three times.

"I'll get the men ready." Alexander strode off.

Andreas stood for a minute, breathing in the humid air. Shallow waves washed across the shingle and wet the toes of his boots before frothing into nothing. He took an ammunition clip from the haversack at his feet and pushed it into the breach with a loud click.

Alexander ran back across the beach, breathing heavily. "There's a small motorboat coming in."

"Right, get them off and send the boat back. How many are there?" Andreas questioned.

"Fifteen men. The fishing boat is laid off further toward the point."

Andreas's heart thumped against his chest. "Good. Now lead them out of here as fast as you can, Alex. I'll cover the rear with two of our men." Both men ran toward the boat. Andreas could make out several figures jumping into the surf as they approached.

Then, in an instant, night suddenly turned into day. A bright searchlight at the top of the cliff cut through the night, illuminating the boat and all around it.

"This is the British Army… Stay where you are… Lay down your arms and walk towards the light." The megaphone voice repeated the order.

"On top of the cliff," shouted Andrea. "The bastards are hidden. Get the light!" He raised his pistol and aimed at the top of the cliffs. A hail of bullets hit the searchlight, but the beach figures still stood out clearly in the moonlight. Both sides fired as Andreas's men tried in vain to find shelter among the few scattered rocks. Tracers from the chattering automatic weapons on the clifftop bounced around, throwing up the shingle. Running men fell screaming, cut down in a hail of bullets sweeping across the beach. Return fire from the beach ricocheted harmlessly off the boulders and cliff top. Within a minute, there was hand-to-hand fighting as soldiers ran out into the open from the two paths on either side of the cove.

Alexander dropped to the ground next to Andreas as a bullet kicked up stones beside him. "We can only swim out from here. We're trapped." Alexander grabbed Andreas. "Come on. You can't do anything for the men now. For God's sake, Andreas, move!"

The launch that landed the men beached itself, engine running. Two lifeless figures lay slumped in the after well. What remained of the forward cabin was riddled with bullets. Splintered wood lay everywhere. Alexander ran to the boat. Occasional bursts of automatic gunfire still shattered the night as a handful of men held the enemy fire on the beach. Another searchlight lit the entire area, and the men fell back across the beach.

"Quick, Andreas."

Alexander clambered up onto the boat and turned. Grabbing Andreas by his arm, he hauled him up and over the gunwale. A single shot rang out, and Andreas slumped across the bow. A photo dropped from his jacket pocket. Caught by the breeze, it fell into the water. The launch moved away from the beach, turned, and motored into the night with a sudden burst of power.

Several minutes later, a British officer walking among the casualties at the water's edge stopped to pick up the photograph as it danced in the ebb and flow of lapping water. He examined it by the light of his flashlight before tucking it into his pocket.

CHAPTER TWO

My BlackBerry rang as I drove around Parliament Square in pouring rain, but I ignored it. If anyone wanted Pete West, he wasn't available until he'd drunk two cups of tea, especially at six on a dark autumnal morning.

Black clouds threatened a day of half dawn as my car joined a long queue of bright taillights choking up London's city centre. The area was an architectural nightmare. Old buildings - weathered and covered in grime, beside tinted glass obelisks - rose to create a confused skyline of historic masonry and vacant office blocks. This day they looked forlorn, huddled in blocks sandwiched between hissing city streets. A sea of black umbrellas joggled for space as crowds hurried along the pavements and down dark passages between the buildings. Each suit was heading for a tedious job in some big business or government office in Whitehall.

Up ahead, the lights changed green. I moved forward, feeling a little depressed. Work for me was an office block in Wapping, another developing area of east London and headquarters for the Hart newspaper group. I was late for an appointment with Max, and by the time I arrived at my space in the labyrinth of cubicles on the fifth floor, there was a note on my desk ordering me upstairs. This meant leaving rows of metal desks on linoleum tiles and rising to the fortieth floor. There I could sink into management's Axminster carpets, relax in soft leather furniture and enjoy the aroma of fresh coffee.

I was heading for Hart's suite on the fortieth floor. Not that he was there. He was in Seattle for the 2004 World Media Conference. That didn't mean he wasn't aware of what went on thousands of miles away. I was betting he'd had a call from D.C. or Whitehall. That's why Max had summoned me.

7

Max wasn't going to pat me on the back. He'd taken the unusual step of inviting me upstairs instead of issuing a summons to his own office. It was because he wanted to shout at me in private. This suggested I might be looking for another job by the time we were through.

I tossed my raincoat over the desk and ran my fingers through wet hair. Brushing some greying black hairs from my shoulder, I made for the elevator that pinged all day long. The damn thing was a few yards from my desk and irritated me intensely, especially at lunchtime.

When the elevator arrived, it was empty. I took a deep breath and stepped inside. The door closed, leaving me in silence. Bad thoughts and nightmarish dreams rebounded off the walls of the metal box from which there was no escape. I concentrated on the changing numbers above my head, willing the elevator to speed up. I tried thinking about the previous day's column and all the names Max was bound to call me. After a minute, I lost the fight as I always did in enclosed spaces. Loosening my tie, I leaned against the wall, closed my eyes, and heard mother and father shouting. Then the smell from thick acrid smoke engulfed me. I could almost taste it. Relief came with a slight bump, a loud ping accompanied by the hum of the doors sliding open. I stepped out onto the Axminster and sucked in a lungful of roasted coffee.

An ex-fellow journalist, Gilbert O'Grady, stood to the side, waiting to go down. He had a silly grin on his face. He got promoted a year earlier and wasn't used to the management dress code yet. His creased trousers looked like they'd been dropped concertina fashion on the floor and stepped into again the following morning. "Good morning to you, Pete." His grin broadened.

He passed me and stood in the elevator with one hand in a pocket, hitching up his pants. His eyes never left me as a nicotine-stained finger stabbed at the button violently, as though hammering a nail into my coffin. I ignored him and straightened my tie. The man made me feel untidy.

It took over a minute to walk to Hart's office, and by the time I got there, I'd decided how to annoy Ms. Linguard. She was Hart's first line of defence, a woman I'd never seen eye to eye with since I had greeted her as Ms Mudguard the first day we met. She never forgave me. I walked in and smiled nicely. In her mid-forties, I guessed, tall with short blonde hair and smartly dressed, Susan Linguard was busy sipping coffee. She sprang from the desk and stood between me and the inner sanctum.

"Well, good morning, Ms Linguard. I believe the fuehrer is waiting for me in the bunker."

She didn't return the smile. She turned her back on me and opened the door to Hart's office. "Mr Pete West, Max." Her nose rose an inch. "Max, can you please refrain from smoking in here? You know Mr Hart doesn't like it."

I didn't wait for her to usher me in. "It's all right, Ms Linguard," I said, making her jump as I brushed lightly past her. "I'll make sure he opens all the windows before I leave - okay?"

She looked me up and down with tightly drawn lips and disappeared back behind the door without slamming it.

I gave Max a limp 'sieg heil' salute. "Since when have you been on first name terms with Doris Day?"

"None of your stupid humour, Pete." He paused and stubbed the cigarette out. "I've been given hell over your column. Hart's furious."

I assumed he was referring to my column two days prior when I just vented a personal opinion and a little name calling over the crash of Amerigo, an American aero manufacturer. I regretted that and guessed I would pay the price. "You mean I didn't stick to writing the truth and nothing but the truth according to Hart?" I glared at him defiantly and stuck both hands deep inside my trouser pockets.

Max was a little bald man in his late fifties. A pair of rimless glasses sat precariously on the end of his nose. He always dressed smartly casually, wearing a suit only when necessary and never loosening his tie like many of his contemporaries. A large red nose and ruddy complexion gave the impression he drank, but he was teetotal. Smart both physically and mentally, Max Edwards had wit but no charm.

"Why can't you remember there are times when you should keep your damn mouth shut?" He leaned forward across Hart's antique rosewood desk, scowling, spreading both palms flat across its surface as if readying himself to pounce at me. He'd survived in the industry since starting an apprenticeship in the print shop, and there wasn't a lot anyone could tell him, especially the likes of me. He had the ear of all those with influence within the news media, the city, and especially the politicians. He waved me to a chair.

I crossed my legs and nonchalantly jiggled a scuffed Italian leather toe in the air as I sat. I told Max the article on the Amerigo scandal was one of my best stories in a long time. It was controversial, well informed, and presented in the style our readers had expected.

"Bollocks." His fist hit the desk hard, making me jump. "You called the American President and the Prime Minister a deceptive double act. While one told Congress what they wanted to hear about falling unemployment, the other convinced parliament he would reap millions from the Amerigo project." The cloud of blue smoke above his head thickened as he puffed on another cigarette.

Max had taken a week's vacation, and while he was away, I slammed the project without worrying about the editor's red pen. His deputy, a long-time buddy of mine with over thirty years on The Herald, loved the piece and left it uncut. Less than a year from retirement, neither Max nor Hart would fire him. I was a different matter.

"The project was a disaster from the start," I answered.

Max reached for a copy of our newspaper from the desk, his angry blue eyes never leaving mine. Political advisors had warned their respective governments that the project was high risk. Now Amerigo had folded after taking a billion dollars from the government.

"Where are the new C25 transporters?" I asked. "Nearly five thousand people staring at redundancies."

Max held his hands up as I spoke. "You can't resist going over the top, can you? Half the population calls our political leaders names, but none of that goes into print, does it? Let the readers make up their fucking minds what they think. You don't tell them." He picked up the newspaper article and waved it at me. "This paper supports the government."

"The owner supports the government."

"Shut up. I haven't finished." Max took a deep breath and coughed before continuing. "Hell, Pete, I don't have to tell you the basics." There was a pregnant pause. I was about to speak when Max spoke again in a low growl. "Hart got a call from the PM. He's on the warpath."

"I-"

"Shut it." Max's hand slapped the desktop with a loud thump. "The White House was in secret negotiations with Pan Air and a European consortium to take over Amerigo. Your financial forecasts have now stalled the talks. It's about time you were slapped down to size."

His words stung me. There wasn't any point arguing with Max. He was right. I'd let the pen flow.

With a worsening economic downturn on Wall Street, caused partly by financial bailouts for some members in the European Union and ten per cent unemployment at home, President Walker was desperate for a miracle before the presidential election. He promised congress five thousand jobs if they voted in a billion dollars for Amerigo.

My sources in DC and Whitehall were whispering. Despite government orders for the new C25 aircraft, the company didn't have a chance. I knew they didn't. Auditors had been into Amerigo the previous year and came away shaking their heads. In Britain, the Prime

Minister told Parliament that the joint trade agreement guaranteed two thousand jobs for assembly workers in the midlands and was worth fifty million pounds in the first two years. He didn't say the new fabrication factories would cost taxpayers at least half that amount. I'd called the two leaders the best deceptive double act since Roosevelt and Churchill signed 'Lend-Lease.'

I sat there taking it all in, wanting to say a lot more, annoyed at Hart and the conservatives he sucked up to.

For a moment, we both stared at each other in silence, my eyes never leaving his. Then Max raised both hands and dropped the bombshell. Until I behaved myself, my column was suspended. "You can thank the lucky stars you still have a job, Pete." He jerked forward, making me jump and slam my mouth shut. "I want you to know I spent over an hour on the phone with Hart telling him to keep you on."

I cringed then sank back into the chair.

"He wanted you out right away." Max waved a hand at the window, indicating how Hart wanted me to go.

The door opened, and Ms Linguard's face appeared around it. "Max, Miss Du-"

"Get out," thundered Max. The door slammed.

I felt a moment of satisfaction. Only a moment, mind. I was too busy grasping at straws.

"Max, I'm sure I could sort things out with Hart. I'll apologise. Maybe I was a little over the top."

"No, absolutely not." Max jumped out of his chair. "You and Hart are like oil and water right now. You'll stay out of his way. You're being reassigned."

I gripped the edge of my chair. "What?" It's a hell of a drop from columnist to a correspondent. I felt sick and angry. Very angry. His words were hitting home, and my face must have shown it.

"If you feel that bad about it, you can resign. I'm not fucking around. I had to crawl to Whitehall this morning."

"Sorry, Max, I didn't know." I was sorry for Max. He was stuck on the great divide, walking a tightrope between management and scribes, trying to keep everyone happy. I wasn't sorry about the article, though. Many honest workers were out of a job because of two politicians.

Max shrugged, picked up a folder and tossed it at me. "What do you know about Hrisacopolis?"

The name sounded familiar. I opened the folder and saw a face staring up at me. He was into merchant shipping, oil tankers and cruise ships. But what I remembered were the rumours of political corruption. Word had it he was not averse to using a little muscle. He supported General Grivas and EOKA during the fifties, fighting for

Greek sovereignty over Cyprus. There were a lot of Turkish Cypriots who died at his men's hands.

"A nasty piece of work worth billions," I concluded.

Max nodded. "He wants the chairmanship of a new EU agricultural and fisheries committee."

I whistled. "I smell a story."

Max scowled. "You concentrate on the man's philanthropic side. He's offered to transport the Elgin Marbles on one of his ships from London to Athens."

I smiled and slowly shook my head. "That old chestnut."

The British Museum had refused to let the Greeks have the marbles back since the turn of the century. Things came to a head when Greece demanded the stones for an exhibition during the last Olympics. An argument ended in a stalemate.

Max updated me. The prime minister negotiated with the Greek Cultural Minister to return the marbles. They were going home for good, but there were no further details. He pointed a short stubby finger at me, his face set with that stern look that dared me to argue. Sometimes it was better to keep quiet, significantly when Max lowered his voice. "Here's your chance to write something nice," he emphasised the word 'nice,' letting it hang in the air, "about the Prime Minister. I want a four-part article covering the history of the marbles."

The series had to be a politically correct and authorised version of the Hrisacopolis family history and the preparations to reinstate the marbles in Athens. The articles were going to run during the month lead-up to the voyage.

Max rose to his feet and walked around the desk, indicating the meeting was over. Patting my back while walking to the door, he said, "I don't want any dirt dragged up or personal opinions, just a nice pull-out article for our Sunday supplement. Got it?"

"Yeah, sure. Is that all?" I nearly choked—Sunday supplement.

"I've also assigned you a photographer who's a damn fine researcher. She specialises in art and antiquities and has already been briefed."

"She?" Things were looking black. First a Sunday supplement article and now a sidekick. What the hell did I want with a female chaperone?

"Jessica Du Rosse - been working for us freelance for five years." The name didn't ring any bells with me. "She doesn't live out of a suitcase or eat at McDonald's," he added.

I let the remark go. Max was tired and in a bad mood, and I was past caring. I still had a job, albeit second best. With luck, I'd get my column back provided I was a good boy for a while. I thought a diplomatic retreat would be in order and reached for the door.

Max went back to thumbing through a bundle of notes he'd been studying. Without looking up, he said, "Don't let me down, Pete."

I opened the door, smiled nicely at Ms Linguard, and glanced back at Max. "Don't forget to open the windows."

He half scowled and waved me out. "Fuck off, Pete."

Ms Linguard wasn't impressed. Neither was the beautiful West Indian with her. Tall and slender with an hourglass figure and dressed in a dark mauve cashmere suit that looked as though it had just walked out of an expensive boutique in Paris. The faint hint of gardenias set my pulse racing. Linguard bared her teeth. "Mr West, this is-"

"Miss du Rosse," I interrupted.

Jessica studied me with unblinking eyes and held out a hand. "Peter, nice to meet you. I'm looking forward to working with you."

We shook hands. "And I you," I replied. "This is the first time I will share a by-line with someone. I need to spell your name correctly, don't I? I don't want to get off on the wrong foot." I looked sideways and smiled. "Isn't that right, Ms Linguard?"

Ms Linguard's face froze and coloured from pink to scarlet. I was beginning to feel a lot better.

CHAPTER THREE

I KNEW LIVER AND ONIONS were on the menu when we stepped from the elevator. The canteen was a pale yellow area in the basement, brightly lit by fluorescent tubes and filled with noisy chatter and smoke. It was the only place in the building where the smoking ban was ignored. Journalists sitting on yellow plastic chairs crowded around ring-stained tabletops scattered with plates, mugs, notebooks and laptops. Cell phones rang periodically, each with its signature tune piercing through laughter and loud debate. I often wondered why we had cubicles when most of our work was done over a cup of tea and curry.

A strong aroma indicated a fresh brew as Jessica and I joined a short queue for the coffee stand. Unfortunately, we found ourselves standing behind O'Grady and one of the junior secretaries from the newsroom. She was bored as the new manager engaged her in conversation. Seeing me, she smiled.

"Afternoon, Mr West." She picked up her coffee and made a hasty retreat after reaching for a napkin.

O'Grady turned. "Still with us then, Pete?" His cup clattered noisily into a saucer. "Well, I guess demotion has its compensation," he said suggestively to Jessica.

"Just get your coffee, Gilbert, and leave us in peace," I replied.

He poured coffee and stood looking at us with a smirk, one hand still holding up his trousers.

Jessica's chin rose a little as she moved past him. Her nose twitched, and she looked away.

After grabbing my coffee, I followed her to a corner table. It wasn't a nice spot. Dirty condensation streaks were marking the wall nearby, but it was an empty table. The disapproving look returned as she stepped carefully over a piece of squashed tandoori chicken stuck to the scratched linoleum floor.

I couldn't help smiling. Old hacks were coming alive as Jessica jostled around them in a pair of Prada stilettos. The table was situated below an open window where fresh air squeezed in under escaping clouds of smoke. One of two filthy windows looked out from our basement to the street outside. Natural light was limited due to the brick retaining wall close by, but there was fresh air.

"What's so amusing?" asked Jessica. She was balancing a coffee in one hand and some papers in the other.

"Sorry," I replied, "but you are so out of place here." Her mauve cashmere suit stood out like a beacon amongst the drab array of dark jackets and grey trousers. Heads were turning as she walked past.

"I go out to lunch most days." She hesitated, then added, "Not to McDonald's either." Max had lost no time in describing some of my finer points.

"I didn't mean to offend," I said.

"No offence taken, Peter, but I have to meet people in art galleries and auction houses such as Sotheby's."

I couldn't make up my mind if she was sarcastic or serious. She brushed the seat with her papers before sitting. She crossed her legs, tugged at the hem of her skirt and raised the cup of coffee to her lips in one smooth movement. Her high cheekbones and aquiline nose gave her a regal presence that could have graced any fashion magazine. But it was the large almond-shaped brown eyes that held my attention when she focused on me. Jessica looked over the rim of her cup and caught me gaping at her. She sipped slowly, her eyes expressionless.

I ran a finger over the scar down my right cheek and turned away. This habit had started at university when I tried to arrange dates. Several girls rejected me. I thought that was because of the scar. I got fed up being asked about my scar and began lying about it. I still don't like talking about it. Finally, my aunt, who'd doted on me since the fire, persuaded me to go to a shrink. The shrink said I had to 'find myself' and 'rise above the guilt' and made me feel more depressed after each session. In the end, I gave up, lost myself in The Herald and rose five floors above the guilt to the newsroom.

Jessica's lips parted slightly, but she said nothing. Raising the cup to her lips, she sipped.

"So, let's talk about the Elgin Marbles," I said.

Jessica paused for a moment. "What do you want to know about them?" She rested a hand on the table, a large red bead bracelet clacking on the surface. I hadn't noticed until then how long and slender her fingers were.

"Oh, just a brief outline on past and present. I know most of the history, but I'm sure you're better informed about past events than me," I said casually.

Of course, we both knew about the marbles, but I wanted to find out what sort of researcher Jessica was. I wanted her opinions to put a new slant on different aspects of the story and the background to Hrisacopolis' great offer. Some sixth sense told me there was a story here, but it wasn't the one about the marbles.

"I think you know more than you make out." She laughed and gazed out of the window. It was an infectious laugh that begged for company. We laughed, but I felt hers was governed more by social expectations than spontaneous reaction. Jessica knew her history but kept to an outline. She paused to sip some coffee, her fingers wrapped around the cup.

"Hi, Jessica, long time no see."

Jessica smiled and nodded at a woman colleague, threading her way through the tables with a loaded tray.

"You too. I'll catch up with you later," she replied. She gave a little wave, Italian style, bending her fingers in rapid unison as several heads turned our way as she spoke. She attracted attention in a crowded room. Her voice intrigued me too. It was soft yet husky, the kind you heard on those late-night radio phone-in shows that dealt with lovers' relationships and musical requests.

As her lips formed each word, it was hard to concentrate on the commentary as the husky tones lulled me into a dreamlike state of mind. Of course, I knew the history of the Elgin Marbles and managed to jump back into reality now and again, nodding in all the right places. Jessica Du Rosse was a lot more than a pretty face with a wealthy background. She earned a degree in art from the Sorbonne and travelled worldwide, spending a lot of time in London and Paris, working for art galleries, before combining her interests in photography and art. I took the trouble to quiz one of Jessica's close colleagues before meeting for coffee. She told me Jessica wanted out of the social merry-go-round and desired something more challenging. That's why she joined Hart Industries in New York. Two years later, she came to London and headed up the art department.

"What about pictures?"

"There are plenty in stock," she answered.

Our conversation was drowned out briefly by a shrill siren as police hurtled down the road. Being in the basement had its drawbacks. Sounds from the traffic just above our heads constantly competed with the general buzz in the cafeteria. Sirens always won, stopping all conversation.

"I take it Max told you they're being shipped back to Athens."

Jessica nodded and leaned forward, tapping the side of her small mug. She'd been holding the mug awkwardly in her left hand, and it wasn't until then I realised there was a crack she was avoiding. "Regardless of legalities over ownership, they are going back where they belong. The Greeks are going to rebuild the Parthenon."

It took several seconds for her remark to sink in, and then I snorted. "What?" The idea bordered on the impossible and sounded like a bureaucratic fantasy. Every time politicians came up with some big scheme, it nearly always ended as a giant cock-up.

"So, who's squeezing the government?" she asked.

My mug hung mid-air as I thought about that. "I'm not sure," I answered, "but I wouldn't mind betting Hrisacopolis is involved." Hrisacopolis was a politically motivated animal. Without a doubt, he had a few skeletons in his closet. "There's an MP speaking at a rally tomorrow about the marbles," I said.

A breeze drifted in from the window, carrying the scent of Jessica's gardenia perfume under my nose. For a brief moment, I was somewhere else, and Greek billionaires and ancient artefacts had evaporated.

Jessica waved to her friend and then said, "In Trafalgar Square. Yes, I'll meet you there." Without another word, she rose and left me sitting there alone with two mugs of coffee and a missed opportunity.

CHAPTER FOUR

A MASS OF SCREECHING seagulls circled, swooped, and dove around the Enchantee as she entered the outer harbour at Villefranche-Sur-Mer. Her nets were drawn up on either side and hung from the side booms. A pile of orange buoys, attached to the net line, lay behind the hatch cover at the stern of the boat. As she made her way around departing vessels, she left a thin trail of diesel smoke hanging in the air and seagulls bobbing up and down on her white effervescent wake.

Several fishing smacks, painted in faded colours, lay at anchor in the outer harbour or tied up to the quayside wall, rising and falling on the swell. The quay ran for a hundred yards until it joined with a steep grass bank skirting the coastal road. Across the road, scarlet geraniums overflowed from flower boxes beneath the upstairs windows of a row of houses bathed in bright sunlight.

Adonis stood in the bow, his bare feet feeling the heat from the wooden deck. His weather-beaten face belied his thirty-two years, as did his calloused hands. A few years at sea had transformed him from a youth to a muscular seaman. His hair was thick and black, comprising of a mass of ringlets cut just below the top of his ears and across the nape of his neck. Hidden beneath were several small scars. Shielding his eyes from the glaring noon sun, he scanned across the bay at the Golden Daffodil, an eighty-foot white luxury yacht moored alongside several other smaller cruisers some two hundred yards away. Under an awning, he could make out Mrs Fitzgerald lying on a lounger on the foredeck.

The Golden Daffodil lay berthed in the quieter waters of Villefranche-Sur-Mer, away from the public eye. In her late fifties, Barbara Fitzgerald a tall, slender and attractive American with influential friends in politics and the art world. She was a careful woman who shunned the press. Across the bay and beyond Mount Albon lay Nice, a short six-kilometre drive to all the expensive shops, boutiques and restaurants she loved.

Adonis met Barbara through Baris, one of the stewards from the Golden Daffodil. After leaving his last ship, Adonis worked in a local bar when Baris, a regular, struck up a conversation with him and became friends.

Baris worked most of his life at sea. Greek police on Crete had slaughtered his family of migrant workers during the seventies. The two men hit it off, and it wasn't long before Adonis gathered a lot of information about Barbara Fitzgerald and her collection of priceless paintings.

He made sure his new friend was aware he was looking for another berth, and when a crew member left the Golden Daffodil, Baris told his captain about Adonis. Barbara attended the interview without getting involved as the captain went through Adonis's service log. She nodded at the end of the interview, and he was signed on to the crew. For Adonis, it was the first time he'd been so close to real money, and he began to hope his dream to acquire a small fortune might become a reality. He needed money to keep a promise made years earlier.

Barbara Fitzgerald spent June and July at Villefranche every year, hosting parties or flying off to see friends in other parts of Europe. Adonis made a point of remembering her likes and dislikes. He learned to make her favourite cocktail, Tequila Sunrise, the way she preferred it and kept her stateroom in the shade to keep the sun from damaging paintings. The curtains were drawn and opened according to the sun's position throughout the day. He was careful to be courteous and called her ma'am with a slight head incline. In front of guests, she was Mrs Fitzgerald. He needed her trust to achieve his goal.

That opportunity presented itself at an evening birthday party for Barbara. The yacht was filled with influential art dealers and artists. Baris, always on the lookout to make money, pointed out one particular dealer, a Monsieur De Sauveterre, as a possible contact should Adonis need him. He paused and gave Adonis a slow wink. Adonis made a point of serving the man several times during the evening.

Another guest, Ioannis Koskotas, a Greek, spent most of the evening at Barbara's side. At one point, he moved away from her, holding a 'kerchief to his mouth as though he was about to be ill, and staggered out onto the foredeck. Adonis returned from the bar with their drinks when he saw Barbara join Ioannis, who was sick over the rail. She grabbed at the Greek's jacket as he slipped further over. At the exact moment, the yacht crested a large wave. Ioannis swayed and lost his balance. He grabbed the rail but missed. In a split second, despite Barbara's frantic effort to hold onto him, he plunged over the side into the water. Light streaming from portholes illuminated the Greek's head and arms as he broke the surface before disappearing into the darkness.

Barbara screamed and turned, panic-stricken. She clutched Adonis's arm. "Please do something," she pleaded. "Oh, my God, help him." Sinking to her knees, she gripped the rail and screamed out to Ioannis. Adonis dropped the tray. Ripping his jacket off, he climbed over the railing and jumped into the water. Adonis surfaced, gulped more air, and dove again against strong currents pushing him toward the yacht. He kicked against the hull and felt a flailing arm strike him across the back. Twisting in the swirling water, he grabbed it and then wrapped an arm around the Greek's neck. A few seconds later, his hand closed over the companionway. A steward and some guests pulled Adonis and Ioannis from the water, coughing and choking. Ioannis couldn't walk. Two men carried him up to the deck.

Sobbing, Barbara followed Ioannis down to the staterooms below. As she disappeared, she called, "Thank you."

Adonis sat on the top step for a moment, gasping for air and coughing. Saltwater stung the back of his throat. He reached for the rope rail and hauled himself upright. Leaning on one steward and shaking, he managed to stagger back to the deck. Guests gathered around him, congratulating him. Some were applauding.

Baris wrapped a blanket around his shoulders and patted Adonis on the back. "Well done, my friend."

"Here, young man, you've earned this and another for good measure." A guest offered a glass of brandy and shook his hand. Adonis gulped the brandy in one mouthful and then coughed as the alcohol warmed his throat and stomach.

The following morning Barbara thanked him again and asked him to drive her to Nice on a shopping trip. Parking in the city centre, Barbara asked him to stay with the Bentley. With nothing better to do, he settled down to read a newspaper. After sitting for two hours, he decided to stretch his legs. He stepped out of the Bentley and stood under a nearby eucalyptus tree, enjoying a cool breeze that played over his back. He heard Barbara calling him from across the road a short while later. Her bright yellow dress, contrasting sharply with a candy-striped canopy behind her, billowed about her legs. A row of shopping bags leaned against each other, and a small box sat next to them on the sidewalk beside her. She dabbed her face with a tissue and then gave him a quick little wave as he crossed the road. He picked up the shopping and accompanied her back to the Bentley.

"Thank you, Adonis."

He flashed a smile. "Pleasure, ma'am." He opened the trunk and lined the shopping up across the floor on reaching the Bentley.

Barbara climbed into the rear seat. Barbara said, "Adonis, I'm in town next weekend as they drove home. I have several errands to run. I hope you'll be available."

Nodding, he said, "Of course, ma'am."

That trip started badly. Barbara's hairstylist was out sick, and for over two hours, Adonis sat in the back of the salon reading magazines while Barbara fussed to the stand-in stylist. Nothing seemed good enough. She adjusted the ties on the bib around her neck, complaining they were too tight, and she brushed the girl aside when she tried to help.

"Are you sure you know what you're doing," she said irritably. "I can't wait for Denise to return. She knows just how I like things. You young girls have no idea about personal service." The worst moment came when the girl rinsed her hair. "Stop, you're burning my scalp. What do you think you're doing? How dare you treat me like this," she shouted. She pushed the rinse tube out of the girl's hands and glared at her. "I'm going to complain about this, and if you think you're getting a gratuity, you can think again."

Later she made the girl go hunt for more sugar. Her coffee needed sweetening. Adonis felt sorry for the girl and grinned broadly whenever she turned his way. She smiled back, but as he opened the door for Barbara, he noticed the girl walking quickly to the restrooms with a hand over her mouth.

The bad day continued at the Rolls Royce dealer's service department. The Bentley was due for a service, and Barbara found her business manager had not booked it. Adonis listened as she insisted the garage made a mistake and should take the limousine in for a service. "This is ridiculous," she shouted, banging a fist on the counter. "My Bentley has been serviced here for the last ten years. The standards of customer care here are falling. Fit me in today. I'll leave the Bentley outside."

When they refused, Barbara asked to see the manager. Adonis sat on a nearby couch, hoping the manager might deal with the problem before Barbara's mood set in for the day.

"I'm sorry, Mrs Fitzgerald," he said, "but we are fully booked today. Can you please bring your Bentley in next week?"

"If I ran my business like you, I'd get nothing done. Attention to detail, careful planning and looking after clients are the cornerstones of any successful business. Yours is going downhill," she snapped. Furious, she left the limousine parked at the rear of the dealership and stormed off to the stores.

One or two errands turned into more than a dozen. Barbara flitted from one store to another, and by the time she finished, Adonis was laden with bags and sweating. Back at the Bentley, he swung the bags into the trunk, lining them up neatly as before. He closed the trunk and stood with both hands on the lid for a moment. Sighing under his breath, he closed his eyes. When he opened them, he caught Barbara's eye. Barbara's stern expression turned briefly into a knowing smile. She touched his arm then said, "I guess today hasn't gone too well for us. I've got such a lot on my mind. I may have to fly to a meeting in Athens tomorrow."

Adonis looked away at a gleaming Rolls Royce standing nearby, then back again, a fixed polite expression on his face.

She breathed deeply. "Let's have lunch. That's the least I can do."

"Oh, no, that's all right, Mrs Fitzgerald."

Barbara shook her head. "I appreciate your help, Adonis. Why don't you drive us to the Negresco Hotel on the Promenade des Anglaise?"

They walked into the Negresco Restaurant ten minutes later, and a waiter showed them to a window seat overlooking the promenade. Traffic glided along the road in a procession of gleaming limousines and sports cars mixed here and there with noisy scooters. Little pockets of pedestrians strolled along the promenade, some with cardigans draped around their shoulders, the arms knotted around their necks. Others walked a poodle or shiatsu on a long colourful leash, wearing shorts and T-shirts. Behind all the activity, the sea looked choppy, small green-grey waves cresting white.

"So tell me, Adonis, what was the first ship you signed on to?" Barbara peered over the top of her reading glasses, usually hanging from a gold chain about her neck. "Did you suffer from seasickness?" She continued browsing through the menu.

Adonis looked away from the scene outside and picked up the menu. "The Caledonian Princess," he replied, "carrying general cargo containers between Seattle and Tokyo." He opened the menu and read the list of entrées, his heel tapping the carpet.

The conversation carried on through lunch, with Barbara showing interest in where he travelled and the cargos he worked. He recounted the worst storm he'd sailed through off Cape Horn in a refrigerated ship carrying mutton from New Zealand. Seasickness claimed nearly half the crew. The most exciting trips, he enthused, were working on banana boats between South America and Liverpool. Bananas were loaded shortly after being picked and arrived in England before turning yellow.

"Are your parents still alive, Adonis?"

Adonis's eyes flickered. The question caught him off guard. "No," he replied, swallowing hard. His fingers played with his cup, turning it in the saucer. "My father left my mother six months before I was born. She… she died giving birth to me."

Barbara lowered her cup and leaned forward, gently placing a hand on his forearm. "I'm so sorry, Adonis."

"Well, I didn't know either of them, so…" He sipped his coffee.

"I don't know what it feels like to have no parents, but I have found out living on your own isn't much fun either. I suppose the men you worked with were your family."

Adonis nodded.

"I don't miss Geoffrey," she said flatly.

Adonis took his cue. "You were married a long time then, Mrs Fitzgerald? Was he already in business when you met?"

"Just about." Barbara gazed out of the window. "It was tough at first, but the hard work began to pay off. Mind you," she said, removing the napkin from her lap, "I sometimes wondered if the long hours were worth it."

Adonis sat, silent. She paused, a faraway look in her eyes. She turned back to him, the hint of a smile on her lips that disappeared as fast as it formed. "There were a lot of bad moments when things didn't go our way, but we overcame them." She sighed and folded the napkin into a square before putting it down. "There were quite a few good times too." Her eyes focused on his, remaining long enough for Adonis to feel uncomfortable.

He lowered his eyes and nodded. When he looked up, he could see she wasn't finished. Geoffrey was Adonis's age when they'd met at some party and shortly after got married. A whirlwind romance, she said. Geoffrey started a small freight business financed with the aid of an inheritance. "The hotel chain came later. Geoffrey turned into a bit of a playboy." The voice rose, each word edged with a little bitterness. She studied Adonis's hair. "He was a real stunner, and you know what they say… money and men. Irresistible." Her head shook as though she were shaking bad memories loose. "Rather funny that Geoffrey at fifty… trying to be a playboy." She shrugged.

After his death, she sold Geoffrey's businesses off but kept the Trafalgar Art Trust they started together. It was all she wanted. A pause followed her recollection. She brushed a jacket sleeve with the back of her hand then picked up her purse. "Well, I suppose we'd better get back."

"Thank you for lunch, Mrs Fitzgerald."

Barbara clicked a finger at the waiter for the check. "That's something else...." She sounded almost absentminded as she handed the waiter a credit card. After he left, she leaned forward and said in a low voice, "You can call me Barbara when no-one's around."

They drove back to the yacht in silence, Barbara sitting in the back seat.

From that moment on, a respectful friendship developed and over the next few weeks, Adonis became her favourite steward.

The Enchantele turned into her berth alongside the quay and bumped against the row of tires, her engine throbbing quietly. Adonis jumped onto the pier, balancing his rod in one hand and a small basket containing baby Tuna. Hemade his way to the promenade and turned onto the road leading to where the Golden Daffodil was docked.

A large Mercedes roared past, kicking up gravel and a cloud of dust. In the second it took for the large car to pass, he caught a glimpse of the driver. It was Ioannis the Greek who'd visited Barbara several times, including attending the cocktail party when he'd fallen overboard and ended up sharing breakfast with Barbara the next day. Adonis spat on the ground and shook a fist at the disappearing car. He ran forward through the cloud of dust, an arm across his face, and spotted Barbara waving to him from the deck of the Golden Daffodil. He waved back and quickened his pace.

When he reached the top of the companionway, she waited for him—dressed in a red sarong over a white bathing suit. Her deep red lips parted slightly, revealing an even row of white teeth. She was Adonis's idea of how a film star looked at Cannes, wearing a gold chain necklace and a pair of pendulum drop diamond earrings.

"How was the fishing?" Her brown eyes settled on the basket, and a look of expectation spread across her face. "Excellent, what did you catch?"

"Baby Tuna," replied Adonis, stepping aboard. He held up the basket.

Barbara took the basket from him. "Thank you, Adonis. I'll fix some salad to go with it after I've changed." She brushed a fly away from the table. "We'll eat out here."

Adonis went below to his cabin. It was small but comfortable, and it held little furniture save a cupboard, dresser, mirror, hand basin, and a walk-in shower and toilet. Above his bed, there was a wooden cross affixed to the wall, and on top of the dresser, there was a small black and white photo of his mother in a silver frame. Adonis tossed his fishing rod onto the bed and undressed. His tanned body showed scars from several fights over the years. Life at sea had kept him fit. He showered and changed into jeans, a T-shirt sporting the Greenpeace logo and a pair of open sandals.

Barbara was laying the table when he returned to the foredeck. The late afternoon sun threw a soft pink haze across the deck and tinged her white trouser suit.

"Let me do that, Mrs Fitz- Sorry, Barbara. I'll fetch the salad."

Raising her eyebrows, Barbara pointed Adonis to a chair. "It may surprise you, but sometimes I like doing things for myself." Her chin jutted out slightly as she raised her head. She rolled her eyes in the direction of the galley and continued, "When Geoffrey was alive, I couldn't find time to do anything. Life was chaotic. Of course, that all stopped the day Geoffrey died. Nowadays, I like to fuss around the kitchen when the chef is off duty." As an afterthought, she added, "Maybe if there were children...." She sighed, finished laying the table, and left to fetch the salad.

Adonis watched her disappear inside, a shock of red hair cascading over her shoulders and across the back of her suit.

Barbara's red hair and good looks had always attracted admirers. Her parents, cattle ranchers from Texas, put her through college and rewarded her with a trip to Europe after graduation. A friend in London invited her to share an apartment in Knightsbridge. Barbara loved the idea and moved in. Shortly after the move, they attended a cocktail party where she met Geoffrey, introduced to her as a man most likely to succeed by her friend. She thought him handsome with his shoulder-length black hair. His blue eyes sparkled within a tanned face painted with a permanent smile just over six feet tall and muscular. They were inseparable by the end of the party, and a short four-month romantic affair ended in marriage.

The early days of the business were full of stress. It was a period of mental anguish and non-existent home life. They spent most of their time apart, snatching quick conversations on the phone or finding rare weekends when they could be together at home in London. Geoffrey attacked business problems with a zeal she admired. He was tenacious, outspoken, and larger than life; he always wanted her opinion yet rarely agreed with her. As the business took off, the financial issues began to recede. Geoffrey showered her with gifts, the result of a guilty conscience he told her, for all the things she went without. On her birthday, the first year after floating the business on the stock exchange, he bought her the Golden Daffodil. For the next three years, they were the 'must have' couple society wanted at dinner parties and charity events. Then Geoffrey bought out a large chain of hotels. It didn't take long for the rumours to start about his affairs. She wasn't too surprised.

Her love for him dissolved, leaving a hollow marriage devoid of trust. She ignored his girlfriends, and he accepted the lover in her life. She learned to be more assertive and organised her life with schedules that kept her busy most of the year. After his death, she spent a comfortable life entertaining her friends and being more involved with her art foundation.

It was pleasant to find Adonis was so like the young Geoffrey in more ways than looks. He was a hard-working and trustworthy man with an even temperament and good manners. She liked him.

———◆○◆———

The corner of a copy of Le Monde newspaper lying on the table fluttered in the breeze. Adonis picked it up and absently turned the pages. He stopped when a picture caught his attention. Greek billionaire, Hrisacopolis, would transport the Elgin Marbles back to Athens on one of his luxury liners. As he read the article, Adonis's breathing became shallow. He gripped the paper, and his heart was racing by the time he'd read it twice. He took deep, measured breaths, folded the paper carefully, and placed it back on the table. He uncorked a bottle of wine, poured two glasses, and then stood gazing across the bay. Holding a glass with trembling fingers, he gulped the wine.

Barbara appeared from the stateroom pushing a small serving trolley. "Well now, that breeze is very welcome, don't you think?" She brushed strands of hair from her eyes.

Adonis nodded. The freshly cooked tuna made his mouth water. Barbara placed the tuna and salad on the table and served Adonis some salad before helping herself from the bowl. Replacing the serving spoons, she waved a limp finger at Adonis. Resting her elbows on the table, she interlaced her fingers and twiddled her thumbs back and forth. "Adonis… I need to speak to you about something important."

Without replying, Adonis continued removing bones from the tuna with the fish knife and placed them, one at a time, onto a side plate. He paused, his knife mid-air. His eyes focused on a bunch of jangling keys as Barbara removed them from her purse.

"I will have to fly to Athens tomorrow." Adonis continued to eat without saying a word.

She placed the keys in front of him and picked up her glass of wine. "Have you heard of a man by the name of Hrisacopolis?"

He appeared to think. "No... I don't think I have."

She tapped the table with her knife and pointed to the newspaper. "Well, you can read all about Hrisacopolis here. I've known him for a long time. I need to sort out some problems with him about the Trust right away. There's an early morning flight to Athens so that you can drive me to the airport." "I need someone to look after the yacht. The crew has gone on leave for a month, as you know."

"I'll be happy to look after the yacht, Barbara. I could get the limousine serviced too if you wish?"

"Good, and perhaps you would check the bilge pumps every...." She gave up competing against the roar of a passing helicopter, tapping her plate with a fork. She waited for the whine of the engine to fade before continuing. "Could you check the bilge pumps now and again? She placed her knife and fork on the side of the plate and reached into her purse. Taking a key from it, she attached it to the bunch of keys. "You'll need the office key as well."

Adonis's stomach knotted. The office contained several paintings. These included two Picasso's and a Renoir.

"Good, we're all settled then."

Later, Adonis sat on the end of his bed. He took an envelope from the bedside table and drew a faded letter from it. He'd read it many times. The feeling of loss was overwhelming, mixed with a sense of injustice. Anger had long since turned to hatred. He replaced the letter and sat with both hands gripping his knees. "Damn you to hell, Hrisacopolis." His hands balled into fists.

CHAPTER FIVE

I**T WAS THE KIND OF MORNING** I loathed. Light rain fell from a dark grey sky, collecting in puddles by the side of the narrow lane outside my mews cottage in Bayswater. Sheltered from the rain by an overhanging chestnut tree, a neighbour's large black tomcat sat hunched on top of an old red brick wall. He stared down at me with darting eyes, watching my feet shushing through piles of yellow leaves. Across the courtyard, more of the same leaves stuck to the asphalt in a montage of webbed ducks' feet.

I was still mad at Hart and Max, but most of all, irritated at having to work with an assistant. I wasn't sure things were going to work out with Jessica. Social airs and graces were okay in the sophisticated atmosphere of art galleries and Sotheby's. Still, a much harder skin and some knowledge of political corruption were required when dealing with men like Hrisacopolis. I was too hard on her; she was only supposed to dig up historical facts.

I couldn't shake the dark mood off. The damn weather wasn't helping either. Loud squeaks from rusty hinges reminded me of the small white picket gate that needed oiling. I pushed it open and stepped out onto the sidewalk. There was a metallic clang as the gate slammed shut behind me. The tomcat stalked me and stopped at the corner of the wall, the end of his tail flicking back and forth. I curled my lip at him, pushed the trilby firmly down on my head, and walked briskly into the stiff breeze. Ahead of me, cars sped past the end of the mews and down Craven Road toward Paddington railway station. There wasn't any point in taking the car; the tube took me straight to the square.

A blast of cold air hit me as I turned the mews corner. I held the ends of my coat collar tight with one hand while keeping the other deep inside a warm pocket. I cursed inwardly. My eyes began to water.

Lara's Secret

If it weren't for Jessica, I'd still be in bed.

A crowd of placard-carrying protesters dressed in colourful raincoats and others sheltering under decorated umbrellas gathered around a makeshift stage beneath Nelson's Column. Under a small marquee, a conservative Member of Parliament extolled the virtues of British culture and argued why the marbles should stay in Britain. Jessica and I listened for half an hour but learned nothing new.

Max insisted we attend, and under normal circumstances, I would have argued against going, but not this time. The last thing I wanted to do was argue with Max. Jobs in the print industry were scarce enough, and he had stuck his neck out for me. Besides, it was because of him I had my column.

Hrisacopolis was a shipping magnate with many political allies in the Greek government, and he'd been involved in a few scandals during the seventies and eighties. Jessica knew this but wanted me to fill in a few gaps, especially on what could soon happen in Brussels. My irritable dark mood began to fade a little.

The rain stopped, and we moved to a vantage point up on the steps of the National Gallery. In the summer, tourists and sightseers packed the place. Apart from the small crowd surrounding the speaker, a few pedestrians were hiding under umbrellas. They hurried across the square to Whitehall, Pall Mall, or Northumberland Avenue. What never changed were the dozens of vehicles, cabs, and buses that rumbled around the square, travelling to and from hundreds of destinations every day and night of the year. This was one part of the city centre I loved.

Jessica yawned behind a half-folded hand. "So, tell me what he's up to now."

I focused on her face, the speaker and the crowd merging into the grey background. Despite jeans and a bright orange sweater, she still caught my eye. A pair of fleece-lined suede boots kept her feet warm, although her toes tapped the ground now and again. Taking a granola bar from her purse, she nibbled on it and then wiped a crumb from the corner of her mouth with the tip of a little finger. Her voice interrupted my train of thought. "Pete?"

"Oh… he's a very active politician with more contacts than Eros has arrows." I already knew a lot about our principal subject. Hrisacopolis wielded more power than ever before and manipulated his political buddies from behind the scenes from what I heard around

Whitehall. I'd been writing an article on the Cypriot unrest in the late nineties when I first came across his name.

Jessica listened with interest. "Enosis and all that, right?"

A small gaggle of students, one carrying a placard with the legend THE STONES MUST GO HOME, jostled past us. They were climbing the steps for a higher point to shout their protests. I mused they might be at the wrong rock concert but kept the joke to myself. Jessica wouldn't find it funny. "Union with Greece is not 'and all that,'" I admonished lightly.

During the fifties, Nico Hrisacopolis poured money into the EOKA terrorist organisation. The troubles rumbled on for years because of a few men like him.

Jessica rolled the granola wrapper into a tight ball between her fingers and deftly pushed it into her jean pocket, using the tips of her fingers. The movement stirred something inside me. I breathed deeply and looked back at the speaker.

"Money seems to have been the root of all evil in this family," she said, looking at more black clouds rolling across the sky.

I nodded. At the end of World War II, Andronis Hrisacopolis' son, eight-year-old Nico, inherited his father's shipping business. At twenty-two, he fought a guerrilla war alongside Archbishop Makarios and General Grivas, mainly against the British. His wealth and connections funded EOKA and kept the Cypriot dream alive. A few years later, he sent his son, Andreas, back. He fought with Grivas, but the cause he fought for faded fast. He died in a skirmish with the British on a beach at Pomos Bay a year later and returned to Athens, a posthumous hero. It was the end of the fight but not the dream. A military coup in Greece led to terrible repercussions for the Turkish Cypriots. Turkey invaded Northern Cyprus shortly after and formed the Turkish Republic of Northern Cyprus.

Jessica gave me a knowing look. "Now everyone agrees not to agree, and the Cypriot question hangs around in a time vacuum."

I marvelled at her neat conclusion. A UN plan, put forward to end partition, still needed agreement.

"So apart from getting himself a pat on the back as a good patriot and plenty of publicity regarding the marbles, what's Hrisacopolis' connection with Enosis today?"

She was asking all the right questions, and I was impressed. "Cyprus is already part of the EU, but one problem remains."

"Sovereignty." Jessica clapped her hands.

I was warming to her. "Got it in one. In the meantime, Nico Hrisacopolis has plans of his own," I said. Another speaker took the stand to loud applause. Nico needed a platform to speak to meet members of the EU and grease some willing hands.

"Do you know that for sure?" asked Jessica. She pulled a small red fold-away umbrella from her bag and flipped it open. The rain had started falling again, quite heavy.

I glanced sideways at her and nodded. "I'm ninety per cent certain."

Nico needed a position from which he could influence decisions about the future of Cyprus. The end of November would be ideal for him to be in that position. It gave him time to make his move and see who might be his new friends.

"Supposing what you say is true. How does Nico get his platform and opportunity to rub shoulders with the power brokers inside Brussels?"

Someone on the stage started shouting amid many cheers from the crowd. Jessica's feet tapped the ground in turn. Taking her by the arm, I guided her away, carefully avoiding a pigeon waddling around my feet. A small restaurant I frequented wasn't far away. Not exactly the Ritz, but it served hot food all day, and the coffee tasted good. We could have a private chat in one of the dingy corner booths. Traffic got heavier, and hissing tires splashed through puddles as rain hit the road and bounced. Jessica took my arm, pulling me under the umbrella. Our conversation carried on while we walked along the sidewalk.

I'd found out something interesting from my Whitehall sources. Plans for forming a committee looking at proposals put forward by Athens and Ankara regarding sovereignty were nearing completion. Nico Hrisacopolis, selected by his political buddies in Greece, supposedly because of his shipping and oil interests and connections with other EU industries, won the vote as their representative. Of course, this development wasn't public.

Jessica stopped, gradual realisation lighting up her face. "Right... platform, opportunity, and position of great influence."

"Precisely." I pulled my collar up. "He's manipulated the system so he can follow his plans. Not only that, but he is also hoping to be voted Chairman of a new EU Agricultural and Fisheries committee."

We pointed the umbrella forward against a blustery wind. "You don't have a very high opinion of him, do you?"

I counted on my fingers. "Terrorism, blackmail, bribery and murder. No, not very much."

"Have you ever met him?" She was almost shouting over the wind. "No. Why?"

"I always reserve my judgment until I've met someone like Hrisacopolis. I'm sure he's all you say he is, but he did fight for a cause he believed in." She took a large stride over a small puddle.

"Yeah, right," I scoffed, "so that gave him the go-ahead to kill innocent people." Why is it women find powerful men attractive?" As soon as I opened my mouth and started to speak, I knew that I should have kept my thoughts to myself.

"Oh, for goodness' sake, Peter, that is so childish." She pulled her hand away from my arm. The rain dribbled past my collar and down my neck.

We continued in silence, Jessica striding on the high moral ground while I shuffled along with embarrassment, soaking wet. After what seemed an eternity, I grabbed hold of her arm. "Sorry," I shouted, half turning toward her.

She shivered and put an arm through mine, pulling me back under cover. "I think you may be right about him." A mischievous grin tugged at the corners of her mouth and raised her eyebrows. Her brown eyes sparkled.

"Why?"

"He's paying for the restoration work on the Parthenon – eighty million plus."

CHAPTER SIX

L ONDON'S UNDERBELLY reminded me of my home, a Southampton
flat in a high-rise grey concrete block, and why my parents moved
to Devon to give me a better life and education. I became a
journalist trying to change an indifferent world. Damn Hart and
Hrisacopolis. I refused to look the other way. Annoyed at both men, I
gunned my car down the approach road to the better side of Wapping
and The Herald building. I drove around a bend and caught sight of
kids from the nearby tower block, kicking a ball up against the doors
of an abandoned warehouse. The ball bounced across the road in front
of my car. I punched the brakes and skidded to a halt. After several
deep breaths, I wound down the window and ordered the kids not to
play on the road. I drove off at a slower pace. A string of four-letter
words and two-fingered salutes followed.

Not the most endearing of neighbourhoods but then the last
thing a newspaper baron worries about is a scenic location. The city
airport bustled a short distance away, and easy access to several major
trunk roads carrying commuters in all directions through the
metropolis lay nearby. Wapping became The Herald headquarters in
the eighties and, whether I liked it or not, the hub of activity for Hart's
empire. I parked close to the building, jumped out of the car, and ran
for cover. Undercover parking existed for management, not the
newsroom.

Inside, a blast of hot air caught me on my neck. The temptation
to stand and dry out faded with the sound of running feet behind me.
I reached the elevator, and five other staff joined me while waiting. We
dripped rain on the marble floor, all of us checking our watches as
though our lives depended on time – a stupid British thing I've never
understood – and nodded to each other without saying a word. I smiled

inwardly, visualising a group of those little dogs you see on the rear shelf of a car, giving you a nod. The elevator arrived, and we all piled in. We remained silent as we ascended to the newsroom. I couldn't get the Greek out of my mind. Something was missing. I'd got a few inquiries to attend to and decided to ask Jessica to follow up on one particular member of the Hrisacopolis family.

A soft pinging bell warned we had arrived at the newsroom. Everyone braced themselves as the doors slid back with a slight judder. Facing us was a herd of journalists on their way out. Beyond them, office staff on their way to meetings clutched folders. I successfully sidestepped them, only to bump into Max's secretary carrying a polystyrene cup of coffee. She gave me a tight smile but declined the piece of crumpled tissue I produced from my pocket to dab her dress.

I walked to my cubicle, crossing the firing line between our deputy editor and a fellow journalist. They were shouting at each other over the news of a plane crash while competing with the buzz of telephone conversations around them. Monday mornings typically started with a couple of aspirin. Before I reached my desk, I could see a long pair of legs stretched out from behind the partition. Dressed in a pleated light blue skirt and navy-blue jacket, Jessica put me to shame in my dull grey suit. Her red beads were gone, replaced with a gold charm bracelet. The gardenias, however, still hung in the air, an invisible man trap.

After our afternoon at Jack's cafe, I'd decided to work a few hours at the office. I lost track of time and finished at ten-thirty. Nico Hrisacopolis turned out to be an interesting man. The more I found out about him, the more I wanted to dig. Call it instinct, but I knew I'd find a great story behind the story despite Max's warning. The results could sit in my drawer for the time being.

Jessica sat in my chair looking at the notes, holding my pen mid-air to correct mistakes. The desk looked clean and tidy. She'd created a mess in my mental comfort zone.

"Hi," I said cheerfully. I shook my raincoat and draped it over the wall. "It looks different around here." I waited until she got to the end of the page. When she turned the page, I got a little more direct. "What the hell have you done with my papers?" I hovered over her, my anger rising. The cubicle contained my cosy little piece of the world, and it only housed one, not two.

She lay the pen on the desk and looked up with wide eyes.

The opportunity to work with Pete West came as a surprise to Jessica. She vaguely remembered seeing him a couple of times on the newsroom floor, but they had never met. Her office, three floors above the newsroom, was a world away. Work sometimes took her out to art galleries, auctions and museums, but never into the newsroom bedlam.

Max asked her to meet him urgently for an assignment, providing research for Pete. She wondered why she would have anything to do with politics. It was a pleasant surprise when Max briefed her on an upcoming project for the Sunday supplement. The 'West Column' was already popular with readers when she joined the Wapping office, and she too admired his in-depth political comment. The prospect of working with him excited her. She looked at the opportunity as a chance to do something more interesting than writing art reviews.

Pete turned out to be very different to the man she expected. Instead of a well-groomed and polite gentleman, she found herself shaking hands with a savvy bachelor. His bright blue eyes looked into hers and gripped her attention while she shook hands. The dry humour aimed at Ms Linguard made her smile. She liked him at the first meeting, a little shorter than herself and almost twice her age. Across one cheek, there was a short, thin scar that gave him a not too rugged look she found attractive. What did surprise her was his wardrobe. A worn jacket, scuffed shoes, and a rumpled shirt. The clothes were expensive, obviously from a bespoke tailor, and the shoes were Italian leather. Max had warned her West was a bachelor.

The last four days proved difficult. Pete was well educated but lacked any practised social graces. Their backgrounds were different, and Pete's witticisms could be annoying. His political views, though, confirmed his expertise. She listened, fascinated and interested in his vast knowledge of world financial and political matters.

Frustration at Pete's comment the day before annoyed her. She realised that his words were not personal. Her observation showed she may not have understood his depth of knowledge of Hrisacopolis history. She resolved not to make a mistake again, although she felt no need to apologise.

Jessica ignored the question. "Although these notes are informative, they do not exactly stay within the agreed research areas." That said, she returned to the notes and read on. I felt an irresistible urge to place both hands around her neck. I sat on the edge of the desk and leaned forward, speaking as calmly as possible.

"There are several things we have to establish here."

She turned her head and held me with a steady gaze.

"First, this is my chair, and this is my desk, and this is my pen, and this is my space." I pointed at each item and ended by waving my hands in the air. "Next, these are my notes." I snatched them from her and leaned closer. "I'd be obliged if you'd refrain from sticking your nose into my work. Last – since when did you decide what we will and won't do?"

I'd apologised for the stupid remark at the rally, but this was different. There were fifty messy desks in the newsroom, and no one touched a thing, not even the cleaners. She should have known that.

Jessica answered my question with silence and a glare.

"Now - get out of my chair and go get your own," I growled.

She rose and left the cubicle without saying a word.

The chair didn't look like much, just a tiny secretarial chair with a worn cloth seat and three squeaky castors. After sitting in it for half an hour, my buttocks ached, and I spent a lot of time shifting from side to side, but somehow it survived the years. It was part and parcel of my workplace, and I didn't like trespassers.

I settled into the chair and opened the file, feeling justified at taking Jessica down a peg or two. After a few minutes, she reappeared, pushing an oversized black leather executive chair before her with one hand. The chair glided in next to mine, filling the space in the cubicle and making it impossible for me to leave. She sat upright with hands clasped in her lap, an expression of superiority set on her face. In all the years I'd been at the office, no one ever owned a chair like that in the newsroom. I guess the way I looked at the chair begged an answer.

"Max, let me have it," she said, her voice clipped and guarded.

"Just like that. You must have been very persuasive."

"Not at all," she snapped, "I asked politely." She brushed an imaginary speck from her skirt.

The bait dangled in front of me, but I wasn't interested. What did interest me lay inside the folder she'd been reading. The previous night's work turned up a lot of material, some relating to the fifties and some to current activity in the Brussel's corridors of power. Nico proved to be a very shrewd and clever man, a bastard too.

The articles about the Elgin Marbles would be as glossy and nice as Max wanted, but that wouldn't deter me from digging deeper than the Greek's smile. I wanted Jessica on my side for various reasons, particularly her connections within the jet set hierarchy. Her father, a colleague informed me, was a retired diplomat with years of experience on the 'garden party merry-go-round.'

"I'm sorry I got angry, but you should have known," I said. "I've written a column in this little hole for the last two years... on my own. My notes are the only things that belong to me around here." I sighed and threw my notes across the desk.

"I suppose I deserved what I got." She cast an eye over the desk. "If you want to live like this… And I shouldn't be looking at your notes. I'm sorry, Peter."

"You can look at anything you like but don't move anything." I wiggled a finger at her. "Call me Pete, okay?"

The smile returned, the hands unwound, and the legs slid across one another. "I guess the urge to purge political stupidity and corruption is too strong for you to ignore, right?" She reached across the desk and picked the file up. "What's the plan then?"

"I don't have a plan, but I feel that unless someone stops Nico in time, his corrupt tentacles will start poisoning the European Union. By coercing and bribing fellow delegates on the Agriculture and Fisheries Committee, he can cause chaos whether Turkey joins the EU or not.'

"Surely Turkey will eventually join now that Cyprus is in the EU?" she asked, placing the folder on her lap.

I shook my head. It depended on a lot of things, including human rights issues. There was a lot the Turks would have to sort out first.

I put two fingers over my mouth as Max scurried by with an armful of folders. A trail of cigar smoke and two managerial lackeys followed him. "Working hard, you two, I hope?" He said it over his shoulder without looking back at us.

Jessica opened the file and looked through a pile of newspaper cuttings I'd collected. Like me, she knew no resolution on sovereignty meant it would be easier to promote public unrest. I agreed. If that were to happen, the Greek Cypriots would have support from the UN Security Council from that moment on.

I could see Nico standing on the sidelines, watching the disintegration of the Turkish Republic. Therefore, strong leadership and a strong trading partner would be a better solution. No doubt whatsoever, the EU would back a declaration of Enosis from the Greek parliament. The Turkish government would have no choice but to agree to yet another condition to join the Union.

Jessica looked up from some photos. "Despite your tough exterior, you have a heart then, not just a journalist's sense of justice?" There was no sarcasm in her voice, although there was a silent question.

"You'd better believe it," I answered. Yes, I care about my fellow ordinary Joe and his family. That's why I love my job. When Whitehall do something right, I sing their praises. When they get it wrong, I like kicking ass on behalf of Joe.

Her eyes never left mine while I spoke. A hint of sarcasm escaped her lips as she answered. "Well, I guess that explains a couple of things."

"What's that?"

"Why you live out of a suitcase and eat at McDonald's. You don't get time to settle down while saving the world. Have you got a red cape?"

We laughed together.

"So, what's next?"

I told her I was going to lunch with a buddy of mine from the Foreign Office whose father worked in Brussels. While I enjoyed lunch, she could dig up as much as possible about Nico's son, Andreas.

I opened a drawer in my desk and took out a press clipping on Andreas's death and a picture of the man. "That's what he looked like."

Jessica took the cutting from me, studied it, and then tapped the picture. "He's quite a handsome young man. I wonder who this woman is?" She held the image up to the light.

Shaded by a tree, Andreas sat on a large rock with an arm around a woman. Only one of her arms and a shoulder showed.

"No idea," I answered, "probably a girlfriend."

CHAPTER SEVEN

SUNLIGHT FILTERED THROUGH the rustling olive leaves in small sparkling points. A chaffinch swooped down and landed by the side of a hole in the gnarled silvery trunk. After perching for several seconds, it flew up through the small, tapered leaves and sat chirping in the shade.

The olive trees stood in a straight line, casting long shadows that cut across the gravel drive and climbed the villa's whitewashed wall. Beyond the wall, the village, a cluster of small white buildings to one side of the dusty road, stood out against the dark-green orange groves that covered the hillside. Some villagers took advantage of the shade under the trees and lay there during the afternoon siesta.

Nico Hrisacopolis, his portly figure wrapped in a blue bathrobe, sat upright on a lounger beneath a white awning that ran the entire length of the veranda. He watched the bird with interest as two more chaffinches joined it singing on the branch. A carriage clock's faint sound of chimes pealed through the still air twice through the open bedroom window. Nico pushed his wide brim straw hat back and wiped his forehead and moustachioed lip with a handkerchief. The shaded veranda kept the sun from burning him. However, there was no escape from the humidity and eighty-plus degrees that would remain long into the afternoon. The cool interior of the villa, with its marble floors, was more comfortable, but he preferred to sit on the veranda watching the birds. The sun's heat was relentless between ten and four, sapping his strength and forcing him to rest.

His doctor advised him to retire after suffering a heart attack the previous year, but he scoffed at the idea. Instead, he rested for the summer before launching into the elections in Brussels. At sixty-four, he was one of the most successful industrialists in Greece. The accolade meant nothing. Recognition as a national hero like his father, a man whose name passed into history forever, moved closer each day to reality. He thought about his destiny as he watched one of the chaffinches flit skyward.

"Lunch." An elderly woman dressed in black stood in the doorway. A silver hair comb held her greying hair tightly in a bun. Of slim build, she stood upright like a governess with feet together and hands folded in front of her. Small dark brown eyes, a small, pointed nose and a prominent chin gave her a stern appearance within an unsmiling face. At her side sat an equally severe Doberman with a dripping tongue. She repeated herself using a more commanding voice.

Nico acknowledged her with a wave of the hand without looking up.

"Does that mean you will eat out here or inside?"

"Out here."

"The doctor said you-"

"Damn the doctor. Just bring the lunch and don't tell me what the doctor said."

The woman's head and chest rose, and with her lips tightly drawn, she turned on her heels and marched back into the villa in quick little steps.

The Doberman padded over to the side of the lounger and crumpled to the wooden floor with a loud thump. He rolled sideways with one raised paw, waiting for a hand to pat his stomach. When it didn't appear, he whined. A hand came down and slapped his nose hard. The dog yelped, scrambled to its feet, sneezed, shook his head, and then loped off to the other end of the veranda. He crashed to the floor again with eyes that never left his master.

"Damn dog," muttered Nico.

The housekeeper reappeared, carrying a cordless telephone. She announced there was an urgent call from his secretary in Athens.

Nico snatched the phone from her hand. "What?" he barked into the phone.

The secretary told him a journalist from the British newspaper, The Herald, asked questions about his family and the Parthenon marbles.

Nico fidgeted with a cigar, rolling it between finger and thumb. "I know about that, and if you read your morning instructions, you would know too," he answered irritably.

The secretary ignored the remark. The woman was inquiring about Andreas and a picture in a Cypriot newspaper.

Nico sat upright. "What picture?" It appeared shortly after his son's death, along with an obituary. The journalist wanted to know about a girl, partially hidden, sitting next to Andreas.

"What did you tell her?" He flicked open a small silver cigarette lighter and lit the cigar.

His secretary had said nothing and ended the conversation.

"Good. Let me think. I'll call you back after lunch."

Nico ended the call and tapped out the number for his Istanbul office. He waited for the connection. The housekeeper appeared again, carrying a small table laden with a bowl of salad, a tzatziki dip, and a plate of lamb and minted baby potatoes. He waved her away after she'd set the table by his side and handed him a fork. A faint voice fused with atmospherics on the line sounded in his ear.

"Damn it, is that you, Ahmet?" There was silence. "Speak up. Do I have to keep telling you this is always a bad connection?"

There was a pause before Ahmet answered more clearly. "Sorry, Sir."

"Well, what news have you? Has there been any progress? You've only got a couple of weeks now." He forked some lettuce into the dip and rotated the fork before lifting it to his mouth. Some sauce dribbled down onto his robe. He brushed it away with the back of his hand.

Ahmet had good news. The grandson, Andreas Jr., was agreeable to reconciliation although reluctant to join the ship on a trip to Athens from London.

"No. He has to be with us on the trip," said Nico irritably. "If the contacts in Athens are comfortable in the knowledge that my grandson will take over, they will support my election. The timing is right. Before any political fanfares about the new European committee, an announcement about my grandson in the world press will be crucial. I am at the crossroads of my life, and I have waited so long to fulfil the promise of Greek sovereignty my father made to the Greek people. I am so close to achieving this, and nothing must stand in my way."

Ahmet listened and said, "Andreas will be made to understand the importance of being present."

"Good, is there anything else?"

Ahmet hesitated, "If I could remind you of two urgent problems, sir. We still have to work out a statement that explains the situation regarding Andreas. Then there is the matter of two people who need persuading to forget certain matters. Perhaps…?"

"Perhaps nothing. I'll take care of things this end. You will find and deal with the girl, something that should have been done a long time ago."

"Yes, sir." There was a faint click on the line.

Nico sat eating the rest of his lunch thoughtfully. Certain things would have to be taken care of, as risky as that might be, rather than have the truth revealed. His dream of national recognition would be gone, as well as the reputation of a family loved and respected throughout Greece. Nothing was going to stop him now. He smoked for several minutes before picking up the phone. Another problem would need attention.

The Athens office answered promptly.

"Nana, call that journalist back and make all information about my political career and the business available. Also, put her in touch with Ioannis about the photo and call him before the journalist does." As an afterthought, he added, "Extend two invitations to the newspaper to join the cruise."

Ahmet replaced the receiver in its cradle. He lit a cigarette and watched the smoke curl up to the ceiling of his second-floor office. The old oak desk, the grey filing cabinets with chipped paint and the comfortable wooden office chair on castors still stood on the same Persian rug. He had moved into the office nearly thirty years before.

From his desk, he looked out of the large windows at the shimmering surface of the Bosporus. Ships of all sizes passed each day, including container ships owned by the Hrisacopolis line. He exhaled smoke and reached across the desk to turn the small fan on.

The Greek would soon have all those beautiful dreams shattered. The man was an arrogant pig. Hrisacopolis had forgotten that it was himself who had hesitated over the girl's fate. Soon, all the years of being a 'yes' man would be over. He picked the telephone receiver up and dialled Cynara's number. He waited, hoping she had not left for her morning job in Nicosia.

"Yes, good morning." Cynara's voice sounded clear.

"I have a job for you," replied Ahmet. "You may be questioned by the press or your neighbours about a Hrisacopolis grandson."

"I don't understand."

"Don't interrupt, Cynara." His soft voice held an edge of threat and domination to it. "Listen to me and do as you are told. I want you to look through the records of recent deaths of widows or spinsters, nothing over six months old. Then let me know what you have found."

"This would be someone on the island?"

"Yes, it will be announced that Nico Hrisacopolis has found a long-lost grandson who will be taking over the Hrisacopolis Industries. This woman will be the mother who confessed to hiding him, frightened of losing him to the old man. On her deathbed, she asked that the young man be reunited with the Hrisacopolis family."

"Why would they come to me with questions?"

"Your name will be mentioned as the source of information. You will be a friend of the woman. There are other small details I will give you later."

"Will you pay me for this?"

"Of course. You can have a one-way ticket back to Istanbul and ten years in prison."

There was a click, and the line went dead.

CHAPTER EIGHT

I WAS ON MY WAY to see an old friend, Roger Askew-Broughton, or 'B' to his friends. We'd met at Oxford, where we studied politics and modern history. Through the assistance of a father in the diplomatic corps, he eventually found a job in the Foreign Office. When I joined The Herald, he became a valuable source of information for all the intrigue and current world affairs, both political and financial. Whitehall lived and breathed statistics.

On reaching Great College Street, I quickened my step as the cold breeze turned into stronger gusts. I made my way to a small, up-market restaurant, Le Petit Dejeuner. It had been our comfortable meeting place over the years. Decorated expensively with peach flock wallpaper and carpeted throughout in burgundy, it looked and felt more like someone's living room. The furniture was highly polished reproduction Georgian. Overlaid with crisp white linen, the tables sat in two straight lines, each complemented with an ornate silver service. Frequented by city types, Le Petit Dejeuner was the place that dared anyone in jeans or those without a sizable bank account to enter. I wasn't a regular.

Roger was already there, a bottle of claret standing open on his table. He was poring over a copy of The Times that lay spread out before him. He was typical of the well-heeled Westminster set, wearing a dark navy suit and sporting his old Oxford tie. He was forty-eight years old with well styled dark hair, thinning on top. His face was young though, belying his age, with ruddy cheeks and bright blue eyes. In his middle age, he had acquired an overweight girth that threatened to pop the buttons on his waistcoat. He wore a gold wedding ring with one inset diamond and an Oyster wristwatch on his left hand. Ash from a cigar he had smoked smudged his waistcoat.

Sitting down opposite Roger, I tapped the side of the bottle. "C'est combien?"

He didn't look up right away but took several seconds to answer, engrossed in whatever he was reading. At length, he said, "Don't worry, old chap, the bottle is on me." Folding the paper, he clicked his fingers at the waiter. "Thought I'd treat you to a drinky today, what?" He guffawed and snorted at the same time, making me cringe. "Now, let's have a look at the menu." He produced two menus from the small rack at the side of the table and handed one to me.

I scanned for the cheapest omelette. We had an arrangement that whoever called the other for a chat over lunch paid. My wallet emptied most of the time, but I didn't mind. Many a story sprang from our conversations. I ordered the cheese omelette, and he ordered the steak. 'B' always ordered the steak, so I have no idea why he studied the menu. I shook my head.

He caught the look on my face as he ordered. "J'ai une allergie – du fromage et des œufs." He patted his chest and screwed his face into a pained expression. "I'm allergic to eggs and anything stuffed inside them." He poured the claret without spilling a drop. "So, what brings the bad boy from Wapping to my table?"

"You heard then," I replied.

Tongue in cheek, 'B' told me some of my great admirers were champing at the bit. The PM was furious, and the word was he'd told Hart to get rid of me, or else it would be long before The Herald got any favours from Number Ten. He raised an eyebrow before burying his nose inside the goblet to capture the bouquet.

I dismissed his remarks. "Stop horsing around. Max is just slapping me on the wrist." There was a pause while Roger sipped the wine. I got the impression there was something more serious he had to say before we discussed what I wanted out of our meeting.

'B' nodded. He leaned forward and put a hand to his mouth. The Americans were flying out to Toulon to talk a new deal with the European consortium in the morning. His opinion was they shouldn't bother unless the price were right.

"The bloody French won't have anything to do with it. You wait and see," he said, his stubby index finger emphasizing the point by tapping the table.

We both knew the Americans stood to lose the most because of my column. I nodded and agreed with him. He joked I wouldn't be welcome back in the west wing for the foreseeable future, then guffawed and snorted, nearly spilling his wine as he raised the glass to his lips.

I waited until he'd finished and brought the reason for my visit up.

Ray C Doyle

"Yes, the bloody Elgin Marble situation." He bowed his head and wagged a finger at me. "Pete, beware… it's fraught with danger, old boy, fer-aught with danger. If Brussels-"

"Hrisacopolis?" I interrupted.

He nodded on the same wavelength. "Have you been digging?"

I nodded. "Can we share?"

"By word of mouth only, old boy. No tape, no memos, no phone calls."

That meant the Foreign Office was briefing intelligence agencies, and Roger would not talk in great detail. However, if I'd figured it all out right, he would nod and agree now and then, adding some unimportant detail that helped push another piece of the Greek jigsaw into place. We talked through lunch, or rather I did, and through coffee until around two o'clock. As I finished my coffee, we wound up the conversation.

Roger gulped down the rest of his wine. "He will dread letting someone else run the company."

"It's a shame Nico Hrisacopolis' son, although a terrorist for a brief moment in time, had not lived to stand in a while his father entered the EU battlefield. Things could have been a lot different."

"That's if Nico makes it to the EU table, old boy," he added.

Before we parted, he warned me to be careful a second time. "Other eyes are watching our Greek. Some are friendly and others not, but neither will be happy if you get in the way."

I walked back to Westminster Station deep in thought. There hadn't been much new information, but it was interesting that the government was so concerned over Nico Hrisacopolis that intelligence scrutinized him, probably checking for any contact with terrorist groups or arms dealers, given his nasty past.

Roger's warning about 'other's eyes' referred to a Turkish terrorist group called KKA, Kaygisiz, Korumak, Aydinlatmak – Care, Protect, and Enlighten. The group had reformed during the last two years since talks on Turkey joining the EU had begun. Now considered active, they operated in Turkey and Cyprus. Whitehall widely believed that the group would cause trouble if Greece and Nico held sway in Brussels over crucial political decisions on the island's future role within Europe. But then I already knew that.

Political rumours did not influence the EU, though. Only concrete proof of corruption would stop Nico from getting his way. Many EU Commissioners and Euro MPs from member countries needed to be convinced that the Greek had hidden agendas if my hunch about him proved correct. That was a pretty hard to do when Whitehall was dragging its heels over the European government's economic policies and Nico, a hero to his countrymen, was spending money on a glorious cultural renaissance.

Since nineteen eighty-one, Greece itself had been a member, enjoying strong diplomatic and trading ties within the Union. The Hrisacopolis shipping empire was part of that strength. The phrase 'political impasse' came to mind.

I was mad at Max and Hart for not having the insight to see what Nico was up to. I decided to tackle Max one last time. I wasn't going to do that alone, though. I'd write the script, and Jessica would help sell it

.

CHAPTER NINE

I WAS SITTING IN THE BACK of a taxi, almost back in Wapping, when Jessica called. She was in the British Museum library and asked me to meet her there. The cabby shrugged when I asked for a change of direction and then shook a fist at a motorist who wouldn't give way as we tried completing an illegal U-turn in East Smithfield.

Twenty-five minutes later, I entered the quirky building. Inside there's a towering three-story curved grey wall that reminds me of the elephant house in London Zoo. From every angle, it surrounds the library and blurs into an invisible vertical horizon against the grey outer concourse wall. The concourse itself reminds me of some grand railway terminal full of travellers, either hurrying to catch a train or waiting to meet arrivals: a Lowry painting – busy, informal, and filled with anonymous people.

It's a different picture inside the library. I stood for a couple of minutes soaking up the atmosphere, gazing at students sitting at the original leather-topped desks with small brass reading lamps illuminating their intent faces. Oxford and all the nice things I associated with university life flooded my mind.

Gazing across the floor, my eyes focused on a face I recognized. Jessica stared back at me, one hand waving tauntingly as I came out of my daydream. I took a deep breath, stuck my hands inside my trouser pockets, and strolled as nonchalantly as possible towards her.

If I thought she was going to be facetious, I was mistaken. She was excited. She had a big juicy bone she couldn't wait to share. "Guess what?" she enthused as I slid into a seat by the next desk.

"I called Athens and spoke to Nico Hrisacopolis' secretary. She didn't let me have much but did react when I mentioned the girl." Jessica paused, waiting for a reaction.

51

"Okay," I said, "so who is she?"

"Don't know. The secretary ended the conversation abruptly."

"So there's a cover-up, a skeleton in the cupboard."

Jessica nodded. "That's not all, though. She called back within a half-hour, authorizing me to receive as much information about the great man's family, business empire, and political career as I liked."

There had to be a punch line. I waited patiently as she rose with an armful of reference books and her notepads. She gazed down at me, beaming.

"Well, I'm not going to move until you tell all. It might earn you a dinner for two." I don't know why I said that. Maybe it was one of those spur-of-the-moment things that present themselves when the more conventional way of asking a girl out seems to get lost in some dark corner of a dormant brain, namely mine.

She sat again and, still clutching the books, bit her bottom lip before telling me. "We are going on an all-expenses-paid cruise." Her face lit up, excited at the prospect.

I didn't know whether to be excited or not. Going on a cruise was great, but my dinner offer didn't match a Greek billionaire's invitation. I swallowed my pride. Not only a cruise, but we had a private meeting as well.

While aboard his flagship, our opportunity to interview him exclusively for The Herald included heads up on a statement being made public twenty-four hours later. According to the secretary, this statement was of great importance to the future of the Hrisacopolis industry, the Greek people, and the European Community.

"It could be a world exclusive," she gushed.

"Crap."

"Pete."

"I said it quietly."

"I don't care."

Too late, I realized I'd gone too far again. Me and my big mouth.

Jessica rose from her chair, very angry, dropping some of the books on the floor. I bent down to pick them up. She brushed my hand away. "I don't think this is going to work. Maybe you should do this assignment with someone else."

I stood and gently tugged her arm as she made to leave. "Jessica, wait a minute, we need to talk."

"No, we don't." she hissed.

Turning on her heel, she faced me, her eyes on fire and her voice full of anger. "For all I know, you could be right about Hrisacopolis and any number of other subjects you care to name. You're on the top table and well-read as a journalist. The British Establishment – the very people you appear to despise – love your column. I wonder what they'd think if they knew about your bad manners and foul language. As a writer, you're one of the best: as a gentleman, a damn disgrace. You need to grow up and stop being so bloody childish. Max was right about you." She glared at me and marched off, leaving me stunned and a couple of nearby students studying me intently over the tops of their reading glasses.

I left the library feeling guilty and embarrassed. Her words stung in much the same way Max's had. She knew me better than I knew myself. I walked across the concourse feeling thoroughly miserable and annoyed at my stupidity. I stopped to pull my collar up at the main entrance. Somewhere inside my head was a self-destruct switch I needed to disarm. The weather matched my mood as I descended the steps to the courtyard. I analysed myself, wondering what I was doing, letting feelings about Jessica get in the way of work. She was right. I did a lot of cursing, and I wasn't much of a gentleman. Why would I ever assume she might find me interesting when I couldn't be polite?

My cell phone rang. Her voice sounded in my ear before I could say a word. "I'm sorry. I shouldn't have been so spiteful. You are truly the most irritating man I've ever known."

My pulse quickened. "I was going to say-" She hung up. Elation turned to disappointment. By the time I reached Great Russell Street, the rain had returned with a vengeance, battering my trilby and soaking the shoulders of my coat. People dived for cover in little book shops or under canopies. I was so full of mixed emotions that I didn't care about getting wet. I didn't care about Hrisacopolis, the paper, Max, Hart, or the rest. She said she was sorry for being hurtful. I tried to read between the lines but couldn't find any hidden message. The tone of her voice was flat and unfeeling despite her apology.

The phone rang again.

"There's a coffee shop in Dyott Street, this side of Oxford Street. Meet me here. Do you want coffee?" Jessica asked.

"Yes… thanks." She hung up again.

I found the coffee shop five minutes later. Opening the door, the hum of conversation accompanied by clattering crockery, a hissing cappuccino machine, and a squeaking overhead fan jangled in my eardrums. Jessica was sitting over in one corner, sipping coffee. I approached cautiously. "Hi," I said and sat down. I felt a sudden urge to throw myself at her feet. "Please don't throw in the towel. You had some great news, and I spoiled the moment."

She was looking down at her coffee, fiddling with the spoon in the saucer. "We both spoiled the moment, Pete. You have a sense of humour that thrives when directed at the establishment or those who grew up more privileged than yourself. Max filled me in on a few details."

Again, I felt annoyed with Max but let it pass. Saying nothing, I picked up my coffee. She wasn't finished, and I had no intention of interrupting her again. The noise around us faded, and her words became loud and clear.

"I'm far too sensitive," she continued. "I was a young black girl brought up predominantly white diplomatic circles. It was hard. My father spent his whole life climbing the diplomatic ladder, serving the British Crown's far-flung territories in the Caribbean and finally the Cayman Islands as Deputy Commissioner."

"My mother taught me to be mindful of the silly British Colonial culture that dictated dress sense for breakfast, afternoon tea, and evening dinner. I was discouraged from talking too much until I could talk like an English lady. Piano lessons and ballet classes were an absolute must. My parents frowned at me if I talked to another child, not my class. Class was significant to father. He was proud and rose from a sugar plantation cropper to a respected government official. Unfortunately, unlike those who arrived in a diplomatic bag directly from London, he was never part of the Westminster club. It took more than appearances and money to become a member."

I sat fascinated. Her upbringing was so different from mine.

"We lived in style others of their colour envied," she continued. "We mixed socially with other staff and their families as long as we knew our place in the pecking order. My father and mother loved the life, though I knew my mother was hurt on many occasions by the sharp tongues of other diplomats' wives who spent half their lives gossiping. There was never any obvious racism, but it was there. For example, one could decipher the hidden messages in conversations and remarks made around the tea-table at four in the afternoon. Surrounded by snobs and having to turn the other cheek constantly, I got bored and eventually convinced father to send me to Europe."

She sighed, seemingly glad to have said what was on her mind.

"It's strange that I get a little touchy now after such an upbringing."

"No, it's not," I said. "You've shaken off the rule book but retained the guidelines. We come from different backgrounds but are rebelling against something we don't like."

"Perhaps, although I think I'm rebelling against more than a childhood, Pete." She held me with her eyes as she spoke. It was almost as though she'd said it to herself.

"Maybe." It could have been my overactive imagination, but I thought I heard more than a reconciliatory tone.

CHAPTER TEN

"**N**O. NO. NO."

Max should have been on the stage. I'd told him that many times. He went into the same routine each time he lost his temper, generally with me, but it was a joy to watch. Arms extended, hands waving in all directions. The mouth overemphasized each word. Wild eyes glared while he paced around the office, stopping briefly now and again to shout out of a window. His voice changed pitch as he grew angrier too. He sounded like a hysterical woman and made me laugh. It was terrific stuff. My reaction made Max even more furious and more expressive.

Jessica sat quietly in one of the armchairs trying hard not to show her true feelings. I don't think she was upset, more amazed, perhaps appreciative of how Max turned temper into a new art form. As soon as she'd opened her mouth, he'd looked at me accusingly. I should have known.

I waited until there was a lull in the storm and tried again. "Max, under normal circumstances, you'd be foaming at the mouth for a story like this. It has all the ingredients of a real political scoop. At least let us present our case so you can-"

"NO." Max turned away and collided with his desk. One large glass ashtray fell to the floor, spilling butts and ash all over the carpet. Jessica moved quickly to avoid the cloud of dust billowing toward her and put a hand over her mouth. She stepped over to the window and opened it.

Max, unconcerned, lit a cigar and sat on the desk. "You two are on a special assignment. Nico Hrisacopolis has made a very generous offer to The Herald for an exclusive interview and hospitality arrangements for staff to cover the cruise and arrival of the Elgin

Marbles in Athens. You will toe the line or no longer work for this paper. Am I getting through to you?"

Jessica and I nodded together.

Max held a hand up. There was going to be an election in Greece. To be seen to or accused of influencing the Greek public by exposing one of the country's most notable industrialists involved in government corruption meant torn relationships in Brussels.

Max blew a cloud of smoke into the air and stared hard at us before continuing.

The Prime Minister was in Brussels with other EU members, trying to reach diplomatic solutions to Greek demands for increased farming subsidies and a decision — albeit one we already knew the answer to — on the future of the marbles.

Max sympathized with us but was adamant. We couldn't embarrass the British or Greek governments. Nico's shady business dealings and political plans were on hold.

"I take it this directive comes from Hart?"

"Leave it alone, Pete. I'm warning you. You're walking on thin ice."

I sat in the car as raindrops dribbled down the windshield. Somewhere another journalist would get the same slant on things as I had and dig for the real reasons the old man was being so generous with his money.

Before a general election, I could see how things would turn out in Greece but disagreed with Max or Hart. The Greeks had a right to know if Nico was corrupting and manipulating the present government. Damn Whitehall and farcical diplomacy.

There was only one bright spot on the horizon. Nico's plans for political muscle would have to wait, regardless of the formation of the new Agriculture and Fisheries Committee in Brussels. All EU member countries voted representatives onto the committee, but Spain and Ireland refused to name their selections. They also vetoed other members' selections as a protest over fishing quotas. I hoped they would continue arguing, giving me more time to unravel the rest of the Hrisacopolis story. I didn't want that honour going to one of my colleagues.

My cell phone rang.

"Hi there, what are you doing?" Jessica asked.

"Sulking and plotting Hart's murder."

"Where are you?"

"In the car park."

"Pete, I left you there almost an hour ago."

"I know, I've been thinking."

"Well, carry on thinking until you get here. Dinner is in forty minutes." She chuckled softly. "You would like to come to dinner, I suppose?"

I was about to excuse myself from dinner because I might make a complete ass of myself.

"Bring some white wine. We have fish. By the way, I have some news regarding the photograph you gave me this morning."

I forgot the excuse and turned the key in the ignition.

Jessica gave me a Hampstead address, and when I arrived, the neighbourhood was like something out of *Town & Country* magazine. The house was a prominent thirties-style place with long bay windows and four bedrooms. It smacked of class and money and showed Daddy loved his daughter. I didn't hang around outside to admire the long lawn or manicured privets with the rain pounding. What I saw through the living room window as I lunged for the porch steps did grab my attention. Jessica, wearing a white cocktail dress, stood with her back to the window, adjusting a place setting. I was so out of place, wearing a pair of grey corduroy trousers, a shabby jacket that should have been thrown out but kept because it was comfortable, and a pair of brown shoes that hadn't seen polish in weeks. Feeling miserable, I punched the bell. The porch light came on, adding to my discomfort. The door opened. If she noticed my dilemma, she said nothing.

She just held out a hand to usher me in. "Hi, did you bring the wine?"

My face said it all. This was beginning to look like the worst week of my life. "No," I said apologetically. "Jessica, I forgot." Some good news about the photograph and the euphoria of spending the evening with her had been enough to cast everything else from my mind.

"Don't worry; you won't get sent to the Tower of London. I've got some sparkling wine." She gave me a playful nudge.

She put her arm through mine and led me toward double doors across the reception hall, an area my mews apartment would fit into comfortably. Her soft breast pressing against my arm was an experience I'd not enjoyed for some time, and when she withdrew her arm to open the doors, I felt a pang of disappointment. The dark green living room stretched from one end to the other of the house.

"Make yourself comfortable while I serve dinner."

I settled on a chair at the table and watched her walk back to the kitchen, her breasts gently moving with each graceful step. It was hard to understand why there wasn't a man in her life. Or maybe there was. She was wearing the same scent. I wondered if she wore anything else. Not too strong, but there whenever she drew near.

After several trips to the kitchen, she announced, "Dinner is served. Enjoy."

Halibut cooked in white wine and a superb tossed salad. I decided that filling my stomach came first, and information came second. A perfect hostess, she soon had me enjoying light conversation on various topics and proved extremely adept at manoeuvring around anything to do with Hart or the newspaper. I waited until she cleared the table, and we were mulling over a glass of port before turning the conversation to Nico Hrisacopolis.

"I had the most extraordinary piece of luck this afternoon," she explained. "I got hold of the editor of the paper that printed the girl's picture."

I nodded. "Great, how did that go?"

"It happened the editor was a staff reporter at the time of Andreas's death. I asked him to wire the complete story and photo. When I asked if he knew Andreas, he told me 'No,' but everyone on the island knew Andreas by reputation if nothing else. He was a popular leader of men."

I saw that tiny glint in Jessica's eye and knew she'd dug up more good news. I settled back in my chair and prompted the conversation while sipping wine.

"I asked about the girl and whether or not the editor had taken a photograph."

"And had he?"

"He told me, no, and he didn't know who the girl was, probably a girlfriend, but I expected that. Denial is a good first line of defence. Again, denying any knowledge of the photo's origin, he said he came by it by bribing an intelligence officer with the British army a week after Andreas's death."

I agreed with Jessica. The chances of an officer taking a bribe were ridiculous.

Jessica raised an eyebrow. "Something wasn't quite right, though."

"What wasn't?"

"I'm not sure. He answered as if the incident were fresh in his mind, not something he was trying to remember."

"Primed, maybe?"

"Yes." Jessica paused. There was something else on her mind. "The requested wire with the story arrived with the accompanying photo. It was a copy of the one you showed me from your file. There was something odd about it, and then I realized the photo had been cropped."

She wondered why someone, even an amateur, would take a photo of Andreas without including the woman sitting next to him.

Indeed, it made sense for Andreas to be photographed on his own, or there would be a shot of him and the woman together.

"Did you call the editor back?"

"Yes. I asked him for a copy of the full photo."

"And?"

"He said the picture in the paper was 'as is.'"

"You didn't believe him, right?"

She nodded. "No. As soon as I got off the phone, I called a friend in the Ministry of Defence for some information regarding intelligence personnel on Cyprus at the time."

"Of course, I forgot, you must know a few of those…" I stopped short as she sent me a warning signal with her eyes.

Without dwelling on my near slide back to sarcasm, she quickly finished the report on her day's inquiries. Her valuable contact supplied her with the retired captain's address who had been in charge of the ambush. After giving the captain a call, she fixed a meeting at his home in Devon for the following day. "I was a little wary after learning he knew why we wanted to see him but was cautiously pleased." Jessica was beginning to see past the Elgin marbles to the real story.

"I don't want to pour water on your achievement, but this wasn't exactly the right thing to do, Jessica. If this gets back to Max, we're finished."

"The captain knows how confidential our inquiry is," she assured me. "I only told him we wanted to talk about Nico and his son." She gently shook her head and raised her glass toward me to emphasize a point. "Nothing more. But he was keen to see us. He blames Nico for many servicemen's deaths and would like nothing better than to settle that score." She paused and sipped her drink. "I think I rekindled bad memories for the old man. He sounded angry." That was fine with me. If the old boy still carried a grudge, he had a story to tell. I wanted to hear that story.

My research revealed that the Greek government loved Hrisacopolis for his industry and money by the eighties. For unity within the EU and many other behind-the-scenes deals, Whitehall decided to love and forgive him.

"Thanks, you did great," I said, giving her arm a light squeeze. "Maybe you should melt his heart tomorrow and ask a few of the questions yourself."

Jessica was happy, and I felt great. She rose and held out a hand. "Now, if you don't mind, I want an early night. Can you pick me up at six in the morning? I told the captain we would be there at noon."

I stood and held her hand, feeling a little irritated that she cut the evening short but also relieved I'd not made a fool of myself. She withdrew her hand hesitantly, then slid both hands behind my neck and pulled me close. Our lips met, gently brushing against one another until I could stand it no longer. I kissed her hard, my hands holding the small of her back. Her bare skin felt warm and smooth.

"Time to go home, Pete." The combination of soft breath in my ear and the faint scent of gardenias under my nose set my heart thumping again. She pulled away, her head bowed, her hands holding my arms. "We should start on the article for Max tomorrow too."

"Taken care of," I said. I gulped and took a deep breath. "I started on it yesterday. The first part will be in the bag by the weekend. I just need some pictures from you and historical notes."

She nodded and led me to the door, her arm through mine. The door closed behind me. Cold air outside dampened my ardour, not my feelings. I looked down at my shoes before stepping off the porch, then walked briskly back to the car. I was determined to clean up my act, starting with my shoes.

CHAPTER ELEVEN

ADONIS TOOK ONE LAST LOOK around the stateroom and felt a deep sense of guilt. Barbara had not called, and that was a relief. He knew she would be upset, not just at losing the paintings but also at him for betraying her trust. Anyway, he would be dead by the time she found out. And she would get the paintings back. It would take the dealer several weeks to find a collector who did not ask too many questions. In the meantime, he would tip the police off from the safety of a boat moored off Malta.

The harbour lights dotted the calm water and reminded Adonis of all he would miss. He turned away, concentrating on the task at hand. It was an hour away from the art dealer, De Sauveterre. The traffic was light at night, and the Rolls would be back in the marina garage before the manager arrived at eight in the morning.

Each painting proved easy to remove from its frame before he rolled it into a cardboard tube. Another twelve paintings hung on the walls of cabins and the stateroom. Money raised on the three he had chosen would be enough.

Baris' tip about De Sauveterre proved invaluable. The man was easy to deal with and very greedy. Adonis's asking price was a fraction of the actual 'backstreet' value, and the dealer didn't argue. Now all he had to do was deliver the paintings and pick up four million American dollars in cash; one million reserved for the Turk. The rest would buy the two patrol boats, arms, and explosives.

Adonis had first heard of the Turk three years back when his ship had to go to Genoa for engine repairs. In conversation with some other seamen in a bar, they had told a story about being mercenaries in North Africa. Their leader, a big Turk, had hired them to fight in Angola. He had a reputation as a gun for hire and arms dealer who, in underworld

61

circles, was a dark legend.

Three years on, Adonis heard rumours in the red-light district that the Petermerie was seeking a man called 'Turk' for a horrific attack on a prostitute. Later, a local prostitute confirmed the Turk was a deserter from the French Legion. It was also rumoured he had a fifty-thousand-franc bounty on his head.

After finding out he would be looking after Barbara's yacht, Adonis seized the chance to plan revenge on Nico Hrisacopolis, the man who had ruined his life. He knew the Turk would be ideal as an accomplice, even if an uncomfortable one.

It took several days to get a message to the Turk. Adonis moved from one bar to another, meeting with past shipmates and prostitutes he'd known, spreading rumours that the Turk's services were required for a million dollars.

He also spent two days asking around in the busy east end of Vieux Port. Nothing turned up except some wary stares from fishermen on Belges quay, and sealed lips in the seafood restaurants huddled between the southern pier and Cours d'Estienne-d'Orves. The Belsunce quarter lay on the other side of the boulevard. Notoriously rough, the quarter was mainly an Arab area. He had walked into the area the day before and made inquiries at some cab ranks where Turkish drivers hung out.

After lunch, Adonis stood smoking outside a restaurant when a cab pulled onto the curb. One of the Turkish drivers Adonis had spoken to called him over. A small unshaven man with balding grey hair drew and exhaled on a Gauloises that drooped from his lips. The pungent odour escaped from the driver's open window.

Adonis climbed into the back of the battered green cab, an old Citroen, without a word. They pulled away from the curb amid squealing tires and a cloud of oily smoke. Five minutes later, they drove up to Rue Tapis Vert, part of Belsunce, and stopped opposite a covered alleyway on the other side of the road.

"There is a large blue door down there," said the driver, pointing across the street. "You'll be met."

The cab sped away, leaving Adonis in a crowd of Arabs. He crossed over, looking around him, and walked hesitantly into the passage. With a shaved head and a small gold cross hanging from an ear, a huge man leaned against the wall with folded arms. Secured behind a wide black leather belt, he wore a sheathed knife. He beckoned Adonis with large fat fingers.

"I've come to see the Turk," said Adonis. He thrust his chin forward without taking his eyes off the man.

The man unfolded his arms

"Well, where is he?" Adonis put his hands on his hips and glared.

The thug grabbed him by the neck and spun him into the wall, running his huge hands down the front of Adonis's body and both sides of his legs.

"I don't have anything. I want to see the Turk," Adonis told him, gasping.

The door opened, and another man appeared, smaller than the first. Jerking his head in the direction of the steps, he disappeared back down the way he had arrived. The first thug tightened his grip on the back of Adonis's neck and pushed him to the stairs. The door closed behind them, and Adonis stumbled several times before reaching the bottom in the gloom. He found himself in a dingy cellar lit by a small bulb hanging from the ceiling. There was no furniture save a desk and one chair. On it, in the dark, sat the Turk.

"Stand in the light. I want to see a man who has balls."

Adonis clenched his fists and took a step forward. A fist smashed into his jaw, sending him sprawling across the floor. Excruciating pain shot across his face as he picked himself up and stood, rubbing his jaw.

"What do you want?"

"I want someone killed."

"You want someone killed. Don't we all?" The Turk laughed, his deep guttural tone echoing off the walls of the small cellar.

"Nico Hrisacopolis is nothing to laugh about if you are a true Turk."

The laughter stopped abruptly. The Turk leaned forward into the light. His shaven head bore a deep red scar that ran slantwise across the top from above his right eye to behind his left ear. His large nose looked as though it might have been broken at some time. Another small scar ran from the corner of his mouth in a downward slope. It left his bottom lip curled permanently to one side. Tattoos that had faded with time covered the rest of his face, neck, and muscular hairy arms. A giant serpent draped its body over one shoulder, its head appearing over the other, mouth open. Both arms bore a cross with 'Death' written across one and 'Honour' across the other. Dark brown eyes bore into Adonis, studying him for several moments. "What's this about Hrisacopolis? Who is he to you?"

Adonis shook his head. "Wouldn't you be more interested in a million dollars and revenge on this murderer of our countrymen?"

"Ah, you are Cypriot." The Turk wanted to hear the story, but Adonis resisted, giving the man a rough outline of the mission and what he required, including twenty men trained in automatic firearms and an explosives expert. Hrisacopolis was to be left for Adonis to deal with.

"You would kill him yourself?" asked the Turk.

Adonis nodded and promised half the money on his next visit. The Turk agreed, and they shook hands, arranging a time and place for the meeting.

Later, Adonis left the Golden Daffodil with the tubes under his arm and climbed down into the Zodiac. The outboard spat into life, and he headed for the pontoon.

Chapter Twelve

As Jessica and I drove through the pleasant countryside, we passed farmworkers burning waste grass and wood in a field. It was hard to concentrate on what she said while images of that terrible night flooded my mind. I could hear my mother screaming and see the flames coming from under the door. Thick black smoke billowed across the landing, blinding and choking me. In the darkness, the door handle banged frantically as she wrenched it back and forth.

"Pete, are you listening to me?"

"Yes," I lied. My mother's screams were drowning out her voice and the steady throb of the engine. I gripped the steering wheel and tried to concentrate.

"No, you're not. For the second time, can you please stop and check the map? I'm lost." She studied the map, tracing a finger along the route we had travelled.

I didn't need to. "We're on the A30, and we need to take a left at Fenoy Bridges… it's coming up shortly. After that, we'll pass through Ottery St. Mary and Wiggaton before reaching Tipton St. John."

"Clever, Pete."

She kept her eyes on the map. I felt a little guilty for not being a better travelling companion. We should have been discussing the second of our articles.

The day had started okay. I picked Jessica up, and we headed for the M4 out of London. We talked about nothing in particular, Max and Hart, and what irritating bastards they were. Neither of us mentioned the goodnight kiss, a moment I still savoured. Then she told me we should head for Devon and Tipton St. John, two miles from Bowd, a cluster of Devonshire cottages and townhouses that I left after the tragedy. That's when the conversation became one-sided.

"Here we are," she said as I turned a corner. "We should be there soon."

"About fifteen minutes," I said, trying to be cheerful. It took a lot longer. I had forgotten what some of the roads in Devon were like in the winter. We sloshed and bumped our way through puddle-filled potholes and stopped by a privet hedge.

Captain John Stevenson's cottage was on the outskirts of Tipton St. Mary, next to three other cottages. It was a small cottage of post-war design that did not have a thatched roof, much to Jessica's disappointment. A small garden fronted the cottage, which lay several yards back off the country lane. Two tall beech trees shaded the whole area.

"Why don't you soften him up first?" I said as her legs swung out of the car.

She glanced sideways at me and gave me a knowing smile but said nothing. I hadn't taken a great deal of notice of her appearance first thing, but as she straightened up and closed the door, I felt a longing in my stomach and my heart thumping against my chest. She was beautiful. A pale yellow two-piece woollen suit loosely followed the contours of her body. She didn't need to pull anything in or push anything out. I followed her down a path worn into the lawn, weaving through a couple of flowerbeds full of forlorn chrysanthemums that needed cutting down for the winter. A rambling rose trailed across a trellis on one side of the front door sprouting dead whiteheads.

"Not much of a gardener, is he?" I remarked.

"You haven't got a garden, Pete, so don't criticize."

I nudged her gently and answered softly, "I'm not a politician, but no one objects to me criticizing them."

The door opened, and Captain John Stevenson, a small elderly man with a shock of grey hair, stood in the doorway with a newspaper in his hand. A pair of old slippers poked out from beneath a pair of brown corduroy trousers. What really caught the attention were the two cardigans, one green and the other red, he wore over a white shirt. However, any thought I might have had that we were looking at an eccentric was dispelled immediately.

"You are Jessica," he said, holding out his hand to shake hers. He kept hold of it.

He turned before Jessica could introduce me and led us into his living room, a small cosy space warmed by an open coal fire. Ushering us into some armchairs, he left us to make tea.

I sat on a chair by the window. Spots of rain began peppering the glass. "It looks like we'll have a miserable time going home," I said.

Jessica winked at me. "It can't be worse than the journey down."

I said nothing.

The captain reappeared, carrying a large tray with the tea things. He set it on a small round table in the middle of the room and sat down. "Tea, Mr West?"

"Yes," I said, "thank you."

He acknowledged me with a mumbled "right-ho" then poured the tea. Once we settled, he turned to me.

"Mr West, I have read your column several times." He placed a spoon into each saucer and then poured milk into the cups. Pouring the tea, he handed a cup to Jessica. Handing me mine, our eyes met and locked. I sensed tension and wondered if he had second thoughts about the interview.

Stevenson settled into an armchair without picking up his tea and tapped a finger on the armrest. "You will forgive me if I seem a little cautious about your visit," he said. He put a finger to his upper lip and held us with piercing blue eyes before he spoke. "I understand you want to know about Nico Hrisacopolis…." He paused, eyebrows raised.

"Yes," I replied. "We're investigating the marbles going to Athens, given the recent developments in the European parliament."

He pursed his lips and looked out of the window. Rain was pouring from a darkened grey sky. "I wonder," he murmured, "given your past editorials if you have disclosed your real reasons for digging into the Greek's past." He may have been retired for some time, but age had not blunted his intelligence.

I explained I'd come across newspaper reports. There were rumours about family connections to the troubles in Cyprus. Hrisacopolis had some explaining to do.

"I agree," he said. "I want you to be honest. His eyes narrowed, and he leaned closer. "Are you planning to bring about his downfall? I'd be pleased to help in any way I can. If not, you can kiss my rear gunner as they say in the army."

Jessica choked on her tea and burst into laughter. I waited until the moment passed. Joking aside, he told us Jessica's inquiry had stirred some embers that still glowed in his mind. He remembered horrific images of the carnage on both sides in the Cypriot Conflict.

I came straight to the point. "What can you tell me about Nico's son, Andreas? I understand you have a photo of him and a girl?"

He sniffed, not that he needed to clear his nose. It was a sniff of disapproval. "Mr West, just because I agree with your sentiment, it doesn't mean I'll start giving you information that might affect the future of Cyprus." I wondered if, indeed, he was retired.

Stevenson made no apology for the inference and pointed out that his service record included three years stationed near the border in County Antrim, where a lot of violence occurred. He reminded us that he had signed the Official Secrets Act. He wanted to speak to our editor before he gave us any information that might get him into trouble.

Jessica and I locked eyes for a fraction of a second. Stevenson saw it.

"Now tell me why I shouldn't call him?" He held his cup mid-air.

Jessica leaned forward. "Captain, in the process...."

I raised a hand to interrupt.

The captain waved at me. "No, Mr West." He waved Jessica on. "I trust her." I wasn't offended. His concerns were understandable.

Jessica explained. "While we were researching for the story of the return of the Elgin Marbles, we came across news articles. There were also whispers about Nico's ambitions within the EU. One of Pete's contacts supported our suspicions that Nico could be a danger in Brussels."

Stevenson reached for a folder on a bookshelf by his chair. He had never met Nico or Andreas Hrisacopolis. EOKA, The National Organization of Cypriot Fighters, hid in the country, mainly carrying out their operations at night. The British Army knew that their HQ was approximately two miles north from Makarios and Kyoko Monastery. They rarely went anywhere near there, both for safety and political reasons.

I chose my words carefully and asked, "Did you come by a photo of Andreas that later appeared in a Cypriot newspaper?"

"Yes," he replied, "I picked it up off the beach. I assumed Andreas dropped it."

Jessica repeated the details of her conversation with Ioannis Koskotas, the editor of The Cypriot. He had told her that he paid the captain for the photo as a reporter at the time. She took my clipping from her purse and handed it to Stevenson.

"No. This is a copy of the photo I found on the beach."

Opening the folder on his knees, he took a small worn photo from an envelope. He admitted taking it from the archives when he retired, a memento of how close he came to serving justice on the Hrisacopolis family. He handed it to Jessica.

I got up to look over her shoulder. It was the same picture, but Jessica was right. Andreas sat on a wall with a rifle across his lap. Next to him and with an arm around his shoulders sat a beautiful young girl.

"I have no idea what happened to her," said Stevenson, "and I don't think you will find anyone on Cyprus willing to talk about her."

I studied the photo more closely. The girl wore a simple loose skirt and a short-sleeved blouse. On her feet, she wore sandals, and a large black scarf covered her head. "Why?" I asked.

"Her name is Lara Akchote."

"My God. She's Turkish," exclaimed Jessica.

Andreas had committed the ultimate family sin. I could hardly contain my excitement. The secret would put a big dent in Hrisacopolis' popularity, even with his closest allies. Greeks mixing with Turks in romantic liaisons would have been unthinkable when Andreas and Lara were together. Religion was another stumbling block. It had become a little more relaxed since then but was still frowned upon in Greek high society. Nico's reputation as one of Greece's heroes would be shattered, given his exploits in the war for Enosis and strong views on the Turkish occupation, not to mention the news's effect on his industry. A disheartened public would drop their support, and his plans might collapse.

The captain agreed. "But supposing the girl is still alive?"

Jessica agreed. "Yes, if we tip our hand too soon, Nico will ensure we never print a word anyway."

I wondered why the editor lied about the photograph and how he came by it. It seemed very odd. It was understandable he played dumb about the girl if he was pro-Hrisacopolis, but why implicate an intelligence officer? Stevenson knew the simple answer. The man had played a trick to throw us off track and stop us from digging for dirt. It also created more time for him to cover up his lies. The question remained. Who took the picture? Koskotas had to know, especially if he had the negative. A very close confidant would have taken it— someone who could be trusted not to tell. I turned the photo over, examining some writing on the back.

"It could be Alexander who took the picture," suggested Jessica.

"Good guess, but I don't think so," replied Stevenson. "There's much more to this. Andreas's love life may be part of the secret, but there has to be something else, something more dramatic."

I took a sheet of paper he was holding out. "What's this?"

"Run your eye down the list of names and see if you recognize anyone."

Koskotas was third on the list of a couple of dozen names. "Who are they?"

The names on the list were prominent troublemakers – both Greek and Turkish. According to Stevenson, they remained under surveillance during the sixties and seventies. By day Koskotas worked for a newspaper. By night he printed The Cypriot Fight, an underground propaganda paper urging rebellion against the 'occupying imperialistic army,' encouraging desecration of Turkish property and rallying support for the military junta in Athens who were at loggerheads with Makarios. Stevenson reminded us they were turbulent times with Greeks fighting each other and the Turks.

"Must have been very confusing," I said. "Your point about Koskotas is what? That he took the picture?"

Stevenson nodded. Koskotas propaganda sheets were the only source for photos of EOKA action. His accounts often implied his presence on the scene. That also suggested he had a camera. There were often quotes from Grivas and Makarios that were more personal than military views of the campaign. Koskotas was more involved than he let on to Jessica.

Jessica recalled Koskotas admitting he was a staunch supporter of The National Organization of Freedom Fighters when he was young. It made sense he would have had access to a darkroom for The Cypriot Fight.

She was probably right, but something more significant than a love affair lay hidden behind a cover-up in the Greek's head office. I was guessing it had a lot to do with the European Parliament and Cyprus was now part of the EU. Something more than a secret girlfriend happened in Cyprus over thirty years ago that, if made public, would have repercussions for Hrisacopolis' political plans.

Stevenson pointed to the photo. "Keep that, but I'd appreciate its return when you've finished with it. You might try making inquiries at villages nearby."

"I spent several years as an intelligence officer, sifting through thousands of photographs and recognizing the shot's location. Aphrodite's baths are on the island's northern coast near the artillery range. I suggest you start making inquiries there. This is near my last skirmish with Andreas."

"How did he die?" I asked. "No one seems to have seen him get killed."

"I saw him shot." Stevenson poured more tea and explained. "The UN intelligence heard an arms shipment was being dropped off. They had heard from their Athens' office. I was with a British and Dutch UN contingent on duty at the time. I had no idea it would turn out the way it did."

I looked at him as he relived the moment he caught up with Andreas. It must have been a bittersweet moment to have gotten so close to capturing the man, only to see his quarry escape into the night. Taking Andreas alive would have been more satisfying. His story intrigued me. I didn't want to break his train of thought. Jessica was attentive as she sat drinking her tea.

The captain shook his head. "It was all over in a matter of

minutes. Seven dead and four injured… and two escaped… one dead. The next time I heard of Andreas was a news item in the newspapers. They were carrying an article about his death. Nico Hrisacopolis hailed his son as a hero and vowed to fight for sovereignty for Cyprus. Thankfully, or should I say, fortuitously, the Turks landed very soon after and stopped further massacres." He paused and breathed deeply. "Unfortunately, the Greeks suffered for a few weeks after, especially the women."

We talked about the situation for another hour and then took our leave, promising to keep Stevenson informed.

Jessica decided she would drive home. While she wrestled with the early evening motorway traffic, I studied the girl in the picture. It was obvious the couple was in love.

"You know what I think?" said Jessica. "Take a good look at her face. She has an unusual expression. Lara might seem happy, but she has sad and lonely eyes."

One name appeared on the back of the photo, written inside a heart – Lara Akchote. I was determined to find out what had happened to her.

CHAPTER THIRTEEN

AHMET ZEKI SAT IN the shade of a red awning that covered half the tables outside the restaurant. A white straw trilby covered his balding head. Small in stature, his rounded shoulders made him appear smaller than he was. His white summer suit was creased, especially the jacket, which suggested he spent most of the day wearing it despite the heat. The square was packed and noisy, with tourists and shoppers taking lunch. He picked up a glass of tea and sipped while fingering a cream baba sitting on a plate in front of him. A gentle breeze blowing off the Bosporus helped to soothe a growing headache. Eren was late, but then the young man was always late.

Ahmet thought about his trip to Cyprus and was under no illusion of the enormity of the task ahead. It was okay for Nico to issue orders from Athens, but it wouldn't be that man's neck in the noose if anything went wrong. Ahmet pulled a large handkerchief from his pocket and mopped his forehead. As soon as the letter arrived, Nico ignored his warning that there was only one solution to the problem. All of them had to be dealt with. Now there was a mess to clean up. The day he predicted had arrived.

A sudden sharp jab of pain shot through his right ankle as he crossed his legs. The pain was a constant reminder of the falaka beatings in Diyarbakir Prison and the detention he endured as a young man.

At a time of heightened tension as Kurds fought for independence from Turkey, he had watched his mother die from starvation. In desperation, he left his wife of two years and baby son for work in the

73

Tuzla shipyard in Istanbul. His employer, a shipping agent, discovered he was Kurdish. Police threw him into prison for carrying forged identity papers. Three days later, government agents came for him.

They dragged him from his cell to a basement and lay him on a table the following day. His feet were tied to a wooden board suspended from the ceiling. With legs raised, the soles of his feet felt the full force of a flexible rubber hose for half an hour. His screams echoed off the walls and reverberated from the whitewashed ceiling.

Three years later, after a chance meeting with another inmate, Ekrem, in the courtyard, he found an escape route from his imprisonment. Ekrem was a captured member of PKK, the Kurdistan Workers Party, awaiting a trial. He talked freely about his family and his fight to create independence for the Kurds. A scared neighbour, hoping to escape arrest, had betrayed him. Ahmet saw an opportunity. By the time his conversation with Ekrem had finished, he knew the informer's name and where he lived.

A week later, he sat in the office of the Director of MIT, the Turkish National Intelligence Service, falsely accusing Ekrem's neighbour of terrorism. MIT rewarded him with freedom and recruited him to work in Istanbul as an informer on Greek business activities.

As a Kurd, Ahmet loathed his paymasters but looked forward to hurting his other traditional enemy, Greece. An advertisement in a newspaper for a senior shipping clerk led him to Nico Hrisacopolis' office in Istanbul with false references.

❖

Ahmet looked at his watch again. High up in the clear blue sky, a jetliner screamed in on its final approach to Ataturk Airport, sixteen miles to the west. He watched it pass behind minarets, standing like sentries across the city skyline. It eventually disappeared behind the large dome of a mosque. A hand touched his shoulder, and he jerked.

"Ahmet, did I catch you asleep?"

Eren grinned and sat in the chair opposite. Crossing his legs, he leaned back casually with one hand in a trouser pocket. Short black curly hair and large hazel eyes set into olive skin complemented a light grey suit and highly polished black leather shoes. He looked like one of the new wealthy young technocrats growing up in the world of future technologies, high fashion, and fast cars.

Ahmet surveyed his creation and smiled. The suit was perfect, and the image was complete. "You are late again."

"Only fifteen minutes. The suit was not ready. I had to wait." Eren

74

reached across the table and pulled the cream baba toward him. "Not hungry?" he asked, taking a bite out of the sweetmeat.

Ahmet glared at Eren.

"You want me to act like a westerner," retorted Eren, flicking a crumb from the sleeve of his jacket, "but how do I do that if I can't behave like one in front of you?"

Ahmet knew he was right. The new society suffered from the influence of western propaganda. Old values of loyalty and family respect were cast aside for the new materialistic world. Even so, bad manners were not acceptable in any society. Eren's grandfather would expect a well-mannered young man trained in all aspects of Greek culture and a graduate in business studies. That was what Pete had charged him to do, and he would expect nothing less.

"I won't let you down. Didn't I graduate well?"

Ahmet thought for a moment. "Have you been to church this week?"

Eren sighed with frustration.

A waiter came to the table, and Ahmet waved him away. He stared at Eren, eyebrows raised. "Well?"

"Not yet. I don't like it. My faith…"

Ahmed leaned forward and spoke in a whisper. "You know how important being familiar with the Greek Orthodox teachings and service is." He touched Eren's hand. He knew what the boy's Muslim faith meant to him and how hard it had been to accept his new role as 'Andreas Jnr.' The faith he felt inside was strong, and the Almighty knew it, Ahmet told him.

Eren beckoned for some tea. "I know."

Ahmet reassured him that when the time came, all of Turkey and their cousins in Cyprus would forgive any of his sins committed in the name of the cause.

Eren relaxed as the waiter poured the tea. "You think I'm ready, don't you?"

Ahmet took a small box from his jacket pocket and pushed it across the table. "Wear this at all times. It's your grandfather's signet ring. He wants you to wear it."

They both grinned. Ahmet reminded Eren that wearing the ring meant acceptance into the Hrisacopolis family.

Ahmet raised a finger and held it steady, pointed at Eren. He was not to allow new-found wealth to steer him away from his goal. He would also need to be cautious about women.

Eren touched the side of his nose. "I have never had trouble with women."

"You will if you get involved with a woman, especially a Greek woman."

Ahmet knew Pete wanted his grandson married by the time he was thirty-five. Another Hrisacopolis generation would keep the shipping empire intact. Eren had to resist the pressure at all costs. It was the only danger he faced.

"Is the *Sea Empress* still leaving London in three weeks?" Eren took another mouthful of the baba. Newspaper headlines stated that the British government was close to a decision over the marbles.

Ahmet reassured him. "The ship is leaving with the marbles aboard. As far as your worries are concerned you only need to know more about your parents and what appears in the press statement. Nothing must be leaked before your grandfather's announcement onboard the ship. At the press conference, you have to portray the image of a slightly bewildered man suddenly thrust into the limelight."

Eren nodded. "You will be aboard?"

"Yes, I will be right at your side but remember when the cruise ends, I will be back here, and you will be in Athens." He paused, seeing the worried look on Eren's face. "Is there anything wrong?"

"Not really. I keep wondering about my face, though."

"Don't," replied Ahmet.

Hrisacopolis knew his grandson had Turkish blood, and he expected some features of the mother in Eren's face. After having the nose cosmetically changed and a few other minor alterations would pass. He was Greek, and Nico Hrisacopolis would tell the press. Ahmet waved for lunch he'd ordered earlier.

He reached inside his jacket pocket for a handkerchief and felt the corner of the note he had been handed earlier by an agent from KKA. The message was not urgent, but the hidden warning was clear. Two British reporters were asking questions about Andreas. Nico had invited them on the cruise and granted them an exclusive interview with his grandson. The reaction was expected as he read it to Andreas.

Andreas looked startled. "No, you have to change that. What if they start digging into my past? I can't go through with that. I can't."

"You will do as you are told," snapped Ahmet.

Ahmet could hear the tension in Erens's voice, but there was too much at stake to pull out just because a couple of reporters wanted to question him. That's if they made the cruise anyway.

"What do you mean?" said Eren.

Ahmet shook his head. "Never mind, concentrate and focus on what I have taught you. I will be with you...."

The waiter arrived with some fried Borek and two glasses of water.

Ahmet picked up a fork and pierced the top of the flaky pastry.

Hot cheese oozed out. He bent over the dish and smelled the spicy aroma rising from the crust. Standing up, he repeated, "I will be with you at all times." He touched Eren's arm.

Hrisacopolis trusted him to accompany the grandson and ensure he didn't let the family down. Eren would be all right. He was a little nervous, but that was to be expected. Once he had met his 'grandfather,' he would be fine. With his background checked thoroughly, the name Hrisacopolis never appeared in medical or army personnel records. For the last three years, he'd lived in isolation, taught in business by private tuition, so no one in the city who knew him would recognize his picture in the newspapers after surgery.

"Come now, let's have lunch," coaxed Ahmet.

Eren snapped his fingers at the waiter and ordered.

As they sat eating, Ahmet contemplated his visit to Cyprus. He was wrong. The woman would be easier to deal with than Eren.

Chapter Fourteen

THE CLOCK ON THE WALL showed two-thirty. Max was still in a meeting, and raised voices indicated he was in full flow. Another ten minutes passed before the meeting came to an abrupt end. From behind the reeded glass panel in the office door, Jessica saw people rise, their chairs scraping on the floor. The door opened. Tired-looking staff and a cloud of smoke escaped into the passage.

"Jessica, sorry darling, come on in," shouted Max.

Jessica fanned her face with a hand and walked to the bookcase in one corner of the office where a fan stood idle on top of it. She turned it on and sat in front of it. "Smoking is your pleasure, Max, not mine. I have no wish to suffer from passive smoke."

Max pursed his lips, nodded, and said, "What can I do for you?"

"Pete has finished the articles, apart from a few finishing touches that need sorting out. You'll have them by the end of the week."

"That's wonderful. So where is Mr Angry?" Max looked toward the door and then back to her. He stubbed the cigarette out and coughed loudly, unable to smoke with the fan's turbulent draft aimed at him.

"Pete asked me to see you. He left earlier to pick up some airline tickets for Cyprus."

"What the hell. What's he up to now?"

"Pete tells me he hasn't had a break in a long time, and he's decided that as the articles are finished, he would take off for a while."

Max sat back in his chair with a worried look on his face. "Is he unwell? This isn't like Pete, you know." He chewed on his bottom lip for a moment, then suddenly slapped his forehead. "Has he been fishing around?"

"Sorry?"

"You know what I mean, Jessica. Has he been looking for another job? Because if he has, let me tell you, he'll be in bloody trouble. He owes this paper, in particular me."

"No, Max, he wants a break, and so do I. I haven't had a break in the last two years, apart from visiting my father on a couple of long weekends."

Max sighed. "Okay, okay, tell him to call the office and make the necessary arrangements. You do the same as long as you don't have anything pending. Have we got a stand-in for you?"

"Yes, Martha, my art assistant will be holding the fort."

"Right, well, have a nice break and give my regards to your father. He's living in Reims now, isn't he?" Max stood as Jessica made to leave.

"Oh, I'm not visiting father this time," she said. "I've decided to go a little further afield."

"Where are you going? Somewhere in the sun, no doubt."

"Cyprus."

"Cyprus?"

"Yes, Pete invited me along."

Max's mouth was wide open. "It won't work, darling. It won't work. I've known Pete a long time and know when he's up to something. So what are you two up to?"

"Nothing, Max. We are going on holiday together."

"You and Pete – I don't believe it. Pete's… well, Pete's…."

"Not my type? Not my class? Too old?" she snapped, one hand resting on a hip.

"I didn't mean anything, Jessica." Max held his hands up in apology. "It's just that Pete's been a confirmed bachelor for as long as I can remember. I'm surprised, that's all."

"You're assuming something is going on. Pete and I are really good friends." Her eyes were wide open with defiance, her breasts rising with emotion.

Max sat on the corner of the desk and ignored her comment. "Is this serious between you two?"

Jessica let the question hang in the air as she stepped to the door and opened it. Over her shoulder, she said, "Nothing is going on, Max." The door closed behind her.

Max shook his head and reached for a fresh cigar. "The hell there is, Jessica," he muttered, "just you make sure you bring that old Irish wolfhound back alive."

CHAPTER FIFTEEN

THE SHORELINE BOULEVARD of Paphos reminded me of other seaside towns I'd visited. Fast food franchises, souvenir kiosks, banks, estate agents, clothes shops, and travel agents all cluttered together in uninteresting little strips. Tourism was an essential income that kept the economy healthy.

We'd arrived three hours earlier at Larnaka airport. While we checked in at one of the more expensive hotels, the clerk informed us there wouldn't be any running water for twelve hours. I left a frustrated Jessica with the manager and took a stroll along the boulevard. I wanted to think.

We chose Paphos for a reason. The cove in which Stevenson and his men had ambushed Andreas showed up as a dot on the map a few miles to the north and could be reached by the road, followed by a two-mile hike. According to various press reports, Andreas operated in the island's northwest. It stood to reason that Lara must have come from the same area, with half a dozen or so thinly populated villages. Armed with just a name and a photo, I hoped we could track the girl or her family down. Jessica had made inquiries about Lara before we left London, but she found nothing. There had been no proper census records kept on the island before nineteen seventy-four.

I walked back to the hotel and made arrangements at reception to hire a car for the next day. It was eight p.m., and the heat made me tired. I wanted a shower, but it didn't look like I would get one unless the hotel had fixed the problem.

"Well, hello, stranger." Jessica appeared from the elevator as I entered the lobby. Slipping an arm through mine, she announced she had a surprise. We were on the top floor, and fabulous views were across the sea. Not only that, there was water. It came from a separate tank on the roof. She moved me away from the desk and whispered, "Actually, it's what they call the penthouse suite. I call it the pits, but at least we have water."

"You changed our rooms?"

"Yes, don't worry, I paid." She pushed the button to summon the elevator back. "There's only one small problem."

The elevator doors opened. "What's that?" I asked.

"There's only one bed." I turned as she pushed me into the elevator. "Sorry, but I must have water. Oh, and that's another thing," she said, absent-mindedly. "We have to conserve what water there is, so we'll bathe together. There's a Jacuzzi."

We travelled up in silence. I was too afraid to speak. The corners of Jessica's mouth twitched as she tried to control herself. I decided to act casually. I didn't want her to think I was expecting any extras if this was a joke.

The penthouse suite turned out to be three rooms A shower and toilet, a sparsely furnished lounge with three easy chairs, a sideboard with a built-in minibar, and a dining table straight out of the sixties. A queen-sized bed dominated the bedroom. In one corner stood a writing table and a couple of old chairs in another. Set into the floor near the balcony doors, a pink Jacuzzi looked out of place but a welcome sight.

Net curtains billowed into the room on a sea breeze that wafted through the open glass doors. White plastic furniture faced the Mediterranean, turning the water a deep blue under the almost set sun.

"Pour the water, Pete. The last one in is a sissy. Isn't that what you say?" Her voice came from the shower room.

"Yes." I was at the taps and turning them before she finished speaking. A small bottle of scented bath oil stood on the soap rack, and I poured the contents into the water. Undressing quickly, I threw my clothes on the bed and stepped into the bath with my socks on in my rush to seek refuge. Sitting back on the end of the bed and feeling bloody stupid, I pulled the socks off and threw them on the floor. I slipped under the bubbles a minute later, just before she appeared with a bottle and two glasses. Still, in her clothes, she ignored my predicament.

"I'm sure you and the wine are at room temperature by now." She chuckled.

My grin covered my embarrassment. "Well, at least I get to bathe first."

I felt humiliated that I'd not acted my age and she had shown me up. What had I promised myself in the lift? I should have known better and guess I got what I deserved.

"Pour the bloody wine before it gets hot," I said, flicking suds at her.

She giggled and put the wine and glasses on the edge of the Jacuzzi. "Just a second…."

She slipped out of her shoes and put one foot over the side of the Jacuzzi and into the water, followed by the other. Allowing her dress to billow about her as she lowered herself into the water, she sat next to me, our bare thighs touching. Our eyes met, and we laughed. As the laughter subsided, I grabbed her by the shoulders and pushed her down under the suds amid screams of protest. When she surfaced, her arms encircled my neck, and we kissed.

The spark of expectation smouldering all evening erupted into a fire. I peeled her wet dress up and over her shoulders and dropped it in a soggy heap on the floor. I ached from head to toe, unable to focus. I'd never experienced that before. Her breasts felt soft against my chest, and her lips hot. We caressed and kissed until her nails dug into my back, pulling me into her.

Later, after lying on the bed together in silence, she said, "Do you think I should call Max and let him know?" She recalled the holiday conversation with Max.

I rolled across the bed and gave her a playful slap. "Yeah, right, make his day."

She raised herself on an elbow and leaned over me, drawing a finger lightly down my chest. "You'll do for me, Pete. Whatever else, you have a big heart and a great sense of justice and that I like." As an afterthought, she said, "The sense of humour isn't too bad either."

Jessica didn't know it, but that was the best compliment any woman ever paid me. It showed how she felt. I kissed her and said, "I'm madly in love with you."

"I know." Shifting to her side, she said, "Let's just say we're really good friends for now, and you're on probation."

The old Ford Escort ran well enough. There being no air conditioning, we kept the windows right down. Jessica wore a long, loose red cotton dress, a pair of sandals, and RayBans. On the other hand, I cursed myself for failing to dress for the occasion. A pair of khaki shorts are great for walking but not for driving. It might have been September, but it's the second hottest month in Cyprus. My thighs were cooking on the hot plastic seat. I loosened several buttons on my shirt and adjusted the ball cap. Sunglasses shaded most of the sun, but my eyes were sensitive in bright light, a legacy from the fire.

Jessica looked down at an unfolded map across her lap. "Let me see now; she traced the road north to the Akamas Peninsula and the town of Polis. "Can we stop near Polis? She wanted to see Aphrodite's Baths, where Akamas, the son of Theseus, surprised the nude bathing Aphrodite when he saw her reflection in the water. She glanced sideways at me. "Please?"

Not wanting to disappoint her, I agreed, although the visit would have to be on the way back. Lara came first. I added, "Wasn't there an unhappy end to that love affair?"

"Yes, Aphrodite returned to her husband, the god Hephaistos." She squeezed my knee. "Did you know that you'll fall hopelessly in love if you drink from the spring that feeds the baths?"

I gave her a little nudge in the side. "Must have been some of that spring water in our Jacuzzi." I drew a deep breath. "In the meantime, where do we go from Polis?" The car lurched to one side as we hit a pothole. Jessica's map fell to the floor. The car juddered for a second, and the engine nearly died. "Bloody roads are useless, and this car isn't much better." I looked sideways, and our eyes met. I went back to complaining about the dust and drove on. Our route took us west of Polis to a village called Dyo Potamoi. Another three or four villages were located to the south.

Andreas operated mainly around Paphos to Polis and the coast near the British firing range. He smuggled arms and men right under the army's nose and moved them east through canyons and gullies into the Paphos Forest.

I hoped someone might recognize Lara and point out how we could find her. She didn't live in the area anymore. All the Turkish Cypriots had moved into the northern enclave after the invasion. The division line meandered between Kato Pyrgos in the west and Famagusta in the east and north.

We drove along the central road north, passing large green, orange, and lemon groves, each carefully tended tree heavy with fruit. Several miles further, we left the road and headed down a dusty track to Dyo Potamoi. The way ended in a square surrounded by dingy hut-like homes caked in whitewashed plaster. Most were windowless, the openings covered by slatted wooden shutters. All had flat roofs where lines of washing dried in minutes.

Further into the village, a long hitching rail, covered by a thatch roof of branches and long thick grass, provided shade for a line of silent donkeys standing with heads bowed. A teenage boy dressed in dirty shorts and a T-shirt sat under a eucalyptus tree in the middle of the square. He held onto a small donkey, its tail swishing the flies away at regular intervals.

The boy stared at us with large brown eyes. As we stopped the car and climbed out, I saw his feet. He wore a faded blue cord slipper on one foot and nothing on the other. I wiped beads of sweat from my eyes and forehead.

Jessica, fanning her face with the folded map, looked across at me. "Let me do the talking."

"He won't speak English," I said.

She walked over to the boy and said a few words. The boy got up and led the donkey away without saying a word while a dozen men appeared from behind some huts and stood in front of us. None of them smiled.

Jessica tried again, although I could sense the tension in her voice. "I want some information about a girl called Lara… She swallowed and started again. "We think she lived around here some time ago. Does anyone know of her?"

The circle around us parted, and a middle-aged man stood pointing a shotgun at us. I'm not a coward, but something about the barrel end of a gun makes me nervous. The man snarled something at us and gestured with the shotgun for us to go. I took a step back, pulling Jessica with me. The man continued shouting obscenities, I'm sure. He kept spitting on the ground.

Jessica spoke to him calmly, asking the same question. This time she tried in broken Turkish.

The reply got even louder. I grabbed her arm and pulled her back.

"Time to go… Let's get out of here," I said, taking another step back.

"Just a minute, Pete."

"No. Now." I wasn't arguing with her.

We walked back to the car with careful steps, followed at a distance by the small crowd led by the man with the gun. I crunched the vehicle into reverse gear, eased my foot on the accelerator, and drove out of the square to the track.

Jessica looked out at the crowd of men. "That was close," she breathed.

"Close? You could have got us shot." I drove forward in a cloud of dust, the car bouncing over the rough ground until we reached the track. The crowd disappeared from view in the driving mirror. "What the hell did the man say anyway? He knew her."

Jessica picked up her map and unfolded it. "Oh yes, he knew her."

I spotted an old man walking out onto the track about twenty yards ahead of us.

"Now what." I slammed the brakes on and stopped short, hoping he didn't have a gun.

"Calm down, Pete. He's just an old man."

"Oh, sorry, I didn't know there was an age limit on firing a gun. If he's got one – what are you going to do?"

"Got your red cape?"

The old man stepped up to Jessica's window. "Go to Bellapais and ask for the whore Jamilya. She can tell you about Lara." He held a leathery hand out for the customary gift, and Jessica reached for her purse.

"Can you tell us where Lara is?" I asked.

He waved us away. "You must go now."

"Bellapais is on the map. I saw it earlier," said Jessica. "it's south of Kyrenia. You were right. This is the area she came from." She looked at her watch. "Thirteen-thirty, time for lunch."

"Okay, lunch it is," I answered. "We'll look for Bellapais tomorrow. At least we've found someone who knew Lara. Now, lead me to the place of gods and lovers."

Chapter Sixteen

A Volvo cruised along the Athens coastal highway. Rays of the setting sun glinted off the car's windshield as it turned a bend. Just a quarter mile out, off the coast and bathed in an incandescent orange, the island of Salamis came into view. In the half-light, a couple of small fishing boats were on their way back to the harbour, followed in their wake by a swarm of noisy gulls. In the distance, the late afternoon lights of Megara twinkled against a hazy blue sky.

Constantine Demetrios was a big man. Cramped in the front seat, the heat made him uncomfortable. His hairy arms glistened, and his shirt stuck to his back. His partner, Stavros, a smaller man of stocky build, sat with his eyes closed.

"Megara coming up."

Stavros adjusted his seat position with closed eyes. "We'll be there in an hour."

"Are you sure you have all you need?" Demetrios looked sideways, nervously.

"Yes. I think so." Stavros opened his eyes and began to issue a deep guttural laugh. "You think I need advice from you?" He rubbed the stubble on his chin and yawned.

Demetrios felt his stomach knot. As he had many times, he wished he'd refused the money. But he knew that he had no choice. His own life would have been in danger. "I didn't mean that."

"You just worry about getting me there and getting me away when the job is done. I'll take care of the business." Stavros grinned.

Demetrios shivered. He licked the perspiration from the top of his lip and drove on in silence. Minutes later, Stavros began to snore.

Italianate balconies, adorned with flowers, hung over either side of the narrow, cobbled street, filling the air with a heavy scent. Several small, terraced home windows glowed with a dull light from within. Music accompanied by loud clapping and raised party voices drifted out into the street from an open doorway.

Demetrios cut the car's engine and glided into the dark space beneath the last balcony. Ahead of them, another street led off to the right. "The apartment is over there," he whispered.

Stavros finished pulling on his gloves and picked up the length of rope and green canvas bag between his feet before carefully opening the door. Both men stood for a moment, looking in both directions along the street before carefully closing the doors with a soft click. Demetrios walked a few feet ahead of Stavros, both men striding silently in soft trainers as they crossed to the other side of the street and turned right at the junction.

They knew Alexander left his studio each night and went to the bar in the town square. Between eight and nine, he returned, normally drunk.

Demetrios' breath came in short nervous gasps as they reached a crossroad. All he had to do was place the bag over Alexander's head and help tie him up.

They walked on in silence until they reached a small block of four apartments and stopped. The block was an old three-story building, the bottom level being two basements that were once garages but now turned into studios. Both were reached by a cracked concrete slope covered with weeds. Set into the white flaking walls were two old wooden double doors. Alexander had the bottom apartment on the left and used his basement for painting.

Both men moved quickly and descended the slope through long shadows cast by another block of apartments next door. Reaching the double door, they stopped, both breathing heavily. Demetrios licked his lips. His mouth was dry. He looked back up the slope and then at Stavros. His stomach was churning. A strip of light shone from under the door, and he could hear someone inside. Nodding to Stavros, he knocked twice.

"What? Who's that?" a gruff voice bellowed.

Demetrious knocked again, louder.

"Just a minute." The sound of a piece of furniture falling over-filtered through the door. "What the hell do you want?" The voice was slurred. The door opened, and Alexander's face appeared, red hair tangled in front of his eyes. "Who are you?"

"Alexander Gravari?"

"Yes."

Stavros pushed the door back with force, throwing Alexander off balance. The instant he hit the floor, Stavros slapped a piece of duct tape over the big man's mouth, and Demetrios placed the bag over his head. While Stavros pinned the man's arms from behind, Demetrious bound the wrists tightly with the rope before paying attention to the legs. Thrashing wildly, one of Alexander's legs caught Stavros a vicious blow to the chest, winding him. Cursing, Stavros released his hold and stood to gain his breath. Demetrious had secured the big man's arms and legs in less than a minute. He lay helpless on the ground, struggling against the ties.

Stavros turned to Demetrios and ordered him to trash the apartment. It didn't take long to overturn the table and throw paintings on the floor and all the other painting materials lying around on the workbench. Demetrios stepped over to the door without a backward glance when he finished.

"And now, you pig, you will pay for insulting the Hrisacopolis name." Stavros pulled him along the floor and sat him on a chair. He took a long-handled razor from his pocket and pulled the hood up enough to expose Gravari's throat.

———◆○◆———

Nico Hrisacopolis sat by the side of the pool, eating from a fruit breakfast. A cigar lay in an ashtray, smoke spiralling into a clear sky. Although seven-thirty a.m., the temperature gauge on the wall showed seventy-five degrees. The Doberman, half asleep in the shade of the awning, panted in time to his chest's rhythmic rise and fall. Hrisacopolis opened his newspaper and scanned the headlines in the business section.

He snatched at the phone the instant it rang. "Yes."

"Pete, it's Alain Boutin."

Pete reached for the cigar and drew on it until it glowed red. Boutin was one of twelve EU members of parliament representing France within Brussels. "How's the weather in Brussels?"

"It's raining."

"Isn't it always? You're up early. You work too hard," said Nico. "Take a break and come out here. The sun will do you good. Bring your beautiful wife as well." He paused. Alain's voice merged into the sound of heavy traffic. Irritated, Nico shook the receiver. "Alain?"

"Yes, Pete, that would be nice. I'm staying in Brussels this week while the House is in session, but I'll give Aurelia your kind invitation when I get back home."

Nico blew smoke and coughed. He knew he had the man where he wanted him, although it would cost. Alain's vote and half a dozen others would secure his seat and Chairmanship on the Agriculture and Fisheries Committee. A veiled threat and money would seal the deal. "Breakfast with your young man then… while you're in town… I've forgotten his name, Eugene, isn't it?"

Boutin ignored the remark that reminded him how vulnerable he would be if Nico didn't get what he wanted. A male prostitute scandal two years earlier nearly ruined his career.

He came straight to the point. The size of Nico's donation to the Montpellier Art Foundation was very generous, particularly if given as an annual gift. However, there were expenses for travelling and accommodation while entertaining and arranging exhibitions; very hard to fund on a limited budget, explained Alain. He sounded worried.

Nico thought for a moment. The man was greedy, but then all the politicians he knew were greedy. It needed to be an amount that bought total loyalty. He couldn't take a chance on the man having second thoughts. "Shall we say half a million?"

"Francs?"

"Dollars."

"Perhaps an advance?"

"Total amount paid into any account tomorrow."

There was a moment's silence, then, "Pardon?"

"Renewable on the same date next year." Nico grinned, then added before Alain could answer, "An annual payment, Alain."

"You will have my vote, Nico."

"On all decisions except those we agree you can disagree on. We don't want anyone getting the wrong idea, do we?"

"Certainly not," replied Alain. "What of the others?"

"There are no others, Alain. There will never be any others. There is only you."

"I understand."

"Do you? If there is any misunderstanding, I want to clear it up now. I would hate to have to remind you." Nico waited for confirmation.

"I understand, Nico."

Nico sighed. One slip, and there would be a disaster. No information about him could be on Alain's computer or any personal notes either at home or at work, nothing to connect them except official EU business. While Boutin was apologizing, an idea occurred to him. Boutin could start earning his money. A Turkish delegate elect was overseeing arrangements for meetings the following month between the Turkish Minister of Trade and his British and French counterparts.

"Mustafa Hamit," said Alain.

"Do you know him well?" asked Nico.

"Yes."

Nico thought for a moment. Suppose Boutin could find an excuse to engage the man in conversation relating to the talks. In that case, he could let it slip that he'd heard a rumour that Hrisacopolis Industries were looking at taking over the Famagusta container complex on Cyprus.

"The British would love that," replied Alain.

Nico agreed. If the British influenced other members to go for the plan, the Greeks' objections to farm subsidies would end.

Nico hung up. The first fish hooked into the net, and soon more would follow. He dialled his office and waited as his housekeeper appeared from the villa and walked towards him with a tray. He looked at her and scowled. "Did I say I'd finished?"

"It's getting hot," she replied.

"I know it's getting hot. I don't need you to tell me."

A voice answered in his ear. "No, not you, stupid," he shouted into the phone. "Idiots surround me. I was talking to my housekeeper." He waved the housekeeper away angrily. "Nana, are there any messages for me?"

"Just two, Sir. A message from someone called Stavros. He sent his respects and asked that thanks be passed on to you for the flowers you sent to his brother's funeral."

Hrisacopolis tapped the cigar. "And the other message?"

"From the police, Sir. I'm afraid it's bad news."

"Spit it out."

"It's one of your chauffeurs, Sir, Constantine Demetrios. He drove your limousine late last night and crashed on the city's outskirts along the coast highway."

"Much damage to the car?"

"It's a write-off. The car went over the cliff." A faint tremor sounded in her voice. "Sir, I'm afraid your driver died in the accident. The police say he smelled of alcohol."

"Damn fool. All right, Nana. Make sure we pay funeral expenses and give his widow a year's salary."

"Yes, Sir. One last thing about the two reporters you asked me to invite on the cruise from London."

"What of them?"

"I called their office yesterday. They're on vacation."

"So?"

"On Cyprus."

Pete threw the cigar into the pool. "Call Koskotas and let him know. Do it right away. Tell him to look our friends up and find out what they are up to."

"Do you want me to cancel their invitation?"

"No."

Pete rose from the chair and called another number. "Be there, you stupid…" he spoke under his breath. "Oh, yes, is Ahmet there." He waited for what seemed an eternity. "Ahmet, I have a little more work for you."

He puffed on the cigar as he spoke. After finishing the conversation, he slumped back down into the chair. He was exhausted.

Being able to pull Boutin's strings made him feel better.

CHAPTER SEVENTEEN

CYPRUS IS A BEAUTIFUL ISLAND but travelling a long distance in a car on a hot day is no treat, especially when there's no air conditioning. There's one main crossing point into the north, and that's in Nicosia at the Ledra Palace.

We left the hotel early, windows rolled down, and we were on our way to Bellapais to try and find Lara's friend, Jamilya. After travelling along the coast for a few miles, we passed Limassol and turned onto the main highway going north.

I planned to get to Bellapais as soon as possible, but Jessica insisted we have a quick lunch on the way before we entered the north. Turkish cuisine did not suit her palate.

"I guess so," I'd answered. "Did you know there's a McDonald's in?"

"No, Pete," she'd retorted, nose in the air.

Jessica went through notes from our previous day's experience as we drove along the highway. She'd written them onto a large pad. According to her translation, the man with the shotgun had bad-mouthed Lara, calling her a 'lady of loose morals.' I accepted her version but knew the man had said something far worse.

Jessica pushed the sunglasses up the bridge of her nose and turned back to her notes. "I expect that's why all the men in the village knew her – or maybe they were just branding her for another reason," she said, more to herself than to me.

A blast of hot air filled the car as a large, covered truck passed us, going the other way. The rush of air brought with it a cloud of swirling dust that blew across my face and settled in my hair. I shook my head and brushed the front of my shirt. Dust was everywhere.

Jessica covered her mouth with a hand and wrinkled her nose at me. She waved the other hand to get me to slow down as we passed an old woman riding a donkey. Large net bags loaded with oranges hung from either side of the animal. Jessica pulled her camera from a bag between her feet and took several shots with practised ease. We continued driving.

Returning to her notes, she asked, "So what of Lara? Do you think she was...? And what about Andreas?"

I shook my head, reading her mind. I explained. If Andreas and Lara were having an affair, they would have broken all social and religious protocols. Her family would have beaten her and disowned her. I hoped for her sake Lara had kept her secret after Andreas died. "I hope she's okay," I muttered.

"Well, look who's got a warm heart?" Jessica patted my knee. She changed the subject. "Have you found out any more about how the marbles will be packed?"

"Some," I said. The marbles needed to be packed and stored safely, their recovery guaranteed if the ship sank. They would be waterproofed, and I was pretty sure some compressed air device would aid them back to the Mediterranean's surface. I still had to make enquiries. I'd thought she might have got onto that.

"I guess you've been on my mind too much lately," I said truthfully.

"Pete, that's feeble." She slapped my arm and gave a short husky laugh.

<hr>

After lunch, we called in at the checkpoint, filled out forms for a pass and were soon through and into the Turkish sector heading north.

Bellapais village overlooks the sea and stands on a sloping terrace a couple of miles inland. To the East, there's a long ravine. Apart from that, the place is pretty spartan.

The natural attraction is the Gothic abbey that stands to the north end of the village. Tourists flock here to join guided tours, armed with a camera and a wallet full of money that's quick to disappear in the tacky souvenir shops and small eateries.

"Where are we going to start?" asked Jessica, stepping out of the car.

I slammed the door behind me and looked around. From the lines of tables and chairs outside the tea house, hundreds of male eyes turned to look at us – actually, Jessica. Small groups of men in doorways stopped talking and stared. If Jessica was worried, she didn't show it.

"I suppose we should make for the dingiest part of town. It would be better if I asked women, although I'll probably get some odd stares."

Jessica shrugged. "I'll ask."

"That could be worse." I imagined the response if she started doing that.

"What about asking a policeman?"

"No, the last thing we do is talk to a man. How about a waitress or shopkeeper?"

The small restaurant we found was full of tourists. Fighting our way through the souvenir festooned frontage, we found an empty table next to a hoard of loud Germans.

There were several waitresses, and our one spoke passable English. After ordering coffee, Jessica asked her about Jamilya. The girl shook her head and replied that her mother, the owner, might know.

With that, she disappeared with our order.

A minute later, a woman with prominent black eyebrows and a remarkable hairy top lip hunched over us and laid both huge hands flat on the dirty wooden table. A bundle of greying hair was tied in a bun, and her grubby black dress stank of grease. The once white apron was marked with a variety of stains.

The woman smiled, showing a row of yellowed teeth. "You want… Jamilya." She waved a finger between the photo, me, and her eyes as she made sure I understood her broken English. "I know you want… see… her." She was looking at the photo and nodding slowly.

"You know her name?" I reached for my wallet, opening it to show my press ID.

Her outstretched hand hovered over my wallet. She nodded again and clicked her fingers.

Jessica was looking out of the window, trying not to laugh. She wasn't trying too hard.

"English pound is okay. Twenty for me… twenty for Ester… son. He will take you… see Jamilya."

I winked, and the smile widened. Her hand remained poised to grab while Lara's photo lay on the table. "You know Lara too?"

I felt conned but pulled the money out. The woman's grubby hand took it, sifted it, and deposited it into the apron pocket with practised ease.

"Lara, yes. She is a good friend… Jamilya."

"Does Lara still live here?"

The woman's smile vanished. "Jamilya?" There followed more hand waving. "She tells you what you want." Her bushy eyebrows rose up and down, and her eyes had a suggestive glint in them. "Everyone know Jamilya. Ester takes you. I fetch him."

She bustled away into the kitchen. Her voice boomed out in Turkish above the general hubbub.

I turned to Jessica and whispered, "If I were him, I'd run. She looks like the cook from hell."

Jessica smothered a laugh. Ester appeared from the kitchen. He didn't say anything, but there was the faintest hint of a sneer as he passed us.

The woman stood in the opening to the kitchen, her hands on hips, indicating we should follow with a slight nod of the head.

"Thank you," I murmured. Jessica and I rose together.

I followed Jessica through the drab tables, pleased we did not have to eat lunch there.

Outside, Ester headed up the street quickly, dodging between tourists and baskets of produce stacked on the pavement. I pulled Jessica by the hand, and half trotted to catch up. "Stay close. You need to keep your eyes open," I said, breathing heavily. I gripped her hand. We were leaving the tourist area for the darker side of town, and I wasn't too keen about Jessica being there. After turning the next corner, my fears were confirmed when we caught up with Ester.

Chapter Eighteen

THE VEINS STOOD OUT on Hrisacopolis' neck. Midday at the villa was not the best time to hear bad news. The journalists from The Herald had been on the island for two days, and he knew nothing of it. For over forty years, information of that kind flowed into the Athens office through Ioannis' journalists at the Cypriot Times.

Nico banged the arm of his recliner and threw his cigar into the pool. He shifted the receiver from one hand to the other and gritted his teeth. "You are the embodiment of stupidity."

Ioannis answered calmly. "Nico, if you're going to shout down the phone, I'll hang up. I don't have to put up with this. They left word with the hotel they were going to Bellapais. Anyone going into the Turkish zone has to inform the hotel. The curfew-"

Nico cut him off impatiently. "Yes, yes, Bellapais, you say... They're looking for Lara?" He wiped a handkerchief across the back of his neck. The heat was unbearable.

"They asked about her."

"Well, they won't find the bitch, will they?" growled Nico.

"No, but supposing they find Lara's friend... the woman Jamilya, just by asking about Lara?"

"Ahmet is there to tidy up."

Ioannis paused before answering. "Yes. He's going to be here tomorrow. I got the message from Athens."

"What. And those two are there already. You make sure Ahmet is picked up from the plane, or I'll close that miserable paper of yours down."

"Nico, don't threaten me. I don't live out of your pocket."

Nico ignored the remark. "Make sure Ahmet is on the next flight out of Istanbul.

Tell him he's to catch the flight for Ercan."

"Ahmet is getting old," said Ioannis calmly, "do you think he's still capable?"

"Ahmet knows the island like the back of his hand," said Nico, "you don't have to worry about him. He'll be very efficient as far as his assignment goes, unlike the one I had to rescue you from."

The line went dead.

Ioannis slapped the phone back into its cradle. Nico couldn't resist reminding him every time there were sharp words between them. Nico's arrogance and the big dream was going to be his downfall. He sat for a moment and then picked the phone up.

Dialling Ahmet's number, he wondered how even Ahmet could have stayed so loyal. Ahmet answered almost at once.

"Ioannis?"

"Yes, are you ready? Nico is getting impatient?"

"Yes. I'll be on the plane tonight. I wanted to make sure she was still where I put her. I should have dealt with this a long time ago."

CHAPTER NINETEEN

THE MIXED AROMA of strong Gauloises cigarettes, alcohol and hot food hung in the air outside the Café ParLaran, an old building in the west corner of place Sadi-Carnot. Its faded green woodwork was bathed in bright sunlight. In front of the old façade, several old men sat at small red and white check covered tables, playing cards while onlookers, mostly locals, sat sipping beer. Inside the smoke-filled cafe, a chess game was in progress, both the players engrossed in stratagem. Despite the loud idle chatter, the players seemed unperturbed.

A little silver-haired man dressed in a grey suit sat across the table from Adonis, frustrated by the chess players' moves. His white eyebrows rose and fell while a low hiss escaped his parted lips. Now and again, he crossed or uncrossed his legs.

Adonis looked at his watch for a second time. Gerard, the Turk's lieutenant, had arranged for a ten o'clock pick up at the cafe. Gerard was to arrive by taxi and take him to the Hotel Concorde, a pension hotel situated on the beachfront at the edge of the city's tourist sector. It was 9.57 am.

Absorbed in watching the square outside, Adonis was unaware that the little man had stood up to face him. He brushed the creases from the front of his trousers and then pulled the corners of his jacket down with a sharp tug. His voice broke Adonis's concentration. "Monsieur," he said congenially, "I'm Pierre - perhaps you would like me to take you to your appointment?"

Adonis's eyes flickered back to find the man standing over him, indicating the entrance behind them with an open hand. "Pierre who? Where's Gerard?" The man seemed amiable enough, but Adonis objected to the open hand.

"My name is not important, Monsieur… certainly not as important as yours. Gerard, you will meet later." He bowed very slightly with both hands by his side. "Now, perhaps you would allow me." He stepped forward and past Adonis, making his way toward the door. Without replying, Adonis picked up his case and followed Pierre out of the café just as a taxi pulled into the curb. The driver beckoned both men into the taxi.

Driving out of the square, Adonis realised they were travelling in the opposite direction, away from the Hotel Concorde. "We are not going to the Hotel Concorde?" Adonis asked.

The driver gave him a long stare in the driving mirror before shaking his head. Pierre said nothing. The taxi sped along Rue Colbert and into Cours Belsunce. Within minutes they were on the Rue de Rome and headed towards the city suburbs. Adonis tried to remember some of the buildings as they flashed past. He was now concerned.

Death would come eventually but not at the hands of the Turk. A debt owed to his mother remained unpaid. His mouth twitched as he recalled the bloody knife, the letter, and the promise he made to himself. Pierre broke into his thoughts.

"Don't worry, Adonis, the Turk always keeps his word, so long as you keep yours," he said. "Do you have the money with you?"

"Yes, I have it here." Adonis tightened his grip on the small attaché balanced on his knees.

"Then I suggest you let me have it." Pierre's eyes darted to the driver, who nodded. Adonis caught the exchange and let his fingers relax. Pierre slid the case to his lap, opened it and checked the contents. A few seconds later, he looked up and nodded toward the driver.

The taxi swerved around several corners into a dilapidated housing estate and pulled up next to a derelict parking lot. A man waved to the driver from a balcony on the third floor of one of the blocks of dingy apartments. Adonis followed the two men into the stairway and up to the apartment. The foul stench of urine on the concrete landing caught in Adonis's throat.

Stepping through the open door, Adonis found himself looking at the same bald thug who was at the first meeting. He held his arms aloft.

"That won't be necessary today," called the Turk. "Come through and let us talk."

Adonis passed the thug and walked into a sparsely furnished living room. Like the cellar where the first meeting took place, a desk and two chairs sat in the middle of a bare wooden floor. A thin spiral of smoke from a recently stubbed out cigarette rose from an ashtray on the corner of the desk. A thicker cloud swirled across the room toward yellowed net curtains covering the opened window.

"Cognac, Cypriot. Let us drink to the successful outcome of our joint venture." The Turk was sitting at the desk, holding up a bottle of cognac. Pointing to a magazine lying on the table, he announced he had been reading about the marbles and wanted to know how Adonis would steal the priceless Frieze. "I want to know how you, a mere little Turkish gigolo, intend to take this great prize from Hrisacopolis." His guttural laugh boomed around the empty room.

Adonis sat across from the Turk, picked up a glass, and held it out. The Turk had been investigating him. It was to be expected. So were taunts. Swapping insults would be easy, but he needed to stay focused. He raised the glass as though toasting the Turk. A grin froze on his face long enough to imply disrespect, but he said nothing.

Behind him, the thug, dressed in a dirty T-shirt, raised a hairy arm, ready to strike. Adonis wrinkled his nose as body odour filled his nostrils.

"No." The Turk waved the thug away and pointed a finger at Adonis. "I said you had balls, and I was right. I admire that, Cypriot, but don't test me."

Adonis let the remark pass. "If we're to work together," he replied, "then the least you can do is lose the violence." He swallowed the cognac in one gulp and held the glass out for more.

The Turk filled the raised glass while making it clear before they got down to business, there had to be an understanding about the operation. "My men are to remain under my control at all times." He shifted and leaned forward, one hand tapping his chest. "You send orders through me… understand?"

Adonis agreed with a shrug if only to please the man. There wasn't any point in arguing about who would give orders. "I agree." He held up a hand.

The Turk was a cautious man, and that was good. Adonis looked around the room at Pierre, sitting in one corner and the thug hovering over him, arms folded. "Perhaps it might be a good idea to talk in private. You can tell your men only what they need to know."

The Turk smiled. "Okay." He looked up but said nothing. The room emptied, and when they were alone, he said, "Have you got the market you spoke of for the marbles?"

"I have an interested party… But first the business at hand," Adonis said, picking up the attaché case. He pulled out some drawings from beneath the money and spread a chart of the Mediterranean and a cross-section sketch of the ship over the table. The *Sea Empress*, he explained, would leave London in two weeks. Hrisacopolis and an assortment of lackeys, politicians and a clutch of dignitaries would be aboard.

The Turk's finger traced the cross-section of the ship and stopped midway between the bridge and the bow. "This is a cargo area where the marbles will be stored." It was more of a statement than a question. Adonis remained silent. The Turk growled, "How will we move these marbles into our boats?" Irritated, he waved a hand across the drawings. He glared at Adonis and thumped the desk with a fist. "You didn't think about that, Cypriot. We can't drop them down into the boats, and we can't take the time to lower them on a derrick. That's if we can get them to the ship's rail." He studied the drawing and shook his head. "Impossible."

"We won't have to take them to the rail," answered Adonis. He paused and sipped cognac. He avoided the Turk's eyes, "The marbles will be in storage. There are double-loading doors on either side of the hull to access stores and baggage. Your men will throw the marbles into the sea from there unless the stones are stored somewhere that has easier access to the sea."

"The sea?"

Adonis ignored the remark as the Turk poured more cognac. "This," explained Adonis, tapping the chart, "is the course of the *Sea Empress*."

Two days after leaving London, Cadiz was the first port of call. Then a short stop to take on more guests and hold a dinner hosted by the Spanish President. The ship sailed through the Strait of Gibraltar and made her way to an anchorage off Nice the following day. She would stay for two nights. A banquet planned for the second night in honour of the British, French, and Spanish ambassadors to Greece highlighted the purpose of the cruise. All ambassadors attending were supposed to have been influential in having the British return the marbles. The Greek ambassador to London was the principal guest.

"Four ambassadors." The Turk rubbed his chin. "Are they staying on board?"

"Why, is that a problem for you?"

"Of course not." There was a quick chuckle. "You better be right about this, Cypriot, or my knife will cut off your balls."

"You are worried about my plan?"

The Turk was silent for a moment, observing him through half-closed eyelids. "The only thing that worries me is your planning," he hissed.

Adonis thought of nothing but the plan. The itinerary for the cruise and the guests attending had been widely advertised in the media. He looked down at the chart. "There is nothing wrong with the plan. There will be at least twenty bodyguards plus more with Hrisacopolis. I want you to have enough men to take care of them."

"You bastard, Cypriot." the Turk exploded. "You think you are better than me? You think you can tell me what I need to do the job?" He grabbed Adonis around the throat and pulled him halfway across the desk. "Maybe, little Cypriot, you should show more respect," he snarled.

Their noses touched, and Adonis smelled cognac and strong cigarettes on the man's breath. "I have planned very carefully," he gasped. "How will you know how many men you want unless you know how much security there is?"

The Turk rose and threw Adonis back into his chair. He walked to the window and looked down at the parking lot. "Perhaps it might be better to take the ship before it reaches Nice."

Adonis straightened his shirt and swallowed hard. "No," he insisted, "I need the ambassadors' on board the ship before we take over."

The following day, the ship arrived in Naples and entertained the Italian Prime Minister at a formal dinner party in the evening. Then it began its final leg of the cruise, south to Sicily, through the Malta Channel, and then Athens.

"I take it you plan to move somewhere between the Malta Channel and Crete?" The Turk was poring over the chart.

"Exactly." Adonis disliked the Turk but respected the man's maritime knowledge.

"The water is deep. How do we retrieve the marbles?"

"That's the easiest part. Let's concentrate on taking the ship first." Adonis unfolded another chart showing the layout of the ship's decks and storage areas. He ran his fingers over the chart, deep in thought. He had studied Hrisacopolis and his life as well as his business interests and had committed everything to memory. The man was part of his daily diet. "We will need more men than I originally asked for."

"That is not a problem." The Turk lit a Gauloises and tapped the chart. "And so?"

"I estimate there should be a hundred crew, perhaps another fifty men on security. Your men will already be on board."

"How?"

"Details later," replied Adonis.

"Okay, so I have two of my men on board." The Turk sat down, his face expressionless. "What next?"

"What happens next depends on whether you have managed to secure two fast cruisers. Getting the two men on board is going to be the hardest part. Getting the rest of you on is simple."

The Turk had two cruisers moored in Nice, and the contact wanted money.

"That's not a problem. I'll have the money tomorrow." Adonis turned his nose up at the dirty apartment. "Your man can pick it up from me in the Café ParLaran. I don't care to come back here."

"I don't suppose you do." The Turk grinned broadly, showing a row of nicotine-stained teeth.

Adonis ignored him. "You will have the cruisers moved to Mgarr Harbour on the island of Gozo. Do you know where that is?"

"Of course I do. It's northwest of Malta." The Turk tapped the side of his nose. "Two strange foreign cruisers, each towing a large inflatable and over twenty men on board, will look very suspicious. Tongues will wag on the island, my friend."

"No, I doubt it. Not on Gozo," replied Adonis.

Careful planning, double-checking and several exploratory trips to Malta and Gozo in the last month had got him this far. Adonis knew as long as the Turk had two men aboard the ship in Naples, nothing could go wrong. Now he was ready to move to Malta.

Adonis reassured the Turk that the cover story was plausible. They were wreck salvage experts if anyone asked. There was prepared paperwork that would satisfy any local authority. Gozo was a quiet place. As for the men, not all of them had to be there until the day before they sailed.

The Turk looked at the ship's layout. "The two men aboard the ship will open one of these store's doors you spoke of?"

CHAPTER TWENTY

"I'M WORRIED, PETE."
I felt uncomfortable too. We'd followed the lad into the Turkish downtown area: a place for locals, away from the tourists and commercialised false rural charm. The narrow, cobbled passage we entered was in shadow from the overhanging balconies. Wash on rope lines hung across the void like dozens of multi-coloured garlands, only they weren't garlands, but tattered T-shirts, jeans, sheets, socks, and God knows what else. Little side passages branched off every so often, and each offered its view of crumbling walls in this decaying place where time had stood still. Hanging in the air was the pungent odour of Turkish cuisine mixed with foul raw sewage. Add to that the constant jangle of Turkish music bouncing off the walls, and you understand why guided tours were not on offer.

But it wasn't any of this that bothered us. It was the silent observers from behind small windows half-hidden by darkness: the balconies where women stood with crossed arms and from doorways where small clusters of men huddled, with eyes fixed upon us. It was an unsettling feeling, and I was worried for Jessica.

I kept a hand on her wrist. "I think I'll pass on the visit to the market."

"Don't joke, Pete." She stumbled on the cobble stones and stooped to adjust her sandal strap. "Let's get on. This place is awful."

The lad suddenly stopped and pointed into a dingy side passage. "You there," he said sullenly. With that, he held out a dirty hand.

"Where?" I asked. The passage, unlike all the others we walked down, was deserted.

"You there," he repeated. He looked at Jessica. "Dogru gidin. Solda in yaninda firin."

"Straight ahead. On the left next to the bakery," interpreted Jessica. "Thank you." She gave the boy a ten-dollar bill.

"I've already paid," I protested.

"He won't see anything from his mother. Anyway, I liked him."

I might have guessed. "Okay, let's get away from here and find Jamilya."

We walked along the street and found the bakery. Either side of it was doorways leading into small living quarters. I knocked at the first door several times but got no response. From the second door came a very positive reaction the moment I knocked.

"Gheet."

In any language, I know when someone tells me politely to go away. I ignored the request and knocked again.

Jessica called her name. "Jamilya?"

After a moment of silence, a bolt slid back. Jessica nervously jumped. The door opened a crack and the outline of a woman's face, cloaked in a headscarf, appeared from the gloom. "You are English?" The voice was old but softly spoken.

"Yes," I replied. "You speak good English."

Slender fingers pulled nervously at the edges of the scarf, tightening the cotton border around the face. "What do you want?"

Jessica spoke slowly. "We came to speak with you, Jamilya, about your friend Lara."

There was a low but audible gasp. "Please go away. There is nothing to discuss." She turned away.

"Jamilya," I said, "we need information about Lara." I decided to play my ace card, relying on her awareness of Lara's romance. "We want to expose Nico Hrisacopolis before he causes more trouble for this island."

The door opened. Two eyes, set in a face that flashed with anger opened wide. She hesitated for a moment, eyes focused past us along the passage, and then beckoned us to enter.

The room was small but colourful. Large white and gold cushions covered with woollen drapes of all shapes and sizes lay scattered around the floor. The walls were covered with an array of Turkish tapestry, mainly geometrical in design and full of vibrant colours. In one corner of the room was a single mattress. Apart from that, there was no other furniture. A beaded curtain covered an archway that presumably accessed the kitchen and bathroom.

"Please be seated."

I hadn't noticed until then that Jamilya walked with a noticeable limp. She wore a simple knee-length black dress and black woollen stockings. The black headscarf knotted under her chin looked frayed, and on her feet, she wore a pair of sandals that had seen better days. Of medium height and weight, her deeply tanned face was weathered, making her seem older than she was. The most noticeable feature was a disfigured nose, probably broken. It had set wrong in an awkward position, bending slightly to the right. I felt sorry for her.

"I cannot tell you much," she said. She sat cross-legged on the mattress with her hands in her lap. Her head bowed; she gave the impression she was a woman too scared to talk. I wouldn't have put it past Pete Hrisacopolis to have threatened her. Yet her initial reaction on hearing Pete's name and the invitation to join her meant her dislike of the man might overcome the reluctance to talk. I was hoping.

"We need to know what happened to Lara," said Jessica. "Tell me about her and how things were back when you lived in the South."

Jamilya nodded slowly. "Are you going to put this in a newspaper?" she asked. "No one must know. They would kill me." She was hesitant.

Jessica and I exchanged glances. I was right. The bastard had worked his evil influence. He could even reach inside his enemy's castle.

"No one will ever know you said a word, I promise you." Jessica reached out and placed a hand over Jamilya's. "We know you were mistreated. Help us to punish him."

Jamilya breathed deeply. Slowly, she said, almost in a whisper, "Things were never good between the Greeks and my people, but we lived side by side, and my family worked the land. My father and mother had some goats and a small piece of land. They were content."

"You shared secrets too?"

Jamilya looked confused.

"You talked about boys?"

Jamilya turned to face Jessica. "Oh yes."

"When did you know about Andreas?"

"The day that Lara met him. That was the day we broke our friendship."

"What happened?"

"I was ill and stayed at home that day. Lara saw me that evening. She was very excited and couldn't wait to tell me she had met a man. He'd spent the night in her father's small donkey stable near the coast. They talked, and she'd fallen in love with him."

"I was excited for her," explained Jamilya. "All girls want a husband."

"Why did he spend the night in the stable?" asked Jessica.

"He told Lara he was hiding from the British," she said. She paused and looked first at Jessica, then me.

107

I listened with interest. Jamilya was upset when Lara told her the man was a Greek and tried to explain that it was a love her friend couldn't have. This man was fighting Turks as well as the British. Lara became angry with her and accused her of being jealous. Jamilya tried to tell her that if her parents found out, they would be disgraced and punish her by beating her, but Lara would not listen.

"I told her I did not want to see her again because I was afraid my parents would find out and beat me too." Jamilya's hands constantly fidgeted in her lap.

"How old were you, Jamilya?"

"Seventeen, Lara was sixteen."

"So, when did you see Lara again?"

"We met most days but didn't speak much until the day Lara visited me, crying. Andreas was dead. It was then I heard who he was. Lara told me that Andreas had written to his father asking for money so he could take her away and marry her. Lara's heart was broken, and I was sad for her."

I was beginning to see how Nico Hrisacopolis would react to the news his son had fallen in love with a Turkish girl. I didn't think he'd have sent money. I smelled something sinister brewing as Jamilya continued, gently coaxed by Jessica.

"So you began to talk to each other again."

"Yes, of course, our parents did not know about Andreas, and Lara had to cry alone."

Jessica leaned closer and spoke in a whisper. "That was hard for her… and you."

"Yes. We would meet in the fields or walk together after work."

"Did she ever hear from Hrisacopolis? Did he send her money?"

Jamilya's face darkened. "No."

"What happened?"

"Lara was visited by one of Andreas's men. He gave her money, a little from Andreas." Jamilya wiped tears from her eyes with a corner of the cloth shawl draped across her shoulders. "He then gave Lara a letter and said it was from Andreas's father who wrote it before Andreas died. Hrisacopolis still wanted Lara to have it because he wanted her to know what he was going to do for her."

Jessica turned to Jamilya. "Do you know what was in the letter?"

"No, but she said things would be all right once she had escaped. The letter, she said, was her secret."

Jessica paused and nudged me.

"Escaped? When was that?" I asked.

"Lara came to me one evening and told me someone had tried to kill her," replied Jamilya. A shot had rung out while she was in the field working with another girl. The bullet grazed her arm, but another hit the girl, who died later. There were some more, and she ran, thinking a Greek gunman was shooting at her. She hid for the rest of the day and visited Jamilya after dark. She avoided her father and begged Jamilya to help her escape to Kyrenia.

Jessica looked puzzled. "Why there?"

"Because by then, the Turks had invaded the north… right?" I asked.

Jamilya shook her head. "No, not then. Soon after, though. Lara wanted to go to Turkey by boat. She would be safe there."

Hrisacopolis wanted her silenced, that was for sure, but he could have killed her in Turkey too, so I asked why she thought she would be safe there. "Was there another reason?" Jessica's elbow stabbed my ribcage.

"So you helped her get to Kyrenia, then what?" Jessica threw me a warning glance.

"We took my father's truck, and I left Lara near the port and returned home. Later, when Jamilya's father found she had taken the truck, I told him what she had done but never told him about Andreas. My father then told Lara's father, and I was beaten. Lara's father went to Kyrenia but could not find Lara. Two weeks later, the Turkish army invaded."

Jessica leaned forward and looked into Jamilya's eyes. "That was the last you saw of Lara, but you did see someone else, didn't you? Someone came to see you about Lara."

Jamilya nodded. "A Turk came from the city and asked me about Lara. I told him I didn't know anything. "Then he did this." She rubbed her right leg. He broke it with an iron pole. Her head lowered, and her voice became barely audible. She hid her head in her hands.

I felt pity for the poor woman, and my anger grew as she continued.

"This man brought Greek youths with him a day later, and I was raped. He informed my parents that I'd been with Greek boys in front of the whole village. My family suffered disgrace, and the village shunned them."

Jessica looked away briefly and took a deep breath. I was feeling the same way. I could see she was getting more upset, but it was better she questioned Jamilya.

After Jamilya's leg healed, the village women grabbed her and beat her until she told them Lara was in Turkey. The Turk paid them well. He told Jamilya if she ever spoke about Lara, he would return and kill her. Shortly after, her father disowned her, and since then, she had sold herself to eat. Jessica's arm went around Jamilya's shoulders as the woman shook with emotion. Tears streamed down her cheeks.

I wanted to get up and get out. Go slap a few heads together. I was angry. This poor woman spent her whole life paying the price for being a friend of Andreas's lover. I wanted Nico to pay for this alone, but I knew more would come. Nico wasn't the kind of thug who forgave or forgot. "Why did you move here?" I asked gently. "Would you have not been better off with the people you knew, even if you were shunned?"

"The man from the city told me I had to move here. He pays for this place."

"So he knows where you are." I knew Jessica was thinking the same as me by the expression on her face. "You must leave here, Jamilya. Look, I'll give you some money, and you can go to Nicosia or Famagusta."

She shook her head. "No, I will stay here. I have no husband, and moving alone will attract too many questions."

I knew we'd done the wrong thing by this woman. In hindsight, we should have been more discreet. A lot of locals saw us. We had to get Jamilya out of Bellapais. 'B' was the obvious answer. I was hoping he had contacts and could get hold of the Turkish authorities. I sat waiting for Jamilya to compose herself. There was still one question I needed to ask before we were through. What happened to Lara, and was she still alive?

Jamilya opened a small leather-bound case at her side and withdrew a newspaper. She said, "Lara's young brother threw it at my feet sixteen years after I last saw Lara. Such was the shame the family still felt. He travelled to Bellapais to deliver the paper to me. The story said she was caught with another man by her husband. It told how she killed her husband and then herself. I knew Lara didn't kill him. It was a lie. Lara was not the kind of girl to go with men."

"Did she ever contact you at all?" asked Jessica.

"Once, when she got to Turkey, she sent a card to my father to say she was all right. She had married a soldier. She knew he would tell me."

"Do you know from the newspaper story if she had any children?"

Jamilya shrugged. "All Turkish girls marry and have children."

I pulled the photo of Lara from my pocket and showed it. The effect was instant. Jamilya burst into tears and wept.

Jessica waited, then said, "She was pregnant when she left this island… She was, wasn't she? That's why she wanted to go to Turkey. It was where the baby would be safe if she had a husband."

Jamilya closed her eyes. "She had a son."

I breathed in deeply. That's what Nico was afraid of. Both of us thought that but having it confirmed made things a lot clearer. I took another photo from my pocket. It showed a group photo of Andreas's men with Andreas in the middle. "Know anyone here?"

She pointed to a tall, muscular man in the back row. "This is the man who gave her the money. I know this because she said he was big with lots of hair and no moustache."

She was right. The man had long curly hair. "Did she tell you his name?"

"She called him Alex."

I was finished. She had told us all. I took the newspaper from her and thanked her for the time and information. As we stood, both Jessica and I emptied our pockets of British and Turkish money. I was worried about Jamilya despite her wish to stay put. I decided to act even if she protested.

"I will have a friend contact your Director General's office in Nicosia. I'm sure they will be able to move you to Nicosia or Famagusta. You'll be safe there." I wasn't sure about that, but she would have a chance. For all his amiable, laid-back personality, 'B' was a formidable diplomat with much influence over many foreign embassy staff officers. If anyone could help Jamilya, he could.

Letting ourselves out, we left her sitting in the corner of her hovel, counting the money. I felt sad, angry and frustrated.

We were now looking for a son. The newspaper confirmed his father's name as Hussein Ishmael and the mothers' name as Lara. A photo of Ishmael in military uniform topped the article. I knew that the son lived in Istanbul when his parents died.

CHAPTER TWENTY-ONE

AHMET WIPED THE BACK of his neck as a simmering orange sun descended slowly toward the horizon. Its warmth penetrated summer clothes despite a stiff breeze that played across the water's surface. In the distance, the general hubbub of city life, peppered every few seconds by impatient drivers blasting their horns, drifted on the breeze. He sat on the varnished bench next to the white railing surrounding the ferry's upper deck and looked to the Asian bank across the Bosporus. The last time he had taken the ferry was nearly three years before on an entirely different mission. Then, as at this moment, he waited for contact. Before, it had been an agent from Hrisacopolis, informing him how important it was to win Baki over.

After years of watching the boy grow up in the slums of Istanbul, working long hours in his stepfather's leather workshop, the opportunity Ahmet had waited for fell into his lap. The boy joined the army with help from a family friend after his mother's and stepfather's sudden deaths.

Ahmet's plans meticulously worked out two years before, went into immediate effect. His first task meant informing Baki who his real father was. Andreas became Baki's chosen new name, acceptable to Nico. Even more important, he was to tell the young man whose estate he would one day inherit. The news caused an argument. Indeed, Baki had ended the meeting by shouting insults. Ahmet remembered the second meeting when Nico had tried to send Baki money. The young man set fire to it and told Ahmet to tell Nico his blood money was not wanted. Ahmet gently stoked the fire each time, pretending to persuade Baki to forgive the old Greek for past sins and take the Hrisacopolis name. Instead, the young soldier cursed Nico for being responsible for his mother's death.

On Nico's orders, Ahmet visited once a week, always trying to convince Baki to change his name. It was apparent Baki hated army life. Upon hearing this, Nico arranged to bribe a medical officer to release Baki on medical grounds. Baki hated Nico with a vengeance, and the offer of early release from service was dismissed out of hand. Ahmet dutifully reported everything to Nico while the next part of his plan took shape.

A tall thin man wearing a light grey suit and red fez sat down next to Ahmet. Mustafa was, in appearance, an astute Turkish businessman. His suit and crisp white shirt were without a crease, his cherry tan leather shoes highly polished. An Arabic nose and chiselled chin gave him a Middle Eastern aristocratic appearance. He crossed his legs and, without acknowledging Ahmet, looked out across the water. "We have decided that he must not reach Athens. Can you handle that?"

Ahmet struggled to keep his composure. "Me. Why? Surely you can let me have at least one man. I can easily get him aboard as a personal aid." He rubbed a handkerchief across his forehead and bit his bottom lip.

"No, I'm afraid that's impossible. Besides, who better than someone he trusts, someone who will be by his side most of the time. You will have plenty of opportunities."

Ahmet felt betrayed. The KKA had put him into a dangerous position, probably on purpose. They trusted no one, especially a comparatively new face. This would show them how loyal he was to the cause. If only they knew. Still, once the task was over, the reward would be a new life of luxury and no more false humble servitude to a bastard like Hrisacopolis.

"Ahmet?"

"Yes, I heard you."

There was a slight vibration as the ferry's propeller bit into the water. Slowly the old boat pulled away from the quay, leaving a frothing mass of bubbles astern.

Ahmet knew precisely how important it was for the KKA to have Hrisacopolis out of the way.

Mustafa took a silver cigarette case from his inside pocket. He opened it and slid a 'Murad' out with well-manicured fingers, then snapped the case shut. Clicking his fingers at a tea boy, he took a book of matches from the boy's tray and lit the cigarette. A stream of pungent smoke escaped from his lips, only to be lost in the breeze.

"The Greek government," he explained, "on Hrisacopolis' death, will inherit his empire by nationalization and gain substantial muscle within the Union, upsetting the balance of economic power and causing irreparable damage to the European government, something that would help their cause. The worst scenario is a young dynamic grandson with a new pair of steady hands bringing further stability to the oil industry. In contrast, his grandfather brings years of trading experience in the world markets to Brussels. The Europeans will prefer to do business with the Hrisacopolis family rather than new faces. While Nico and his grandson are still alive, the Greek government will dare not oppose them. Nico has too many ministers in his pocket, both in the EU and the Greek government. Once our organisation's biggest headache has gone, we can arm Turkish patriots and take over Cyprus."

Ahmet could only hear, 'While Hrisacopolis and his grandson are still alive,' ringing in his ears. "Only Hrisacopolis is to die, surely?" He turned toward Mustapha, a worried look on his face. "I have spent years waiting for this moment."

Mustafa sympathised with him but carefully considered before deciding what to do. Initially, they went along with using the grandson, through Ahmet, to feed finance back into the organisation's hands for men and munitions. However, there was always a chance this arrangement would be compromised. After all, Mustafa mused, the grandson did have Greek blood. There were too many loose ends to worry about. Besides, the Syrians agreed to finance the year's operation and more if successful. Hrisacopolis would be dealt with in Athens by other agents. Andreas was Ahmet's problem.

Mustafa ran a finger, first one way and then the other, over his moustache. "Placed, as you are in the local office here, you will be playing a key role in Hrisacopolis' eventual demise. Of course, you are to be well rewarded." He took an envelope from his pocket and placed it in Ahmet's hand.

Ahmet took the envelope and fingered it nervously. His plan was going wrong. He could see sense in what they were going to do. Why hadn't he thought of that? He'd made no contingency plan. If the grandson wasn't dead by the time they reached Athens, he knew what would happen. He was thankful he had not told them everything. There had to be a way. "Thank you," he said and put the envelope in his pocket. "You do realise that I will be suspected."

"Of course, you will, so make sure the body goes over the side. And no blood. Strangulation will suffice. I know you are particularly good at that."

Ahmet looked nervously at his watch.

Mustafa drummed his fingers on the rail and pursed his lips. "Don't worry, Ahmet, you will catch the plane. A car is waiting for you at Anadolu Kavagi." He drew deeply on the cigarette and then asked about Ahmet's visit to the island.

The inquiry was expected, and Ahmet replied there were some

shipping people to meet in Famagusta. He sighed inwardly. He could hardly tell Mustafa that he was about to kill a Turkish woman. A sudden thought occurred to him. The quickest way to get rid of the two journalists upsetting, he planned to goad Mustafa into taking care of them. "I also have to find out what the two reporters are doing poking around in Nico's past," he added. "The same two your agent sent me a warning about."

Mustafa thought for a moment. "You know them?"

"They have written a series of articles on the Hrisacopolis plan to rebuild the Parthenon."

"And do you know where they are now?"

"Yes," Ahmet, "my contacts tell me they are on Cyprus and went up north."

"They will cause us trouble."

Ahmet nodded.

He felt Mustafa straighten in his seat. "One of them is a political columnist."

He glanced sideways. Mustafa's eyes closed, and his jaw set firm. Mustafa wanted details.

"I only found out a few hours ago," replied Ahmet, turning away.

Mustafa opened his eyes and slapped a hand on the rail behind Ahmet's back. Ahmet's shoulders jumped involuntarily. "Did it not occur to you that such an important piece of information should be reported at once?"

"As I said-"

"When did they arrive on the island?"

"Three days ago."

"Three." Mustafa checked himself as a young couple walked past. Then in a lowered voice, he said, "Three days, and you're only just going there?"

"Nico wants me to check up on them while I am there."

"I'm sure he does. Are you aware that these people may be British Intelligence? They have little time for either Hrisacopolis or us. I am very disappointed in you, Ahmet. I trust you will redeem yourself very shortly."

"I'll write their details down for you."

Mustafa uncrossed his legs and folded his arms, annoyed. "You will leave them to us."

Ahmet frowned. He could deal with Jamilya, the whore quickly while Mustafa silenced the journalists. British Intelligence – something else he hadn't thought of. It was time to retire. There would be a way to turn the situation to his advantage. It would come to him.

Ahmet awoke as the sun's rays spilt through the slatted wooden blinds, illuminating the white room in a diagonal pattern of light and dark stripes. A bus went past in the street below, its diesel engine shattering the peace and spewing thick clouds of diesel smoke. The Lapethos Hotel stood on the main road through Nicosia, walking distance from the bus station. It wasn't where Ahmet would have liked to stay. The Saray was more expensive and comfortable but much further away.

After showering and dressing as quickly as possible, Ahmet breakfasted on two croissants and a glass of orange juice, declining a newspaper and coffee. A short while later, he headed for the hotel lobby and paid his bill. Outside he found the heat was already climbing, and by the time he reached the bus terminal, he was carrying his jacket over his arm.

Ahmet looked for the district stand first, where coaches ran through three designated areas -Kyrenia, Nicosia and Famagusta. Ahmet looked for the Kyrenia district and then where each coach route was. Finding what he was looking for, he waited in line.

The covered terminal was oppressively hot. A warm breeze blew through the large opening at one end but did nothing to relieve the dozens of waiting passengers who stood around in noisy groups fanning themselves with newspapers. Ahmet waited patiently, flapping a newspaper in front of his face. A taxi would have been quicker but would have aroused a lot of suspicion in Bellapais. By bus, no one would take a second glance at a weary Turkish traveller.

There was a hiss of air as the dirty yellow coach door opened, heralding the arrival of the coach driver. Ahmet gratefully trudged along behind a woman and two small noisy boys. He found a spot near the rear of the coach and settled next to the window, hoping the seat next to him would remain vacant. It did. As the coach left the terminal, Ahmet closed his eyes and concentrated.

His peace of mind was the secret that would one day bring shame and disgrace to the Hrisacopolis name. Contacting KKA had been Andreas's idea. By ensuring funds passed onto the organisation after Nico's death, they provided their own safety from retaliation or blackmail from anyone who might expose them. That would hardly be possible and difficult to prove, but even a slim chance had to be covered. KKA was good insurance. The trouble was that the organisation was taking over and changing the plan. The idea to involve them was turning sour. They both wanted the same things, a Turkish Republic of Cyprus and Nico dead. One goal was nearly impossible, but he wouldn't tell a fanatical guerrilla organisation that. The other was a certainty. It was just that his way, the wealth and power would be his and not the Greek governments. There was, of course, Eren, who stood to gain too.

The coach bounced over a curb, jolting Ahmet's elbow resting on the windowsill. The city soon faded into the countryside, and he watched one file of field workers after another walking along the side of the road. Nothing had changed except the people. Gone were thousands of Turkish Cypriots to Great Britain, North America, and Australia, angry at the significant influx after the invasion. Ankara, in its wisdom, allowed tens of thousands of impoverished Turks to settle on the island. It wasn't only an island split in two.

Fifteen minutes later, the coach came to a dusty stop in the market town of Kioneli. Ahmet still pondered how best to deal with Mustafa's order. One thing was for sure. Andreas was not going to die.

A young boy climbed into the coach carrying a tray of bottled water. "Sisede. Sisede."

Ahmet waved a hand at the boy and bought a bottle. It was warm, but at least it eased a dry throat. The nervousness was there again. He could feel a knot in his stomach, and his head was beginning to ache. Closing his eyes again, he focused on the whore.

Twenty past nine. Ahmet wanted the job out of the way. He stood on the corner of the narrow passage and looked to see if there were many people at the bakery. Pulling the Panama down lower, he walked up the passage and past Jamilya's door. All seemed clear. He stopped, turned around and walked quickly back to her door. Facing the street, he saw no one and then knocked lightly four times. "Ingilizce konusuyor musunuz?" he called.

The door bolts slid back, and the door opened a crack. "Yes, I speak Eng-"

Jamilya fell backwards as the door crashed against her. Ahmet stepped into the room and closed the door in one swift movement. Pouncing on her as she tried to rise, he fell on top of her with one hand around her mouth. "Now, bitch, how much did you tell the British bastards? You scream, and I'll kill you. Tell me what I want to know, and I'll spare your miserable life." He took his hand from her mouth but continued to pin her down.

"I told them everything, you pig," she screamed. "May you die in pain with your master."

Ahmet grabbed her by the throat with both hands and squeezed.

"And so will you," he hissed through gritted teeth. "Can you feel the air going out of your lungs?" As he throttled her, he pulled her head up and backwards. Then, releasing the pressure from her throat, he let her breathe again. Seconds later, he squeezed again and repeated the process. He turned her as she gasped for air and sat astride her body. Releasing his grip on her throat, he smashed both fists into her face.

"The Greek is not my master, you bitch. Do you hear? He is not my master. Like you, he is going to die." Jamilya's eyes stared defiantly into his. He grabbed her throat as she spat at him.

"Die, you whore."

Chapter Twenty-Two

THE SUMMIT OF OLYMPUS was never on my list of 'must see' places. A TV tower and an RAF golf ball-radar dome sat on top. There wasn't much to see except rock, dust and more rock. In the winter, the place got covered in snow.

Jessica wanted to look at two ruins just below the summit. There was a Venetian watchtower and an ancient temple of Aphrodite. Despite a tarmac side road to the summit, she insisted we take a hike from Troodos Resort and follow a well beaten trail most of the way. My bare arms and legs glistened, and despite a warm breeze, I felt uncomfortably hot. We finished the hike near the summit and sat on a large rock within minutes, eating lunch.

"You look bored," said Jessica from under the wide brim of a straw hat while fanning flies from her sandwich with a napkin.

I chewed on a chicken salad sandwich and waited until the urge to be sarcastic had passed. "Not really. I was thinking about the cruise." It was a little white lie. The cruise had been on my mind. We were ten days away from departure and, more importantly, weeks away from the first round of talks at the EU on forming the new Agriculture and Fisheries Committee.

Something 'B' had said kept coming back to me. It was one of those silly little asides he was good at making that sometimes hid a more serious message. "I'm just admiring the view," I said, staring at Jessica's legs.

"Drink your wine." She tapped the back of my head and offered a full glass.

I remembered 'B' was nodding at something I had said. I can't remember what, and then he remarked while our coffee arrived. 'That's if Nico makes it to the table.' Why I hadn't picked up on it while it was fresh in my mind I don't know. I sat for several minutes trying to figure out what had triggered the remark but drew a blank.

"I'm going to Istanbul," I said, sitting bolt upright. "I'm going to find out what happened to the boy."

"What? When?" She moved closer and put an arm around my neck. A little shiver ran through me as her lips touched my ear. She said, "I guess I should have known you'd be off to look for the boy, right?"

My thoughts far away, I could see the haunting look in Lara's eyes staring at me from Captain Stevenson's photo.

"So we pack tonight?"

"Yes. I can catch a flight from Ercan tomorrow, I answered."

"Wait a minute," protested Jessica, "I thought we were in this together. You want me to go home when we're getting our teeth into it."

"Have you ever been to Turkey, in particular Istanbul?" I asked.

"No, but-"

"I'd be worrying myself silly about you. You know how women are looked upon there. I want space and freedom to move in places I wouldn't take a London call-girl."

"Very funny." She pouted as she packed away the picnic.

"Darling, I'm sorry, but I want you safe, and Max kept at bay. Tell him the truth but let him know we're not upsetting Nico, and we are still on leave. He'll be all right, you'll see."

She smiled. "Thank you."

I frowned. "For what?"

"That's the first time you called me darling."

I felt a twinge of panic. Something about the smile and how Jessica spoke made me think I was losing my independence. I shrugged and avoided her eyes. "Let's have dinner out along the seafront tonight. There's that expensive-looking hotel at the end of the beach road." I sounded enthusiastic but was far from happy. We'd only been on the island three nights, and I'd spent all of them with Jessica. The following two or three were going to be sleepless.

We headed down the road towards Troodos Resort, a one-and-a-half-hour walk from the peak. By the time we arrived back at the car, we had looked forward to a cool shower. With all the windows rolled down, I drove with my head tipped to one side to catch as much breeze as possible.

"So, where will you start when you get to Istanbul?"

I didn't know. There wasn't much to go on in the newspaper article, although it did give out what district Lara was living in. "I guess I'll start from where she lived," I answered. "Maybe you could dig something up back at the Turkish Embassy in Belgrave Square."

The sun shone into our eyes as we went around a rocky outcrop.

We both grabbed the sunshades and pulled them down. The gradient became steeper. The view was breath-taking.

"I'll call Max in the morning before I catch a flight," replied Jessica. "I'm sure he might get me an appointment with the appropriate member of staff." She threw her hands in the air and imitated Max. "No. No. Watch my lips, NO."

We were both laughing when a coach came around the bend below. I braked slightly and changed gear. As the coach passed, I let go of the brake pedal and cruised down, enjoying the rush of air filling the car. "So, what do you say we get a swim in before dinner?"

Jessica nodded. "Take it easy, Pete. The road is getting steeper."

I glanced at the speedometer. "Don't worry. I've driven on worse roads than this and survived." I braked again. "That's funny."

"What is?"

I pushed my foot down on the brake again, and the car slowed. I released it and braked again. The brake was spongy. "Hold on, there's something wrong with the brakes," I said, looking for a pull-in spot.

"Pete, if this is your idea of a joke, I don't find it funny." Jessica grabbed the strap at the top of the door. She panicked. "Pete! Pete! Stop the car – stop!"

"No joke, Jessica, I'll pull in as soon as the road widens."

I tried to stay calm and kept a foot on the brake, keeping the speed to around twenty-five miles an hour. The pace increased, and I pressed harder. Nothing happened. I jammed down on the pedal as hard as I could. "Get into the back seat and sit behind me," I shouted. My heart pounded. I started to panic.

"Don't be stupid! Use the handbrake!" She leaned toward me and gripped my wrist for a brief moment. "Do it, or we're going over the top, Pete." Her wide eyes frightened me.

The car was gathering speed. Rock face and brush by the side of the road became a blur. With no crash barriers, we had no chance of surviving a fall. I crunched the gearbox down. The engine screamed. A Mercedes suddenly appeared in front of us. Instinctively, I pulled the handbrake up sharply. We narrowly missed it.

"Let the handbrake off. Use it to slow us down, not stop!" Jessica shrieked.

Too late, I realised my mistake. The car's rear slewed sideways across the asphalt at an alarming speed. The car juddered, and rubber squealed. I released the handbrake and tried to correct the skid. Desperately, I yanked at the wheel and watched, horrified as we slid into the narrow band of brush.

"Do something! Arghhhhh! Peter, Peter, do something!"

The rear nearside wheel dropped over the yawning chasm, and the chassis hit a large rock with a sickening, bone-jarring crash. We rocked once before resting at an angle in a cloud of choking dust. It was then, as reality returned, I became aware that Jessica was screaming. I grabbed her arm.

"Get off me!" She pushed my hand away. "Get off me. How cou-?" She coughed and burst into tears. Furious, she grappled with the door handle but couldn't open the door. The car was leaning toward the drop. She thumped her fists against the dashboard and finally slumped back into her seat, sobbing loudly. "Get me out of here - now."

This wasn't the moment to offer any apologies to Jessica or explanations. Not that I owed any, although, from the way Jessica reacted, it looked as though she thought otherwise. I would have acted similarly if I hadn't had the wheel in my hand.

I reached across her and pulled the door handle down while pushing the door out with the other. It was a struggle, but I managed to pry it lose a couple of inches. "It would help," I said as calmly as possible, "if you could give the door a shove, Jessica."

She obliged by swiftly pushing the door with both hands. It swung back, and she clambered out. I managed to push myself across to her seat, cracking an ankle against the gear stick on the way. Just in time, I grabbed the door as it began to swing back. Jessica was walking - or should I say, marching - determinedly across the road with arms folded.

I stepped down onto the waste strip and walked to the front of the car. We were lucky to be alive. A large boulder was all that prevented the vehicle from a long dive. Turning, I was in time to see Jessica disappear from view. She wouldn't get far, and I wasn't going to chase after her. It was better she cooled down on her own.

What was immediately urgent was an inspection of the car. After looking underneath for any tell-tale signs of leaking brake fluid from the two brake cylinders I could get to, I tried tracing the pipes. It didn't take long to find what I suspected. Above a small patch of fluid in the grass, I found a neat cut in the pipe to the rear brakes. I sat on the grass and could only think of one thing – our visit to Jamilya. Someone knew. Intuitively, I knew she was dead.

"Someone cut the pipe." It was a statement, not a question.

I didn't see her walk back. She must have watched me inspecting the car.

"I'm sorry I lost my temper. I was terrified. I've never been so scared in all my life."

I waved a hand and nodded in agreement. "At least we're still alive, although I fear for someone else. Whoever tried to kill us…"

Jessica sank to her knees beside me. "Oh God no, do you think..?

I mean, would they have? Surely not. We only left her yesterday."
"Yes, of course, they bloody well would have." I exploded. "They must have followed us." I had a lump in my throat as guilt racked me. I felt like throwing up. "I might as well have put a bloody bullet in her head myself." I choked.

I got up and turned away, fighting the emotion. Opening the back door to remove our rucksacks, I stood with fists clenched around the shoulder straps. "You know something?" I said calmly. "Max was right. I'm too damn big for my boots. I don't know when to stop." Throwing the rucksacks on the ground, I rounded on Jessica. "Well, I'll tell you this. I don't care what it takes. I'm going to get that bastard Hrisacopolis. I will pull all the crap out of his closet and let the world know he's not the bloody hero he's been made out to be." I sank to the ground again, sad and very angry. My eyes were tearing up, and I fisted the ground in frustration.

Jessica knelt beside me and put an arm around my shoulders. "You – we, did no more than any of our colleagues would have. If we hadn't got to Jamilya, I guess she would have had a visit from the Turk she told us about anyway." She came close and kissed me. "You could be over-reacting too."

I kissed her back. Her comment made sense. 'B' had been a little put out when I called him after returning from Bellapais but agreed to call his Turkish buddies in their London Embassy and have them arrange through the Turkish Director General in Cyprus to have Jamilya arrested and taken to Nicosia for her safety. As Jessica said, I hoped I was over-reacting and decided to call 'B' as soon as possible.

"I suppose we'd better be getting back. We'll have to hitch a ride on one of the coaches coming down. I think one of them came from Paphos," I said.

Jessica winked. "Don't worry; I'll stand in the middle of the road and show a bit of thigh." I know she was putting a brave face on things, but I didn't feel like smiling.

We started down the road. I was thankful we were going down. The heat was unbearable, and my ankle hurt like hell. I tried again to remember my conversation with 'B'.

I knew we were waiting for dessert around the time of the remark. I tried going back to the main course. I commented that Hrisacopolis should be content to be a billionaire shipping magnate. Then I said… what was it… that it was a shame about something, but what?

Jessica put her arm through mine as we walked. "I think you should book your flight as soon as we get back, Pete."

The remark hit me like a bolt of lightning. "Eureka."

I explained the problem. Then I told Jessica I had said that it was a shame the old boy's son had not lived to take over the shipping business years beforehand. Perhaps things might have turned out differently. Then he made that comment about dreading letting another captain steer his ship.

"I don't understand, Pete."

"You reminded me why I was going to Istanbul – to find Lara's son, Pete's grandson. Don't you see? 'B' was telling me something, but I wasn't paying attention."

"Okay, so what was the message?"

I wasn't sure, but my fingers were almost touching a piece of the puzzle.

Jessica stopped walking. "Your comment about Andreas made him say two things. One… that he, Nico, would be dreading letting someone else run his shipping business, and two… that he might not make it to the table in Brussels because of… what?"

"Because of the new captain running his industry… whoever that is."

"Or isn't."

It was my turn to look mystified. "Or isn't?"

Jessica theorised Nico had to have some corrupt crony in mind, but that person might not accept the post. It would have to be someone who already knew about the business and all the dirty tricks going on. There had to be trusted staff in the know.

If she was right and Nico went to Brussels, he would have to convince some nervous mandarins that all would be okay and the good life would continue.

Nico Hrisacopolis probably had half the Greek government in his pocket, and I needed to find out who he had in mind and who was powerful enough to oppose him.

I decided to call 'B' as soon as I returned to London. I was sure I had the answer but said nothing.

Chapter Twenty-Three

THREE LARGE FISHING VESSELS lay tied against the harbour wall, all freshly painted about the superstructure, but the fresh coat did not hide the pitted metalwork beneath that showed their actual age. Two pontoons running parallel to the quay were full of traditional Luzzus. The fishing boats lay moored in four rows, a colourful splash of blue, green, red, and yellow against the stone wall and white sheds that lined the shore. Behind the sheds, dozens of coaches stood in the vast parking lot, their drivers and guides waiting for the incoming ferry from Malta to disgorge hundreds of tourists.

It was unusually windy for the time of the year, yet the temperature climbed into the 80s. The sun reflected off the water and through the porthole to bathe the cabin roof in incandescent light.

Adonis knelt and pushed the wires beneath the edge of the carpet that ran alongside the bulkhead bench seat. He worked quickly, double checking every inch. If one of the men came back unexpectedly, the whole plan would fold.

"Damn." He dropped the long-nosed pliers and held his finger. Blood seeped from a small wound in a finger pinched by the pliers. Wiping the finger on his shorts, he picked the pliers up from the deck and continued his work. Minutes later, he finished pushing the edge of the carpet back into place and dabbed his face and neck with a rag. The heat below deck was oppressive. Making his way back to the small engine room, he pushed one hand beneath the engine mounting and felt for the duct tape holding the explosive in place, then wiped the surrounding deck clean.

The cruisers had arrived on time, towing the sizeable inflatable craft. At first, they attracted some interest from the locals, but that was all. The authorities examined the paperwork and stamped them with no more than a cursory glance at the cruisers. Everything was set. The time was near. In two hours, the Turk was arriving.

Adonis returned to his work, checking and double-checking the wiring to the Semtex as he progressed. After finishing his work an hour later, he showered and returned to the stateroom. Later, he felt the cruiser rock, followed by loud footsteps along the deck as he rested.

"Hey, Cypriot, are you in there?"

Adonis's jaw set firm. He picked up a magazine without answering and consoled himself, knowing that he wouldn't have to listen to the Turk's voice for much longer. He swallowed hard and gripped the magazine.

The Turk appeared, his huge body framed in the stateroom entrance. "Are you happy with the boat?" He grinned broadly.

"Did you get the job done?" snapped Adonis.

A huge hand waved his question away. "Don't worry."

"What do you mean, don't worry? Didn't Rublev contact you?"

There was no answer. A strong smell of cognac wafted through the stateroom on a breeze blowing through the open door. Unable to contain his anger, Adonis threw the magazine across the stateroom. "Forget everything. Go to hell."

He stood with his back to the Turk, hands clenched by his sides, shaking with rage. The man was repulsive. He hadn't washed or shaved in days and always reeked body odour. More importantly, Adonis could see their relationship was deteriorating to the point where the operation would be in jeopardy. He breathed deeply, annoyed at himself for losing his temper. This was no time to show weakness.

A huge hand grabbed him by one arm and spun him around. He looked into the Turk's face, creased in a snarl, inches from his own.

"I have killed men for lesser insults." He snapped his fingers in Adonis's face. "Better I help you into hell by letting you achieve success than kill you myself." He pulled Adonis closer and grinned menacingly. "I shall phone Aleksey right now and make sure all is well," he said slowly. He placed a finger on Adonis's chest. "When this is over, I may still send you to hell anyway. Nobody tells the Turk to go to hell." He thumped his chest.

"Perhaps we will go together," answered Adonis, his nose twitching. He turned his head away from the heavy odour of Gauloises and sweat. "But until we do, you will follow my instructions," he said, his voice rising. "This is my operation, not yours."

"Ha. Now that would be an interesting journey. I'll return shortly," replied the Turk. He waved a hand in mock salute and disappeared back through the door, bowing his head.

Adonis watched him leave the cruiser and jump up onto the harbour wall. For a big man, he was very agile. On the ship or shortly after, the Turk would indeed go to hell. Adonis wondered which one of them would see the other off first. He stooped to pick the magazine up and breathed a sigh of relief. He had faced the man and asserted his authority. Now he would have to follow through and gain a little more respect by producing a plan so carefully conceived that it guaranteed success and freedom to enjoy that success. That was, of course, as far as the Turk was concerned.

It was a full fifteen minutes before the Turk returned, a bottle of cognac in his hand. "I have good news. Aleksey has done the job; our men will soon be aboard." He pulled a small tumbler from a shelf above his head, blew into it, and poured some cognac.

The smell of cognac filled the cabin as Adonis announced a change to his plan. Initially, the idea was to go out each day to various locations and dive, creating the impression that they were searching for an old wreck. He decided not to wait until the night of the hijack but to take up the actual position where they intended to start, make several trips into the area by inflatables each day and be part of the scenery when *Sea Empress* made her way past them to the north.

The Turk thought for a moment. "You know, I was going to suggest something very similar. Yes, I agree. We will do that," he said, wiping sweat from his bald head and rubbing his hands down his trousers.

Adonis did not comment but continued. The men were to buy enough supplies and fuel to last until after the operation without returning to Gozo. He pulled charts and drawings from the overhead locker. "Okay, this is what will happen," he said, waving smoke away from his face.

At that moment, *Sea Empress* lay docked in Naples. The Turk had contacted Aleksey in Naples, and two men would soon be aboard, despite the crew having already been picked and vetted through security. The crew would be getting the ship ready for her VIPs. The Turk's men had to be aboard when she sailed for England. Security was going to be strict, and there were going to be more checks before Hrisacopolis boarded. Naples was a straightforward port to gain access onto a ship. The men had kidnapped two stewards on shore leave and taken their ID cards to Aleksey Rublev.

"What about the head steward? He's bound to know his staff?" said the Turk.

"Don't worry. The men need the ID for boarding purposes. Once aboard, they will hide… here." Adonis pointed to a sizeable forward locker room, a store for provisions, kept on the lower deck. Forward of it, a smaller room stretched across the whole width of the bow, a twelve-foot store for carts and work savers. No one entered it once the ship left port. The men would have to stay there, except for checks when they could get some fresh air.

The Turk rubbed his chin. "And what of the two missing stewards?"

"I'll leave that up to you." Adonis knew the men's fate was sealed. He dismissed the thought from his mind.

<hr />

A small beetle scampered across the decking and stopped in front of a chair leg. It changed direction and started back the way it had come. A large sandaled foot crushed it with a loud bang. The Doberman awoke from his afternoon siesta with a start and yelped.

"Yes, that's fine, minister." Pete Hrisacopolis eyed the dog. "Yes, I'll take care of it. Don't I always? Right then, I'll see you Thursday." He put the phone back on the table. Irritated, he momentarily closed his eyes and then picked it up again. It rang before he could dial. He answered and was relieved to hear Ahmet's voice.

"I just got back. Everything has been taken care of."

"Thank you, Ahmet. Will you be seeing my grandson today?"

"Yes, we will have dinner at the Ciragan Palace tonight."

Nico took the half-smoked cigar from the glass ashtray by his side and put it to his lips. He coughed several times. "Has his nose healed completely?"

"The nose healed some time ago. Andreas Junior will pass the test; you have my word." There was a pause. Ahmet's voice lowered. "There's was one small detail neither he nor I am too happy about. Two journalists have an exclusive interview, and it has been assumed Andreas junior is included. He is afraid of letting you down at such a critical moment and didn't want an embarrassing situation if they started digging into his army life or where he lived in Cyprus."

"You could be right, although I want him to come across as a strong man ready to take on my role. Remember, we have people to impress at home and in Brussels. What did you have in mind?"

"I suggest the Athens office could prepare a statement for Andreas about the shipping industry and where he saw the company going in the next three years," replied Ahmet. "We could come up with a few safe predictions that would steer Andreas away from any suggestion that his grandfather in Brussels would have any influence on company policy. Indeed, Andreas could hint that the company had got stuck in the old ways, and he hoped to revitalise company policies and introduce younger minds into the boardroom. He could even threaten – in a nice way – not to renew as many trade contracts with EU members. That would suggest that some member countries enjoy a larger slice of the tanker and container business, especially the French and Germans."

"A statement is already prepared for him, but you have raised an interesting point, Ahmet. I like the idea that he would give more business to the other members. It shows business strategy, a mind on the bigger picture and a feeling of change. Good." Nico coughed again and threw the cigar into the pool. "And what about the journalists? Where are they now?"

"They were sightseeing as far as I can make out."

"No, they were not, Ahmet, no, they were not. You did not locate them, did you? You got there too late, long after I first told you to go and find them. Now, God knows what they are up to because of your inefficiency. They got to the girl before you, didn't they?"

"No, sir, they did not. The girl told me the truth before I silenced her. I have not located the journalists but found out they booked out of their hotel in Paphos this morning. I checked with Ioannis and found that Jessica Du Rosse had left for Larnaka. According to the hotel clerk, she was flying to London.

"What do you mean, 'obviously'? And where was the other one. . ." He waved a hand.

"Pete West."

"Yes, West, where was he?"

"They were staying in Paphos, but there is only one flight from there a week during this time of year. Ioannis says West booked out, probably by the woman. I assume he left with her."

Hrisacopolis sat fuming, unable to speak.

"Sir, are you there? Hello…? Hello?"

"Yes, I'm here." thundered Nico. "Am I the only one to see something is going on?"

"Sir?"

"You are a fool. Ioannis is an even bigger fool. Surely if they flew into and stayed at Paphos, they would be flying out of Paphos on a flight a week or two later. Why would they drive across to the other side of the island to fly home? What about the man? Did he leave, or is he still on the island? What is he up to?"

Ahmet knew the woman had taken West's luggage with her. West may have been in the car for all Ioannis knew or buying some last-minute souvenir. He had no reason to stay on the island. The girl was dead. Perhaps West had found that out, but they had been unable to trace the girl more than likely.

"I hope to God you are right, Ahmet. If my plans are upset because of you two bungling idiots, I'll personally throttle the pair of you."

CHAPTER TWENTY-FOUR

I STOOD HALFWAY UP the white stone steps leading into the elegant Ciragan Palace hotel. A faint odour of pollution from traffic crossing the Bosphorus Bridge spoiled the invigorating fresh sea air. The view across to the other half of the city on the European bank reminded me of my first trip many years before as a student.

The distant noise of the opposite waterfront and a skyline of minarets and golden domes injected mixed memories. For just a moment, I was a graduate again. It was still a vibrant city, boasting architecture through Roman, Byzantine and Ottoman periods and an intriguing mixed ethnic culture. That same excitement I felt the last time filled my senses again, but there was a sense of purpose this time. This wasn't a nostalgic trip, more a trip into an uncertain future.

My watch showed 2:30 p.m. Turning, I climbed the rest of the steps and went into reception. My mind wanted to unravel the mystery, but my body didn't. I needed quiet.

The place was expensive, but I thought it a good investment for a couple of nights in town. The last thing I wanted was an unofficial room search. Besides, I had to buy a few necessities. Jessica had taken my luggage back to London, and all I had was an overnight bag with very little in it.

The immaculately dressed clerk smirked at me as I approached the desk. It always fascinated me how Middle Easterners have a talent for making just one facial expression that conveys genuine sincerity, suspicion, happiness, and boredom.

"You have a reservation, sir?" he asked, folding his hands on the desk.

The fawning yet annoying smile froze on his face. He reminded me of 'Dickens' Uriah Heap. "Pete West. I booked last night."

His thin little fingers traced straight lines down the columns of the guest book and stopped with a tap of the index finger. "Yes, Mr West... You are on your own?"

I looked sideways and then smiled back at him. "Yes, just me."

He held a hand in the air. "Room four thirty-one." Before his fingers had clicked, a young, uniformed baggage boy appeared by my side.

I followed the boy to the open lift and then up to the fourth floor. After tipping him, I closed my room door and promptly sprawled across the bed. I was tired. Jessica made love like we were never going to see each other again. Neither of us got much sleep.

I rolled over and reached for the phone. After making a wake-up call for 7:00 p.m. and ordering some toiletries, I closed my eyes. I needed a couple of hours of sleep.

———◇———

A traditional silk and wool carpet, woven with a mass of geometric designs in red, blue, gold, and yellow, covered the entire floor. My room could have been right from the pages of a brochure. I felt as though I'd just woken up in the past. The Ciragan Palace originated from the Ottoman period. Jessica was going to scold me for not being there. The place was a treasure trove of history.

A breeze off the straits kept the room cool and played with long net curtains that fluttered over the carpet from the tall open windows. The bathroom included a Jacuzzi I could fall asleep in and a cold marble floor cooling my feet.

By the time the telephone rang, I was already up and pouring water for a bath. I decided to eat downstairs in a restaurant noted in the city for its fine cuisine and expensive menu. The thought of going out on the town didn't appeal. Besides, it was a balmy evening, and I wanted to spend some time sitting out on the long stone veranda that ran the length of the hotel. I needed to turn things over in my mind. A picture was forming, but the blurred images didn't fit yet.

'B's cryptic message, Jamilya's story, the attempt on our lives; most of the story was there except the one piece I knew would make sense of it all. Then there was the photograph. Lara's face haunted me, or rather her sad eyes did. The story was in there too. I let all thoughts of my mission fade away and sank into a deep bath of warm soapy water. Then the phone rang. Conveniently, a gold extension sat on the bath's marble surround. I picked it up.

The clerk with the friendly smirk spoke into my ear with a well-rehearsed actor's voice. "Good evening, Mr West, you have a call from London from a Miss Du Rosse."

I thanked him and waited for the line to connect. "Jessica?"

"Pete?"

"My father called from Paris today. Two days ago, he spoke to a friend, an art dealer in Greece who told him of a particularly gruesome murder a few miles outside Athens. Someone we know. I don't sup-?"

"No, it wasn't Hrisacopolis, but it was someone just as interesting. It was an artist by the name of Alexander Gravari."

"Christ. Andreas's right-hand man... The one who visited Lara."

Alexander's death was a gruesome affair. The police attributed his death to the Turkish terrorists from the KKA group. I knew what that meant in more ways than one. Alexander suffered in the same way others did in the seventies. The killer put a sack over his head and cut his throat. I was willing to bet it wasn't the KKA who killed him. Following close on Jamilya's death, this was no coincidence. Nico had been at work. First, Jamilya and now Alexander; both knew something from way back that Nico needed to keep quiet.

"Pity we didn't try to track him down first. He knew Lara," said Jessica.

"Maybe, but I know someone you could track down and talk with over lunch. He'd jump at the chance to take you to lunch."

"I assume you are referring to 'B'?"

I wanted her to give him a ring and inform him she had something regarding Nico to discuss. I wanted her to drop Lara's name in his lap during that conversation and see any reaction. It would also be good to let him know about the accident. I had a feeling he would be interested.

"You know something, and you're not telling me."

"Not at all," I replied. As I had started to tell Jessica to ring 'B', the fuzzy picture had cleared for a split second and with it came an answer, preposterous yet convincing. It occurred to me that 'B' should know where I was. He would know what I was doing and why. "So, how are things over there?" I asked.

"I have an appointment at the Turkish Embassy tomorrow. I'll see what I can dig up then. Until then, I have to put up with Max."

"How so?"

"Max wants to know if you're still alive. I think your sense of humour is rubbing off on him. Max told me I would be the first woman charged with loving a man to death and commented on our relationship. I told him to mind his own damn business."

"He has no sense of humour. He's a little jealous." I paused purposefully before saying, "Who could blame him."

"Thank you, darling. I miss you too."

Our conversation ended, and I took a bath. The tiredness I felt from the flight was gone. Nico was clearing up some loose ends. Whatever it was all about, it was from the past and, if I wasn't mistaken, to do with Andreas and Lara's son. I dressed and left my room. Downstairs, the reception area was alive, with little groups taking tea in various enclaves with sofas and armchairs positioned beneath palms. Although audible, the conversations were little more than a general buzz compared with the mad clamour of the bazaars.

I walked to the restaurant entrance and stood by the gold podium. A tall suave man dressed in an evening suit, the maître d'hôtel, advanced on me armed with a familiar plastic look on his face. As he did so, he took a menu from a rack. "Perhaps Sir would follow - oh, excuse me for just a moment."

Unceremoniously, he pushed past me to welcome another guest, someone he knew well and a regular. The guest was a small man in stature, balding, and wore a white suit. With him, a youngish man, good looking and dressed immaculately. The two walked past me with the maître d' gabbling as he led them to a table. For a brief moment, the little man's eyes met mine. Small piercing brown eyes, cold as ice, and the kind you never forgot. I watched him as he made his way to a window table, and then I turned my attention to a waiter beckoning me to the other side of the room.

<hr />

Ahmet sat at the window table observing West as a waiter led the man to the other side of the restaurant. He waited until the maître d' had left. "Andreas, take a look at this." He took a folded newspaper from his jacket pocket and pushed it across the table. "Study the face in the picture at the top of the column."

Andreas unfolded the clipping. He looked at the small picture. Under it was a name – Peter West. "Who is this?"

"This is one of the journalists interviewing you on the ship. He has a daily column in this newspaper." Ahmet tapped the clipping. "We are going to have to be very careful about him. He is a political journalist here in the city."

"What for?"

Ahmet had no idea West was in Istanbul. Fortunately, West did not know them, which was to their advantage. Their plans had to proceed. As it was, they might have to alter them due to some last-minute changes.

"You can't change things now." hissed Eren. "Not after all I've been through. You can't do this to me."

"There is nothing for you to worry about. Just minor details."

"That's all very well for you to say. It's not you that's changing a whole lifestyle and religion to please an old man. God. How I hate him. I wish he were dead already."

"Precisely, and that is what we must think about." Ahmet folded the clipping and placed it back in his pocket while a waiter hovered over them. Ordering a fresh vegetable meze, he waved the waiter away. Eren would not be doing anything different to what they agreed on. When Nico Hrisacopolis signed his will and placed the company into Andreas's name, he would never get into office.

Eren was silent for a moment. "You're going to kill him so soon?"

"Why not? Does it matter to us whether he goes to Brussels or not?" Ahmet drummed his fingers on the table.

"But what about the others on the board of directors? They have to stay to run the company. There will be a free for all with Hrisacopolis out of the way. Without him, no one will ensure I retain control."

Ahmet reassured him. Nico Hrisacopolis had many friends in government who would be only too willing to make sure Eren did not inherit any problems. It would be in their interest to see that things remained as they were for the future. Their bank balance and power relied on it.

"All right, but supposing this government falls at the elections? What happens then?"

Ahmet knew he was right. If the present government fell, there would be grave consequences for the company but not before Eren had the company secretary transfer millions from the business into several Swiss accounts Nico had set up, including one for his grandson. The timing was everything, and there was little time to get things done. The idea came to him one night as he lay in bed. It was simple and effective. Most of all, it was a way around the organisation's call for Eren – AKA, Andreas, to die.

Ahmet patted Eren's hand. "It will not matter. Trust me. We'll discuss your grandfather's tragic death later." He saw the waiter returning with the meze. "For now, let us enjoy his generosity."

"What of the journalist?"

"I think he may be too busy very soon to worry about us."

CHAPTER TWENTY-FIVE

THE SUN ROSE ABOVE the city rooftops, throwing silvery yellow rays between the pillars of the Fatih Sultan Mehmet Bridge, creating a shimmering pattern across the rippling Bosporus. One of the old passenger ferries slowly made its way from the European side, its white superstructure bathed in orange. Three men sat in white shirts and sunglasses on the stern upper deck.

I stood for a minute enjoying the picture book start to the day before venturing into the noisy bazaar, searching for someone who knew Lara's husband, Ishmael. Hailing a taxi, I headed for the Grand Bazaar across the bridge. Within ten minutes, I was in the thick of a scrum, battling wandering tourists, stepping over yesterday's discarded fast-food containers and trying to speak to shopkeepers.

"This is the only picture I have of her. She had a son, Baki." I held the newspaper up a little closer, trying to get the little man to concentrate. It was a losing battle against tourists looking through his leather goods' display.

"No, no, no. I do not...." He turned to me briefly, "Excuse me, please." Then he turned back to the tourist with a toothy grin. "You like to see more." He was on his prey in two short steps, palms up, showing his honesty and respect for a stranger. "I have many bags for pretty ladies."

I left him telling a plump lady with a red face and sunburned arms how the bag she held in her hand would enhance her beauty. Good liars make good salesmen.

The Grand Bazaar covers a maze of sixty streets with hundreds of shops. I was quickly getting lost. Emerging from the claustrophobic and noisy interior, I made for a line of workshops surrounding the place. According to the newspaper, Ishmael was a leatherworker who made various goods for the bazaar. The sun was warm for the time of year, and my mouth was dry. There was a small teahouse a little further up the bazaar, and when I got there, it was, as I suspected, crowded. I must have looked like a lost lamb because a couple of old men watching the crowds go by motioned me to join them. Say what you like about a male-dominated society, but the men are friendly and like nothing better than talking when the opportunity arises. My new companions spoke broken English which didn't surprise me. Most European countries teach English as a second language. That's why we British are lazy about learning a foreign tongue.

I waited for the server to finish clearing the table before pitching the photo at them. One of them, a small man with thinning white hair and a black moustache, recognised Hussein Ishmael's photograph. "Yes, I am a friend of his neighbour," he said. The old man turned both hands palm up on the table. "He met with friends most nights before going home." As an afterthought, he added, "A very generous and good man."

On my first visit to Istanbul, I learned that when you buy a man a raki, an aniseed-based alcoholic beverage, you immediately become a good man. Muslims don't, as a rule, drink, but in Turkey, raki is the national drink most men find hard to resist. "Would it be wrong for me to offer you something to go with your tea?" I asked.

Both faces lit up as one. "It would be very generous of you," replied the other man. He was of similar age to his friend but smaller and extremely overweight. On both hands, gold rings adorned every finger. I made the mistake of admiring them too long.

"You would like to buy one of my rings? I have many in stock. I also sell all other kinds of jewellery and brassware."

"Perhaps," I offered, "but first, let's drink to our friendship." I ordered raki for them and tea for me. They seemed surprised. "I do not drink anything but tea." They both nodded. "And now, could you give me the neighbour's address so that I might talk to him?"

The server arrived a couple of minutes later with our drinks.

"You will have to be introduced," said the man with the moustache. He sipped the raki then drank some water from another glass. "I would be happy to do this for you." He showed me that confident smile I was getting from Uriah back at the hotel.

"That is very kind of you. Perhaps you would like…?"

Both men gulped down the rest of their drink and politely placed their glasses in the centre of the table. The waiter, on cue, removed the glasses and within a minute returned with two fresh drinks and a glass of tea, even though I had not finished the first cup.

After another refill, we set out to meet Hussein Ishmael's neighbour. It took twenty minutes, moving slowly through the bustling crowds before coming to a busy intersection. The tourists were long gone. Here was the real Istanbul. Rows of white sandy coloured abodes, some no bigger than my tiny place in the mews back home.

"This is the place," said my companion. "Let me see if he is in."

He left me standing inside a small dark courtyard dominated by a tall plane tree. A gentle breeze wafted through its branches, rustling the leaves. Grateful for the shade, I turned, so the breeze blew into my face.

"You are not used to the climate yet?"

The voice was soft and perfect in articulation. I turned to see my companion and a tall, distinguished-looking Turk dressed in a dark suit. The stark contrast between the suit and the old man's loose-fitting robe reminded how old and new cultures and lifestyles blended, particularly in the east. "I only got here yesterday." I held out a hand.

The old man stepped forward between us. "Mr Mehmet... Mr Pete."

We shook hands. "You're welcome, Mr Pete."

"Thank you," I replied. "I'm sorry I can't be as courteous as you and wish you well in Turkish."

"No matter what the language, you just have, Mr Pete. Please." He motioned me to some seats beneath the plane tree. After saying goodbye to his neighbour, he re-joined me. "And so, Mr Pete, you wish for information about an old acquaintance?"

"Yes, in particular, Mr Hussein Ishmael."

"Ah, yes, Ishmael. A sad, sad story. But tell me, why do you inquire about him?"

I handed him the newspaper and tapped the headline. I needed to know what had happened. The paper gave very few facts. My paper wanted an article about Turkish Cypriots and what happened in the seventies. During my inquiries, a colleague told me of the story of one Turkish soldier who fell in love with a beautiful girl and brought her back to Istanbul. My colleague sent me the story, recounting how the woman had murdered her husband and committed suicide. I believed they had a son who, at the time, would have been fifteen years old. It was a human-interest story that I could use, showing what happened to some Cypriots as they returned to their homeland after the invasion.

Mehmet clapped his hands, and a young girl appeared from inside the house. "Let us have tea, Mr Pete, and while we drink, you can tell me the real reason for your inquiry."

I decided to throw caution to the wind. "I believe Mr Ishmael's wife knew Andreas Hrisacopolis before fleeing Cyprus."

Mehmet waited for several seconds before answering. It was a well-known fact that Nico Hrisacopolis, Andreas's father, had few friends in Turkey. His son died a supposed hero, but he was nothing more than a coward who killed many Turks. Mehmet stared deeply into my eyes without blinking.

"I do not like the implications of what you are saying, but if your purpose is to tell the truth... and you seem an honest man to me... about Andreas Hrisacopolis, then far better you know the real truth of a sad story. The question is, Mr Pete, can I trust you?"

I was impressed. Mehmet was open and honest. He made me feel guilty that I had accepted his hospitality then lied to him. "My apologies," I said. "I assure you my intentions toward the Turkish people are honourable. I believe Nico Hrisacopolis has hidden agendas behind his generous offer to rebuild the Parthenon. I would like nothing better than to expose him for the corrupt man he is. Unfortunately, I cannot get to that hidden agenda unless I know about Ishmael and his wife Lara, as painful as it may be to dig up the past, especially for their son."

"Do not worry about their son, Mr Pete."

The tea arrived. I waited until the girl had left and then asked, "Why not worry about him?"

Mehmet poured tea and offered me a glass. We sipped in silence. "He's dead."

"Pardon?"

"The son, Baki, is dead and has been for some time."

CHAPTER TWENTY-SIX

A HMET SAT CROSS-LEGGED and watched the foyer lift over his newspaper's top. Too much was happening at once, and there was no one he could trust to help. Eren remained confined to his apartment and was instructed to study the Greek Orthodox teachings. The last thing they needed was a failure of understanding the church. Every time Eren opened his mouth, he had to be Andreas junior, the Greek.

West had returned to his room some thirty minutes earlier after taking breakfast. Keeping an eye on him was crucial. The man emerged from a lift a few minutes later with a small computer case slung over one shoulder. Ahmet followed discreetly, neatly folding his newspaper and holding it like a baton under one arm.

Wherever West was going, he was walking and appeared to be interested in the sights. Ahmet cursed him and fell in behind a group of Germans walking along the waterfront. He hated walking, especially during the day when tourists and shoppers filled the bazaars and jostled on the sidewalks. West hailed a taxi without warning, and Ahmet ran to catch another turning into the street up ahead. It was easy getting a taxi before noon but after that, impossible.

The journey took them over the Fatih Bridge spanning the Golden Horn, and onto the noisy Grand Bazaar. It was already humid and the crowds thronging the narrow passageways didn't help. Ahmet took a handkerchief from his pocket and wiped the top of his lip. Up ahead, West stopped and appeared to be asking directions. He was looking for someone, which meant he was after information about Hussein Ishmael and Baki.

Standing under an awning that shaded the front of a leather workshop, Ahmet watched West drinking tea with two men. He cursed at the prickly heat and dabbed his forehead.

When West finally rose to leave, Ahmet was surprised to see him accompanied by one of the men. His surprise turned to apprehension when they arrived at the house of one of the city's well-known financiers by the name of Mehmet. Ahmet's fears were coming true. Mehmet had financed Hussein Ishmael and enlisted Baki in the army after the parents' deaths.

As he sat at a table under the awning of a nearby tea house waiting for West to come out, Ahmet made a decision. The man was getting too close. Mehmet's influence in Turkish society equalled a highly respected and 'untouchable 'status. On the other hand, West was a nuisance and had to be taken care of; the sooner, the better. He brushed a fly away from his glass of tea and tried to relax.

Half an hour later, West left Mehmet's house after the two men shook hands at the entrance to the courtyard. Ahmet rose to follow. He left payment on the table and walked across the street, some fifty feet behind West.

CHAPTER TWENTY-SEVEN

EHMET WAS NOT THE KIND of man to manufacture such a story, particularly one so full of detail. If Baki died, my guess was his figuring as part of the big surprise announcement was wrong. I was back at square one. There was, however, one piece of the story I wanted to check out. Mehmet told me of a friend of Baki's who was present when the lad died and now lived in an apartment about a mile away. I decided to walk there and find him.

I unfolded a street map from the hotel and pored over it for several minutes. The map was next to useless, but I could get an approximate fix on the address Mehmet had given me after finding the street I was on.

Murat Kemal lived in a tall block of apartments that stank of stale food and housed hundreds of kids. The place wasn't different from all the other inner cities I'd experienced. Lost in my thoughts, I climbed three flights of concrete stairs and was halfway up the next when I smelled smoke. Suddenly awake, I froze. A door opened on the next landing, and a child ran out, followed by a rather large screaming mother dressed in sweatpants and what looked like flour on her hands. The smell was more pungent and was obviously from something she was cooking.

Pushing my way past the woman, I climbed the next steps and found Murat's door. I knocked once and waited. The woman continued to scream, and the hordes of kids were still running around, adding to the din. I knocked again, and the door opened almost at once to my relief.

"Murat Kemal?'

"Yes, and you must be Pete West."

Mehmet had called in advance and told him that we should talk. I might have known. Mehmet was a man who had influence. Murat would probably have been less than helpful; gaining trust in Turkish society takes time.

"That was kind of him." I shook hands as Murat showed me into his small living quarters.

The room was dominated by a long divan, covered in a colourful drape edged with dark red tassels. Large cushions, some embroidered with geometric patterns and others with Turkish flowers, lay across the bare wooden floor.

I guessed Murat to be in his thirties. He was dressed in a white open-neck shirt, creased black slacks and open-toed leather sandals. Like most Turkish men, he wore a thick black handlebar moustache. For some reason, Turks love rings. Murat wore three big chunky gold rings on the fingers of his right hand.

I sat by the side of a small ornate wooden coffee table on which tea things had been placed. He poured and offered me a glass, then sat back. Sipping tea, he surprised me. "I hope you are going to catch Baki's killer."

That was a new one on me. I didn't know Baki had been murdered and was sure Mehmet would have told me if he suspected murder. I acted surprised.

"Oh yes, Mr West, although you might say that the hands of the killer never touched Baki, the consequences of his actions did."

I watched as Murat drank his tea, one finger tapping the side of the glass nervously. Whatever happened was still painful for him, and memories of Baki's death stirred anger. "How did you first meet Baki?" I took a small notebook out of my pocket.

Murat put his cup down. He paused and then answered, "You're a journalist-I forgot."

I felt a little insensitive and explained I was writing an article on Nico Hrisacopolis when Baki's name came up. That wasn't a lie but only half the truth. Mehmet might have told him the real reason I was there, but I decided not to go into more detail. Nonetheless, Murat appeared to be in the mood to expose Nico and made it clear he would be happy to help in any way he could.

His eyes narrowed. "I am sure Nico Hrisacopolis was part of the plot. I know his treacherous underling visited Baki all the time." He spat the words out, and his face darkened with anger.

There was a huge story here. I could feel it.

"I'll tell you, Mr West, I knew Baki was in trouble the first day he came into the garrison."

I agreed with him but probably not for the same reason. It must have come as a shock to find his grandson joining the Turkish Army. With his political plans in their infancy concerning the EU, it was easy to see Nico wanted Baki out, mainly if those plans involved Baki being a figurehead for the Hrisacopolis Empire.

I reached for my tape and placed it on the table. "Do you mind?"

He was wary of the machine and snatched it from me. Examining it before laying it on a cushion next to his chair, he tapped it and became a little agitated. "It's not that I don't trust you," he exclaimed, "but If anything happens to you and the tape gets into the wrong hands, I could be killed."

I understood his concern but knew nothing would happen to him. Nico and his agent would not know who the voice belonged to; I never exposed an interviewee's name on the tape. His story was crucial, so I picked my notebook up without a word and put the tape back in my pocket.

He nodded and settled back into his chair.

"Okay, what about that day he first met you?"

Baki was a rebel, he remembered. 'I liked Baki from the start. The two of us were standing together in a line, receiving our uniforms and being told which barrack hut we were in.

"So you were both in the same barracks?"

Murat poured more tea. Baki was reserved like he was hiding something. He would spend long hours at weekends just sitting around looking out of the windows. It was sometimes impossible to talk to him. Murat knew a tragedy had occurred in Baki's family and that joining the army a year earlier than usual had kept him out of trouble. There was another rumour that he had killed someone, but he doubted that. Baki wasn't the type.

"So, how long were you together before he died?" I offered a cigarette and left the packet on the table.

"Eleven months almost to the day. Baki hated every day he served, yet he could have got out whenever he wanted."

"How so?"

"A man came to visit him every month. Baki called him an evil traitor."

"Can you recall his name?"

Murat shook his head. Baki told me very little except that the man kept offering to buy him out of the army."

I didn't understand. "If Baki hated the army so much, why did he turn the man's offer down."

"I believe there were, as you say, strings attached," said Murat.

"Which were?"

"I didn't know all the details, but I knew Baki had to change his name. That upset him. It was the only time he spoke about that particular meeting. It was not until I talked with Mehmet after leaving the army that the name Hrisacopolis came up. After Baki died, Mehmet asked for a meeting, and it was then that I found out that Mehmet was the man who put Baki into the army."

I hesitated before asking the next question. "So, is this traitor the killer?"

Murat raised his hands in the air. I'm not sure, but I wouldn't be surprised if the visitor were involved. He certainly had influence and money, and it was not until I met with Mehmet that I found out the visitor was an agent for Hrisacopolis.

"Why do you say that?" I asked.

"Baki never told me anything directly, but I read between the lines. At first, when the man arrived, he offered money to Baki: lots of money. Baki stormed into the barracks shouting that he could not be bought."

I was a little confused. "If Baki didn't like the man, why would he see him again after their first meeting?"

"Captain Abbas." Murat sat forward and pointed the finger at me. "He was the killer. He is the man who should be shot."

Our conversation was getting interesting. "And how was he involved?"

"The captain received money from Baki's visitor every time he visited," answered Murat. "Baki was forced to meet the visitor in the main courtyard of the barracks. If he didn't, he received extra work detail at weekends and twice had a beating at the hands of Abbas and his henchman, a sergeant."

"So things got out of hand? Is that how Baki died?"

Murat lit a cigarette. "I have spent many hours trying to put things together. I am sure that Abbas and Baki's visitor were both involved." He blew a stream of smoke into the air. "If I could get my hands on Abbas, I'd make him talk."

I was beginning to like Murat. He was a little different to the usual middle-aged Turk. His loose black curly hair hung tangled over the collar of his shirt. His attitude towards the army defined him as a rebel, especially his dark eyes that pierced me each time he emphasised his point. I could imagine him and Baki as good friends. "Is the Captain still in the army?" I asked.

Murat shook his head. After the explosion during a training exercise, Abbas deserted. The family of the other killed soldier had put a price on the captain's head even though they were paid handsomely to keep quiet.

It was my turn to sit back. Mehmet had told me Baki died in an army exercise. I made a note of the names involved. For nearly a year, Abbas bullied Baki and was urged by his visitor to change his name. Curious, I asked Murat how the news of Baki's death was received in Athens.

Murat waved a hand in the air dismissively. "After Baki died, I expected trouble, but things were kept low key. Of course, I didn't know that Nico was Baki's grandfather at that time. I wondered why there had not been plenty of publicity in the world press with hindsight. There was nothing except a small item in the Turkish press. A story appeared about a week after the incident, telling of an unfortunate explosion that occurred during a training exercise, resulting in the deaths of two soldiers. No names were ever printed."

I was drawing pictures in my mind. "And the army paid compensation to the family of the other dead soldier?"

Murat's eyelids flickered. His hands balled into fists. "I believe so," he replied.

"And what about the visitor? Did he ever appear again?"

He shook his head. "No, he never came back."

I thought for a moment. How could it be possible that Nico did not know his grandson was dead? Or was it that he did know, perhaps in advance. Had he got fed up waiting for Baki to fall in with his plans, whatever they were?

Murat continued. "They were inside a hut that was a duplicate of our barracks with a squad of fourteen soldiers. The exercise was a fire drill. Abbas liked to make it realistic. A small incendiary device that created much smoke would be dropped through a window by the sergeant. The squad would evacuate through two exits, one was the main door, and the other was a back entrance for anyone caught in the toilet or storeroom at the rear. The object of the exercise was to evacuate in less than fifteen seconds. Now and again, they would lock one of the exits to make things more difficult. Once out, the soldiers had to run one hundred yards to an assembly point."

"Let me guess. They locked one of the exits."

"Yes, but not only that, Mr West." Murat's face darkened. "We were in the storage area where the sergeant had put us. We started for the main door when we found the rear exit locked. I remember the swirling black smoke was so thick we were choking. Then there was a second explosion just as we reached the main door, more powerful than the first, accompanied by a bright flash and flames. I can't remember any more. A doctor told me later that Baki had caught the full force of the explosion, and I was lucky to be alive.

I guessed either Abbas or the sergeant threw the incendiary device into the hut after all the others had got out. No one saw what happened, but I was curious about Abbas and how he escaped the scene. Surely an explosion would lead to the staff running to help from all directions, and he would have to be accountable as the officer in charge.

Murat shrugged his shoulders, reminding me we were not talking about the strictly disciplined British army. Abbas was an officer, and the garrison very big. He had a car and could have driven out of any gate by showing his pass.

"Who identified Baki's body?"

"I am sorry, I do not know."

"Do you know if Mehmet visited Baki at all?"

"I am not sure of that either. If he did, he did not tell me about it, and I never saw him myself."

Murat leaned forward; his voice lowered. "He came to see me in hospital and later invited me to his home. He wanted to know all about Baki's death, just like you."

I wondered if Mehmet had visited Baki, he might have found out who the visitor was.

Murat breathed in deeply. "Mr West, if Mehmet knew the identity of the Turk who visited Baki, he would not tell you and neither would I. It would not be to protect the man more to take care of our own in our way."

I could believe that, but it didn't help. I decided there wasn't anything else to learn, and an early night before flying home was in order. I thanked Murat and assured him I would get to the bottom of things, and he would read about it.

In England, there's an old saying – 'If you want to know the way, ask a policeman.' If you want to know the way in Turkey – don't.

I had decided to take a leisurely walk through the local Kasbah to buy a gift for Jessica. I found two: a beautiful silk scarf and a small leather purse. By the time I had finished my wanderings, I was lost. A policeman, who spoke no English, waved his arms in so many directions after I gave him the name of my hotel that I ended up more confused. The map didn't help either. I decided to follow my instincts and head in one direction until I crossed the main thoroughfare. That's how I had got about the last time, although I wasn't looking for a hotel then, just another bar.

My watch said it was lunchtime, but my stomach defied me to swallow anything I could smell right then. Turkish cuisine can be mouth-watering, but the aroma doesn't always do it justice.

I hurried down one narrow road after another before coming to a T-junction. I turned right and started down a steep cobbled area, just wide enough for single traffic. The road was in deep shadow, and I was thankful for the cool air.

"Dikkat. Dikkat."

I had no idea of the word's precise meaning but knew instinctively that it was a warning. A hand grabbed me from behind. I fell backwards into a doorway and landed on top of my saviour. As I fell, I was aware of an old grey car shooting past and a rush of air on my face.

There was a loud crunch of metal on brick as the vehicle continued down the road. Hitting the ground with a clatter, the front fender flipped back up into the air. It cartwheeled into a doorway with a crash next to an astonished woman, whose shopping bag fell to the ground, spilling its contents. Oranges and a variety of vegetables rolled across the cobbles. Behind the car, as fast as they could run, came a bunch of screaming kids enjoying themselves. Several men followed the kids in hot pursuit, leaving a trail of squashed food and a screaming woman waving her fists in the air. A loud crash signalled the car had come to a halt at the bottom of the road. It had come to rest against a concrete wall.

Call me superstitious, but it crossed my mind that someone was after me. I turned to thank the man who saved me and came face to face with an old man half my size clucking at me through a white moustache, stained brown across the edge with nicotine. We shook hands, and I thanked him with a hug. In return, he went up on tiptoe and kissed my cheek.

I jogged away to the bottom of the hill where the car had come to rest, causing a traffic jam. A large, noisy crowd surrounded the vehicle. Noticing some American tourists, I fell in with them. "How's the driver?" I asked.

"Damnedest thing," a large man replied, "there ain't no driver." He pointed back up the hill. "Must have had a hand-brake failure or somethin'."

'Or something' was right. If enemies could reach us in Cyprus and Turkey, they could easily find us in London. I looked around for a taxi to get me to my hotel. I needed to call Jessica.

———◈———

Cool air wafted through the net curtains and into the room. I was slowly walking up and down in front of the windows with a glass of iced water in one hand and a telephone in the other. Jessica was doing most of the talking.

"I don't understand how Nico doesn't know about his grandson. Surely someone would have told him. His agent, whoever that was, was visiting Baki on his behalf. What about him?"

"He had a personal agenda, whatever that was." I told her the story as I knew it. I also told her about the car and added it could have been an accident. There again, it could have been the KKA group. They had all the reasons to see Nico dead and might see us as a threat. The last thing they wanted was publicity.

"And we've been digging around Cyprus and Istanbul," said Jessica, thoughtfully. "'B' warned me about them too."

I remembered that she had met him for lunch. "How did you get on?"

"He was not surprised when I mentioned Lara and Jamilya." She paused. "Sorry, darling. Police confirmed Jamilya's death. A customer found her strangled. 'B's concern centred on the car crash and the terrorist group he thought might be behind it. He also knew that Baki was dead and was positive that Nico was behind Alexander and Jamilya. We are probably the last ones to know about the true identity of Lara's son."

"No, not quite," I replied. "Murat and Mehmet know that although they are quite safe, what about the editor chap?"

"Ioannis Koskotas."

"Yes, him. If he was that close to Andreas…." I realised something I had overlooked as I spoke, but Jessica beat me to it – naturally.

"He must have known about Baki's death, being close to world news and especially the Turkish press. I'm sure there are Turkish newspapers on the island."

I thought for a moment. Of course, Koskotas knew. "Maybe, and you might be able to find out soon." In a press release, Nico's secretary had sent out a list of dignitaries going on the cruise. Koskotas was on it. I stopped to look out of the windows. Her voice was so near, yet she was so far away. "Thank you. I miss you."

"I miss you too. Come home."

I sat on the end of the bed. There was a lump in my throat and a longing in my heart.

CHAPTER TWENTY-EIGHT

T HE CRUISERS ROLLED GENTLY on the swell. There was a splash as a diver jumped into the sea from one of the transoms. Far out on the clear horizon, a smudge of smoke revealed the nearest ship. Adonis stood facing the stateroom window for some time before turning his attention back to the chart on the table. Everything had to go like clockwork, details checked again and again. He sipped from a glass of water, a determined look on his face.

There was a knock on the door. Adonis straightened the chart and placed another on top of it. "Come in."

A burly Frenchman dressed in the bottom half of a diving suit entered, followed by another much taller man, also French, wearing jeans and a grubby T-shirt. The Turk followed them, holding a large cigar in one hand and a glass of vodka in the other. Still wearing the same oil-stained T-shirt and filthy jeans from the previous day, the breeze blowing through the door brought a strong smell of body odour. Adonis turned away and wrinkled his nose.

"Well, Cypriot, here we are, all together." The Turk grinned broadly and held both arms outstretched. "Okay, take a seat," he said to the men. Touching each, in turn, he introduced them. "Here is Joseph, our explosives expert, and there is Louis in charge of the boarding party. Louis is also a legionnaire – that is, until they catch him. Like me, he's on leave from the bastards."

His deep guttural laugh boomed out while his stomach, exposed below the filthy T-shirt, wobbled grotesquely. A small drop of saliva dribbled from the corner of his mouth, and he wiped it away with the back of the large hairy hand that held the cigar. Ash dropped onto his chest.

Adonis felt utter disgust as he waited for them to settle. "Okay, now I'll tell you what we're going to do and how we will do it." He spread both hands on the chart table and drew attention to the drawing. "There will be no alterations or deviations from the plan." As he spoke, his eyes rose and met the Turk's.

Joseph and Louis glanced at the Turk, who said nothing, standing with arms crossed against his chest. A cigar stub gripped between his bared teeth.

Adonis pointed to a course he had plotted on the chart that *Sea Empress* would take as she sailed northwest of Malta. He traced a finger from their present position to the point of interception where they would change position and come up astern of *Sea Empress*, letting the two cruisers take up the chase. Louis and his men had to reach her quickly.

"They will pick up the cruisers on their radar," protested Louis. He stepped away from the chart and threw a hand up in protest. "Impossible. This is not going to work."

Ignoring him, Adonis continued. "You must make sure we show the appropriate night-time warning lights."

The Turk moved closer. "Never mind the lights, what about the ship's radar? Even the smallest of craft can be picked up on radar. Your plan is flawed." He turned to Louis. "Louis is right. This won't work."

If they closed the cruisers up one behind the other, no one on the liner's bridge would notice a tiny blip on the radar screen, persisted Adonis. They weren't dealing with the military. Louis would be climbing aboard within minutes.

"You stupid bastard. Did you hear what I said? You think we're going to risk our lives on this stupid plan?" The Turk threw his cigar stub on the deck and stamped on it. His fist thumped the table.

"It will work… unless you're getting worried. Who the hell do you think is going to come to their rescue? Now let me finish."

"You're pushing your luck, Cypriot."

Louis lit a cigarette. "What about the two men who will be aboard? Do they know when to expect us?"

Adonis rolled the chart away to reveal another chart showing the ship's layout. The Turk had contacted Alexey Rublev with instructions for the men before they boarded. They would be in position, one of them on the starboard side from where he could see the cruisers as the liner passed. Ten minutes later, the men were going to make their way to the cargo doors and open them.

"Okay, Cypriot, so now they are aboard. I still think they should board at two places."

"Believe me, it will not matter," answered Adonis.

"But-"

Adonis slapped the table and glared at Louis, then at the Turk. The last thing he wanted right then was a voice edged with doubt. Louis glared back, unfolding his arms. Turning back to the chart, Adonis continued. Two hours later, he sat alone with his thoughts. The Turk and his men were aboard the other vessel, playing cards.

CHAPTER TWENTY-NINE

RISACOPOLIS STOOD ON THE podium in a light grey suit sporting a red rose buttonhole, making the odd gesture with his big fat hands. He emphasised how his dream of bringing the Parthenon frieze back to its rightful home was fulfilled. His contribution was nothing compared to the enormous efforts of the Greek and British governments. The Whitehall officials and Greek embassy staff applauded in the right places, cuing the rest of the assembled guests to follow suit. His deep voice droned on for nearly half an hour, clearly boring others and me. I spotted several ladies stifling a yawn with a gloved hand. When he had finished, Nico dismissed the gathering with a wave and gave a quick smile for the cameras.

A small Whitehall flunky from the Ministry of the Arts entourage grabbed at the microphone to direct guests as Nico turned away from the applause. VIPs, he announced, should follow the platform party and board right away while guests with gold invitations should make their way to the afternoon greeting reception in the ballroom on deck B. All other guests, including friends in the press, could check into their cabins, where they would find a brochure listing a full itinerary of functions and meetings.

I turned to Jessica with raised eyebrows. "So we're not important enough to be invited for drinkies?"

She dug me in the ribs. "You're on the unwelcome list, remember?"

We turned away from the quayside platform as Nico and his

'friends' filed away and disappeared into a covered walkway up to the ship.

I'd never been on a cruise ship. *Sea Empress* looked like a giant white warehouse topped with an office block. There were no classic nautical lines in the hull or superstructure, more the modernistic Lego layout of a suburban shopping mall. But then, what did I know. All I did have was an instant feeling of dislike. A few ferry trips across the English Channel and one unforgettable experience in a rowing boat on the Serpentine in Hyde Park were the total of my seafaring adventures.

"It's not very big, is it?" I said.

"What were you expecting, the Queen Mary?" Jessica sounded annoyed. I thought a cruise ship would be bigger, especially this one, which was the distinguished flagship of the line. She gave me one of her looks. "I intend to enjoy myself without listening to you complaining."

I ignored the remark and changed the subject. "I hope we are in the same cabin."

"I hope not." Her nose was in the air.

"Meaning?" I asked.

"We're not married, and there will be guests my father knows."

"How about . . .?"

"No." She smiled without looking at me.

That was the end of the subject. She gave me a sharp poke in the ribs as we neared the boarding line of guests not invited to the reception. Although only joking about sharing, I did hope we were on the same deck. I wanted Jessica where I could see her.

When I got into my cabin, I found a folder lying on the bedside table. It was packed with information about our ship. There was also an envelope with my name scrawled across the front. A neatly written short note, signed by Nico, was inside. I read it several times before sitting on the edge of the bed. There was a knock at the cabin door, and Jessica appeared without waiting for a reply.

"I've just had a strange phone call." She dropped down next to me.

"Really," I replied. "Well, I've just received this."

She took the note and read it out loud. "Welcome aboard, Mr West. I hope you and your colleague find everything to your liking. This reminds you that a private interview has been arranged for you in my quarters. My secretary will arrange the time. Please bring your beautiful colleague with you. I know my grandson…" wide-eyed, she jumped up off the bed. "Grandson!" She finished reading. "He would never forgive me if he were not introduced to her."

I took the note back and tossed it on the table. We sat in silence for a moment.

Jessica interrupted my thoughts. "If Baki is still alive, where has he been since he left the army?"

I shook my head. I picked the note up again and looked at it, trying to read something that wasn't there. Jessica rose from the bed and walked to the window while I scanned the itinerary. There was a general get-together party for all guests after we put to sea. I decided that would be the time to track down our elusive Cypriot editor.

"I'd like to ask him about the photo of Andreas."

"No." I joined her at the window and put my arms around her. "Let's keep our secret a little longer. What was the strange phone call about?"

While Jessica's father looked into the death of Alexander, he discovered Alexander had a one-time association with a little-known art foundation formed by Nico. I'd read about the foundation in the Hrisacopolis file Max gave me. Alexander was a bit of a painter. Nothing really good, but the Greek public loved him. He painted scenes of Cyprus.

Jessica turned from the window. "Some years ago, there was a row over a painting Alexander wanted returned from the foundation. He had loaned it to them years earlier. Nico refused, and Alexander never forgave him. He threatened to write a book about Andreas."

I opened my mouth to speak, but her raised hand silenced me.

Her father spent some time looking into the foundation's history called the 'Hrisacopolis Grecian Cultural Art Foundation' and came across a list of board members. I recognised several: Two Greeks, Jason Simonides and Admes Silas, both politicians and a Belgian lady, Adelheid with an unpronounceable name who was something with the World Health Organization. The other two were French.

She pointed to the newspaper clipping with the picture of Lara that I had placed on the bedside table with my notebook. "Guess who the treasurer is?"

My jaw dropped. "You're kidding… Koskotas?"

Jessica was fast becoming a 'can't do without' asset. I reached out and pulled her close. There was that faint smell of gardenias again, and I kissed her. She spun away. "Have you unpacked yet?"

"No, there's plenty of time." I tried kissing her again, but she pushed me away.

"Pete, I need to unpack. My gowns will crease." She walked to the door and turned. "If I thought you'd be a gentleman, I'd kiss you again." Her hand was on the door handle.

I crossed my heart with my fingers. "I've been nothing but today."

She raised one beautiful eyebrow and slowly walked back.

I have never got used to wearing evening dress. The stiff collar bit into my neck, and the cuffs felt too long even though the cufflinks stopped my sleeves from travelling past my wrists. Adjusting the suspenders holding up my pants, I opened the cabin door and stepped out into the corridor just as a couple, well turned out like fashion mannequins, strolled by. I looked at my shining shoes as they passed me and then took a deep breath. I stepped across the carpet and knocked on Jessica's door. She appeared, looking like a film star.

I was amazed. "You're the most beautiful woman I've ever known."

Some of the women I have interviewed have been stunningly beautiful, but there have been few who could compare to Jessica. Her beauty was natural. Apart from her nails, lipstick, and a hint of eye shadow, she wore no makeup. Her hair had been transformed. It was brushed long and lay on her shoulders, complimenting a long red Grecian style evening gown that clung to her figure. She looked truly amazing.

"Thank you." She winked and took my arm. "Let's see how well we can fish, eh?"

"The editor – Koskotas?"

"Yes, Ioannis Koskotas." She pinched my arm. "Quite a name to get your tongue around."

I sometimes had trouble pronouncing the odd name but had no problem spelling them when I needed to.

We walked to the elevator and rode up to the banqueting suite. A couple of hundred or so guests were milling around in formal dress. I recognised a few colleagues. Most of us were used to jeans, a London Fog raincoat or shorts and a T-shirt. Apart from Jessica, we all seemed out of place. The usual buzz was interrupted now and again by an excessively loud laugh. A waiter slid up from nowhere, offering champagne from a silver tray. I motioned him away after Jessica had taken a glass.

"Let's see who we can spot in the crowd," I said, wondering what Koskotas looked like. I imagined a relatively old man who was small in stature, business-like and a little loud like Max.

"Looking very Greek and with a lapel name tag spelling his name correctly."

"Very funny, I must be rubbing off on you," I remarked.

A soft voice came from behind us. "Ah, Mr West and this lovely lady must be Miss Du Rosse."

I turned to face a tall suave man, dressed in a white evening jacket, mauve cumber band, and yes, his tag identified him as Koskotas. A cigarette held securely in a short ivory holder between well-manicured fingers hovered mid-air. "I overheard you were looking for me," he said pleasantly.

If Jessica was embarrassed, she didn't show it. "My apologies, Mr Koskotas. I hope you will forgive me." Her eyelids lowered, and her voice softened. "We are pleased to be here, and I wanted to meet you, especially after speaking to you on the telephone." She extended a long, smooth arm and arched her fingers upwards with practised ease, red beads dangling from her wrist.

"Please call me Ioannis." Koskotas gently held the hand offered and bent to kiss her fingers. "The pleasure is entirely mine. I take no offence but am happy that you should be looking for me."

Jessica gave him that coy smile that all women reserve for a man they are about to overwhelm. "Please, Ioannis, call me Jessica." She turned. "May I introduce Mr Peter West?"

While shaking hands with him, I wondered if he'd been trailing us. I told him it was a pleasure to meet a director on the board of the Art Foundation that was partly responsible for the acquisition of the marbles. He must have been pleased to be taking them home.

"Indeed, I am Mr West. I have long been an admirer and read your column regularly... Although I have not seen it lately."

I loved how his eyebrows rose over enquiring eyes and the intonation of speech that suggested a little playful sarcasm. "It's a temporary thing," I told him. "Besides, I'm far too busy writing about Mr Hrisacopolis and those, like himself, who were helping to restore some of Greece's past glory."

Sometimes I can get carried away.

"All Greece will be rejoicing soon and then...."

Jessica interrupted right on cue and slid an arm through the Greek's. "Well, before you two men start talking politics, I will abscond with Ioannis and have him show me around."

"We'll meet again shortly, Mr West." He winked as Jessica led him away.

I was glad we hadn't got into a conversation about Nico. That would come later.

CHAPTER THIRTY

I WAS BORED SITTING IN Jessica's cabin. She spent some time whispering into Koskotas' ear before 'doing the rounds' with practised ease. There are times when I have to admire someone who can spend an entire evening talking politics or high society small talk with like-minded people, especially when they do this for me. Jessica was unique as she'd chosen to distance herself just far enough away from the life she loathed but kept near enough to slip back into the fray whenever needed.

The evening was not uneventful. I'd met several politicians and members of the diplomatic corps who were either old sparring partners or nodding acquaintances. I didn't have any friends in parliament or Whitehall; even 'B' wasn't what you might call 'close.' It didn't pay to have a friend in the corridors of power if you were going to kick them one day.

I looked at my watch. I'd promised Jessica I would wait for her to exchange any news and plan our interview for the following day, but I got annoyed with her. It was way past midnight when the telephone buzzed, making me jump. Jessica sounded positive. She was on her way back with a bottle of champagne. I lay back on the bed and hoped the champagne might mean I would stay for the night. Five minutes later, the door opened, and I heard Koskotas wishing her goodnight in an oily tone.

"What happened with him?" I asked as Jessica rustled past me. "Did you find any little dark secrets?"

Jessica hadn't. The man spent most of their conversation enthusing about Nico and the man's ambitions. She paused and looked at me with an air of apprehension. "I don't know if you'll be mad with me, but-"

"But what…? What?" I shrugged impatiently as she paused. "I've been here for almost two hours, Jessica. Tell me."

Her face darkened. She tossed her purse onto the bed and glared at me. "It's not my fault you decided to leave early. I was doing my job," she snapped.

I took a deep breath. "Okay, so what is it you hope I won't be mad about?" She turned away from me, kicking off her shoes.

"Well, I assumed that as we had been told about the grandson, he would know too. I asked him how we – the world – had not known about the young man." She turned, taking out her earrings. "He said it was as much a surprise to them as it would be to everyone else when they were told. We are two of the privileged few."

I jumped off the bed and grabbed her by the arms, wide awake. "Who was 'them'…? Who?"

She'd caught that too and asked him to elaborate. He meant the old man and himself. It appeared, according to Koskotas, that Nico was stunned to hear he had a grandson and couldn't wait to share the great news with the world, especially the European Union.

Nico was lying. Jamilya had told us the truth; she couldn't make up her story. What would be the point? I thought for a moment. Nico wanted Brussels to share in his good fortune meant only one thing. I remembered 'B's strange warning.

"I'll just bet Whitehall has heard rumours," I said, "hence 'B's warning. This grandson will shortly be the new captain at the ship's wheel."

"Or maybe not," said Jessica, upending the empty bottle and pouting.

"Or maybe not," I repeated. "But knowing Brussels, I'm sure he will be."

Knowing that another member of the Hrisacopolis family was ready to keep a steady hand on the empire, Brussels would look more kindly on acceding to rubber-stamp the old boy's appointment he wanted without worrying.

Jessica yawned. "What are we going to do?" She pulled a notebook off the bedside table.

"Forget it," I said. "I want some fresh air and time to think."

"You need some time to get over yourself."

I looked at her while she yawned and let the comment pass. "You need some beauty sleep." I bent to kiss her forehead, but she turned away, eyes closed. I left her yawning and closed the door.

Several things didn't make sense, and I needed a walk around the deck. Apart from that, Jessica had annoyed me, or was it Koskotas? Either way, I wasn't in the mood to worry about her right then. I went into my cabin and picked up my coat.

Outside, there was quite a breeze blowing. We were nearing the Bay of Biscay, and the cold air was clearing the cobwebs away. As I strolled unsteadily along the deck, I couldn't get the grandson, Baki, out of my mind. Pulling my coat around me, I sat on a recliner next to some steps leading down to the deck below. The slow melodic rhythm of a guitar playing Jazz drifted out of the cocktail bar just below me at the foot of the stairs as someone came out to or in from the main deck. I closed my eyes and relaxed despite the chilly breeze.

I hadn't been sitting for more than a minute when I heard voices, quite close, coming from the deck below. I didn't recognise either male but did catch enough of the conversation to realise it was strictly private.

"We have to succeed or face failure..."

"There is another way."

"No."

"As I said, we have other options. There are others that I would gladly see over the side before we reach Athens. Why he invited those journalists, I will never know."

Silence followed this last statement, and I assumed they had moved back inside. I started to rise when the conversation continued in harsh whispers.

"I will meet him as arranged and take him to his cabin."

"Our orders were quite clear."

I sat quite still, waiting for more, but again, there was silence.

Then I heard the splash. It wasn't very loud but discernible, even against the noise of the waves and the wind. I raced across the deck. Looking below, I was just in time to see a hand withdrawn from the rail. Whoever it belonged to was aware I was above him. I made for the stairs and bounded down them. There was no one around. Then I leaned back over the side and saw a large white motor catamaran.

Sea Empress slowed, and I hadn't noticed. A short gangplank extended from an opening lower down on the ship and attached to the catamaran. A figure walked across and disappeared into the 'crew only' entrance. Within moments, the catamaran moved away and disappeared into the night. A red ensign fluttered from the stern, but I saw no crew.

"I'm telling you: I don't *think* I heard a splash. I did."

Jessica was sceptical. She held her fingers up, one at a time, as she spoke. I'd overheard a murder plot, a disagreement, a splash, and then silence. "It all sounded like an Agatha Christie plot."

We were in the restaurant having breakfast. I didn't care what it sounded like. During the conversation, the two conspirators mentioned us.

Jessica almost laughed. There were other pairs of journalists on board.

I was getting pretty mad at her. "Jessica, I know it all sounds far-fetched but remember who we're talking about here. Remember what's at stake."

There was only one way to settle my concern that someone went over the side during the night. She wanted me to ask the captain to check the crew and passengers.

"I already have. The officer I spoke to informed me there were no reports of anyone missing."

"There you are then." Irritated, she dismissed the subject and asked, "What are we going to do about the interview?"

I thought for a moment. If we started asking leading questions about Baki, Nico would know our information came from his enemies. We were going to have to be very careful. I'd ask some general questions about his upbringing, why he finally decided to declare his parentage, and what the future held for him.

"Good idea," said Jessica. "I thought I might take the camera along and get some pictures. I could email them off to the office. They could search to see if our Baki is someone else. You never know."

Jessica handed me a coffee. "Do you think it was Baki who came aboard last night?"

"I think so. Nico probably doesn't want the lad swamped with the press at the embarkation. I don't understand why anyone would call him a fool for inviting us on the cruise unless they knew we'd already been asking awkward questions, which means they have to be close to him."

Jessica tapped her cup. "No. If they were close, why would they want Baki dead? Who else wants Baki or Nico or both dead?" Her cup clattered into the saucer. "KKA." She put a hand to her mouth as she answered her own question. "You don't honestly think they would be on board?"

"It's a possibility." I waved a finger at her. "And if they are, we will be in the middle of it all."

Jessica surveyed the restaurant and then back at me. She whispered in a low cryptic voice, "I think we should tell someone."

I gave her a frosty stare as a waiter hurried past with a loaded tray. "No, we will not do that," I assured her secret services of about six countries scoured the ship, so a terrorist attack was pretty slim. No one would be that reckless. Not wanting to frighten her, I knew a boatload of secret agents wouldn't stop a determined terrorist. Besides, the last thing I wanted was to attract attention.

CHAPTER THIRTY-ONE

HRISACOPOLIS TURNED AS the door closed and looked puzzled. "What the hell was my grandson on about?"

Ahmet drew his lips tightly in anger and settled back into the chair. He steepled his fingers, deep in thought. The first meeting had gone well. Hrisacopolis was delighted that his dead son's name had passed on to his grandson. Whether or not he required a bodyguard, Eren's innocent remark was the kind of remark Ahmet had warned Eren not to make in front of grandfather. In itself, it meant nothing but Nico wouldn't think so. He saw problems with everyone and everything around him.

The KKA were on board. Ahmet cursed them for changing his plans. Whatever KKA's aim was, Nico Hrisacopolis would die- not the pretend Andreas Junior. They had to be dealt with, and he needed a few hours of breathing space. That night's earlier encounter was too close to home. He thought quickly. He could arrange for protection, but it would be impossible to stay by Eren's side and care about the KKA situation.

"We have a problem," he answered.

"It's hard to keep such a big secret for too long," he explained. "One of my contacts let me know that the KKA heard Andreas Junior was attending religious lessons from a Greek priest, something they will learn from the news conference anyway. Andreas knows all that, hence his inquiry."

Nico sank into his chair, dabbing his forehead. "Damn them."

"If I can make a suggestion, sir," said Ahmet.

A specific tone of voice and just the right amount of persuasion was required; insight into Nico's way of thinking always proved valuable in getting him what he wanted. Andreas needed to be a problem for Nico to worry about right then.

Ahmet chose his words with care. After the news conference, it might be good to keep Andreas in close contact with a couple of Nico security guards. The last thing they needed was a mob following him everywhere on the ship. He would, of course, attend the official public appearances with his grandfather during the voyage. Ahmet glanced sideways to gauge the old man's reaction as he spoke. "We need to do this just in case there are agents on board."

Nico thought for a moment and blew smoke into the air. "This is supposed to be the most glorious moment of my life, and already I am making a prisoner of my grandson." He rolled the cigar back and forth between his fingers.

Ahmet frowned and shrugged. Precautions were necessary on the ship, but Andreas junior would be able to move around more freely once back home.

"You're right, of course. All right, I will make arrangements."

Ahmet walked to the door. "I shall see you at the meeting, sir."

———◆———

It wasn't the sudden bang of a door or the shrill ring of an alarm clock that woke me. My subconscious was in survival mode before the thought processes had tuned in. The hairs on the back of my neck were tingling. Half-awake, I leapt from my bed and ran for the cabin door, falling with a loud thump over a pair of shoes that I'd discarded the night before. Picking myself up, I grabbed for the handle and swung the door open. Outside, I bent over double, gulping air and unable to move.

"You all right, sir?"

Sheepishly, I said, "Yes, just a little light-headed after a late night," I lied.

"Would you like me to get you anything?"

"No, no." I waved him away.

He walked to the end of the passage, and I then stepped back inside my cabin. There was no smell, no wafting smoke, and no flames. Sitting on the edge of the bed I realised my nightmare wasn't getting any better but worse. There was a single tap on the door. "Anyone at home?"

"Sort of," I answered weakly.

Jessica sat down beside me and put an arm around my shoulder. "What's up?" A finger stroked me lightly on the lips as I began to speak. "And don't tell me there's nothing wrong when I know there is."

I had dreaded this moment. How the hell did I tell her the truth when I wasn't sure I was telling the truth? The psychiatrist's report said a different story, which everyone believed – except me. "Please leave it. We'll discuss it later."

She gave me a quizzical look. "Tell me about it," she insisted.

I could feel my heart beating against my ribcage as I tried to keep calm. I gave Jessica's arm a playful punch and replied calmly, "Let's just leave it for now, please." I felt irritated by her but more annoyed at myself for being in a bad mood.

A knock at the door interrupted us. "Excuse me, sir. Mr Hrisacopolis sends his regards and would like to remind you that you have an appointment with him at ten this morning." The steward waited for an answer.

I rose from the bed. "Yes, thank you, I'll be there."

Turning to Jessica, I said, "Let's get ready and talk about the other things later."

"Promise?"

"Yes, yes, later." I ushered her out and was glad to see her leave. I needed space to think, yet I felt awful at treating her in such an offhand manner. "Ring you when I'm ready," I called after her.

I looked at the notes she had left for me while I ran the electric razor over the stubble. There was a listing of all the essential questions to be asked, mixed up with what I call nice guys: the kind of questions about nothing in particular that put the interviewee into a false sense of security. The phone rang as I dressed and I guessed correctly it was her.

'Don't wear a suit."

"Why?"

"You are interviewing a young man, so be casual and make him feel relaxed."

"I know that," I replied testily. "Look after yourself. I'm fine."

I replaced the handset and started looking for something more casual. She was right. I took the jacket off and threw it at the chair. Why couldn't I tell her she was right? Ten minutes later, we were ushered into Nico's stateroom, but not before I'd apologised to Jessica and told her she was right about the dress code. She said nothing. Even so, I sensed tension and left matters there.

"Welcome, Mr West."

Nico Hrisacopolis moved across the thick carpet toward us. His stomach wobbled grotesquely. Dressed in a pair of white slacks and a light blue shirt, he looked more like a man on holiday than an industrial mogul at a press interview.

I shook his outstretched hand while a sickly grin spread over his face as he recognised Jessica. An even row of polished teeth showed behind parted thick lips. Sidestepping, he took hold of Jessica's hand with his stubby fingers and stooped to kiss the back of her hand.

"And, of course, the charming Miss Du Rosse. Welcome, my dear." He raised his head, his eyes following the contours of her figure while his hand held hers just a moment too long.

Jessica politely withdrew her fingers from his grip. "Thank you for inviting us."

"Perhaps it should be me thanking you for writing such interesting articles about my family."

While they were exchanging pleasantries, I glanced around the spacious stateroom. A large concert piano adorned with framed photos of the Hrisacopolis family and friends stood in one corner. Some of the subjects were of particular interest.

Nico directed us into some large leather armchairs before settling himself behind an enormous mahogany desk and pressing a buzzer. The door to the stateroom opened immediately. Andreas junior appeared, young and handsome. He cut a dashing figure, unlike his grandfather, dressed in a dark suit and white polo neck jersey. A small Turkish man in a white suit followed him. He looked familiar, but I couldn't remember where from. I rose to greet them.

Nico lit a cigar as he introduced us. "This is Ahmet, my agent in Istanbul who has been looking after Andreas since we found him."

"Really," I said, shaking hands, "how long ago was that?"

Before Andreas could answer, Nico, interrupted. "Why don't we have coffee…? And please, feel free to ask my grandson anything." He held his hands out, palms up, as Andreas sat down.

I pulled Jessica's list out before asking, "I guess the most obvious question is, where you have been for the best part of your life?"

I saw Andreas's eyes flicker momentarily before he replied. "I didn't know who my real father was until my mother told me on her death bed. A cousin in Nicosia raised me before I moved to Athens for work."

"I assume you took your father's name, but what was your name before you learned about him from your mother?" I found myself more interested in Ahmet. The man never took his eyes off Andreas.

Andreas's eyes flickered again. There was a short pause before he answered, prompted with a facial expression from Ahmet. "My name has always been Andreas." He coughed to clear his throat.

"You sound educated, Andreas. Did you attend college in Athens?" Jessica asked.

"Yes."

"So what did you-?"

"I think it is fair to say," interjected Ahmet, "that he studied after

I found him." He paused then added, "I put him on a crash course in business management and economic studies. He came through with distinction."

"Where…?"

"At Athens University. They have short courses for an industry that run two days a week for day release students," answered Ahmet. He looked smug as he sipped his coffee, little finger raised in the air. I took an instant dislike to him.

"So, tell me about your father," I asked. "Were you aware that he was a Greek national hero? Did your mother ever speak about him?"

Andreas beamed. "I was told very little by my mother, but Ahmet has since educated me on my father's life."

"He wears his father's ring with pride," said Nico through a cloud of smoke. He tapped the cigar on the edge of the glass ashtray.

Andreas showed the ring as though it were a trophy. I was fast concluding that the interview was stage-managed. It was a public relations disaster on the old man's part. It all seemed too correct- no hesitation, and most answers came too quickly.

There was a knock on the door. Ahmet, standing at the back of the old man's chair like a hovering falcon, moved across the stateroom. At that moment, I knew where I had seen him and Andreas before - the hotel in Istanbul. I had a question burning a hole in my tongue, but I couldn't ask, not at that moment. I was sure I'd heard that voice before too.

As Ahmet ushered in a steward pushing a cart loaded with coffee and pastries, Jessica asked, "Did you think of joining the army while you were in Athens?"

"No, not at all. Of course, I would have considered this if I had known about my father at that time."

Nico leaned forward. "I am sure you would have, Andreas, but if he could see you now, I know he would be very proud."

I picked up a coffee and sipped. We were not going to get any helpful information from Andreas other than what he had been told to say; I was sure. Why say anything else? He was an heir to a fortune and a lot of power. Nico was happy too. He had a grandson to run the empire so he could turn his attentions to Cyprus and Enosis 'and all that.'

"So what does the future hold for you, Andreas, especially now that your grandfather will be busy in Brussels?"

I thought Nico might get nervous and interrupt, but there was no reaction. His face had frozen in a smile. There was a long silence.

"Andreas will-"

Andreas raised a hand to quiet Ahmet. "I see myself as being guided by those already in executive positions. Call it my apprenticeship. I have a lot to learn and will hopefully fill my grandfather's shoes when he is ready to hand over."

"Then all the rumours are true, Mr Hrisacopolis, you will be putting your name forward for a position within the European government?" I jotted something down in my notebook, pretending to be unconcerned.

There was a pause. "I have indicated that should my country need my services; I would not hesitate to serve. However, Mr West, nothing has been decided yet."

"But you would serve if asked?"

"Mr West, we are here to talk about my grandson, not my politics."

"None-the-less his future is tied up with yours, sir, and-"

"Please do not think me rude, but I would like you to forget my life and concentrate on Andreas's." Nico waggled a little fat finger at me.

Jessica intervened. "What about religion, Andreas? Are you Greek Orthodox like your grandfather?"

"Yes, of course, although I did not go to church as often as I should when I was growing up, now I attend often."

The rest of the interview took another half hour before we wrapped it up. I was bored. I couldn't wait to get Jessica alone but not before taking a couple of photos of Andreas and his grandfather. Just as we were leaving, I pointed to the photographs on top of the piano. "Tell me," I turned to Nico, "are all these people related to you?"

He shrugged. "And a lot more besides."

I shot the last question at Andreas. "Have you ever been to Cyprus?"

"No," he replied, "Ahmet tells me how nice it is. He only just-"

Hrisacopolis interrupted. "Come, come, Andreas, we must not keep our luncheon guests waiting and don't forget we have another news conference after that." He shook hands with us. "Please enjoy the rest of the cruise."

"We certainly will." Jessica shook his hand.

I followed her outside, but my smile hid a lot of anger. I needed fresh air and time to decide what to do about Ahmet.

Chapter Thirty-Two

W E WERE HAVING LUNCH, and all I could think of was Jamilya. I wasn't sure if Jessica had grasped the significance of Andreas junior's last interrupted conversation with me. I didn't want to spoil her lunch and had decided to wait until we were strolling around the deck. However, being Jessica, she stopped eating and asked, "What's up? You're very quiet?"

"Nothing," I answered curtly, "just deep in thought." I forced a half-hearted cheeky grin that disappeared almost at once. I avoided her eyes and munched from a plate loaded with salmon salad. The conversation would lead to the one question I didn't want to address with her. It was unfortunate she had walked into my cabin early. I wanted my problem to stay until Jessica stopped eating and dabbed the corner of her mouth with a napkin. She just nodded and picked up her coffee.

It was not until we walked the deck that I confided in her. Call it a delayed emotional reaction, but Jamilya's death and coming face to face with the man I suspected of murdering her had gotten to me.

When I had finished talking, we were on our third trip around the deck. We walked on in silence until we reached the swimming pool area. I found a quiet spot and leaned against the rail, looking at white-topped waves and filling my lungs with sea air. Jessica defied the breeze and the gentle roll of the ship to keep her balance with one hand on the rail while the other tried vainly to keep hair out of her eyes. She turned to face me and drew close, her voice barely audible.

Jamilya's safety was lost the moment Nico decided to run for the European Parliament. We had given her the chance to tell someone about the monsters in her life, and that must have brought her some satisfaction. Her murderer was already on his way, and 'B' had done all he could but had been too late, despite our urgent request. There wasn't anything to say, but I did feel better.

Jessica put her arm through mine and squeezed my hand. She had seen another side of me. I wasn't too happy about that but sharing some mental burden did feel good. However, one thing was sure; I was determined to continue despite Max and Hart applying the brake on my investigation. I thought I owed that to Jamilya.

Jessica nodded and turned her head away from the wind to wipe her watery eyes. "I agree. We can't just leave things as they are. Jamilya deserves some justice."

"Okay," I said, "so let's have a meeting and look at what we've got."

She winked at me suggestively as we started to walk back. "My room or yours?" she asked.

Not realising the significance of her remark, I absent-mindedly replied, "It doesn't matter."

I have never been to Cadiz and felt disappointed that we could not get ashore. Apart from a few dignitaries coming aboard the following day, the ship would only be in port for four hours.

Jessica stood by the doors leading onto the veranda. She looked beautiful, with a pale pink silk gown flowing loose from the shoulder. Her warmth and softness had most certainly put me in a better mood. "Never mind, Pete, we've got two days in Nice. I'll show you where all the nice girls go shopping." She turned her head and winked at me.

"Okay funny girl, let's get down to it."

We needed to go through everything we had and try to make sense of it. I marvelled at Jessica's figure outlined by the sun as she stood in the veranda doorway and bounced off the bed. "For goodness' sake, get dressed. I can't think."

She laughed that deep, rich, husky laugh that I loved so much and disappeared into the bathroom while I made the coffee. Something kept going round in my head. It had something to do with Andreas, but I didn't know what. By the time Jessica came back, I had filled our cups with an awful instant coffee that smelled good but tasted foul.

"Pete, let's sit outside." As an afterthought, she added, "You'd better get some clothes on too."

I grabbed my trousers. "No, our conversation can carry out here."

She didn't argue but stepped sideways while I wrestled with the trousers to slide the door half open before walking to the bed where I'd laid my notes out. Arranging them by date, I had devised two columns: one for the Hrisacopolis family and the other for all of his victims

"Quite a list," said Jessica, looking over my shoulder. "Where do we start?"

I decided to start in the middle of the muddle. The grandson was the key to it all, but something didn't add up. It had to do with Mehmet, the businessman who put Baki, now Andreas, into the army.

Jessica wrinkled her nose after tasting the coffee. "Yes, but we have a grandson on board who has never been in the army."

"Not in the Greek army, no," I replied, "but if this is Baki."

"Who Mehmet said was killed in an accident at the barracks." Jessica interrupted my train of thought.

"Why didn't Nico know about his death?" I asked.

"Because someone used influence to keep it out of the papers," she suggested.

"No," I said, grabbing my shirt.

I didn't think that would stop the old man from finding out. The answer, I thought, might be more straightforward. Perhaps Baki didn't die. Murat, Baki's friend, told me that he didn't see Baki die.

Jessica's face lit up. We were on the same wavelength. "Captain Abbas."

I agreed. There were two dead bodies, regardless of who they were. One was an unfortunate private, and the other could have been Abbas. Whether Baki or Abbas died or if Baki murdered Abbas and deserted remained the mystery.

Jessica sat cross-legged on the bed and studied the list of Nico's associates while I finished dressing. I could understand Nico sending an agent to persuade Baki to change his name and join him. It was apparent why the Hrisacopolis family kept everything about Andreas senior's affair. I didn't understand why Nico would hand over his empire, albeit still under his watchful eye, to an imposter if he knew or someone told him that Baki was dead?

Jessica looked confused. "You lost me there. I thought we agreed that Baki survived. Surely then, we just met him?"

I shrugged. It wasn't necessarily true we had met Baki, but at the same time, it was hard not to believe we had. The old man was proud and gushing with enthusiasm. If he'd plotted to have an imposter take the place of the real Baki, he wouldn't have reacted in the same way.

"So, someone else, possibly Ahmet, is involved in a conspiracy for what – money?"

"Maybe," I said. It was more than likely that there was more to it than a few greedy men. Other possibilities could involve the KKA.

"So, if Baki were alive now and we have an imposter on board, wouldn't Baki come forward to denounce the imposter?"

That made me more confident that Nico knew nothing about any imposter. I looked down the list. If our imposter theory was correct, we looked for a traitor within the camp. My guess was Ahmet, but there had to be someone else, and there had to be another reason besides wealth and power, possibly something personal.

Jessica held the list up and pointed to one name. "What about Koskotas?"

He lied to her about the photo and his connection to EOKA and was not forthcoming about his position with the art foundation. We needed to check him out.

I thought so too. He was someone who had been associated with Nico for many years, long enough for him to be part of the inner circle that knew a lot about the corrupt business dealings and dark ambitions of Nico.

"While we're about it," I mused, "how about this guy... Boutin?"

Jessica shifted behind me on the bed and put her arms around my neck. Looking over my shoulder, she gave me a little kiss on my ear and, together with her gentle breathing, sent a shiver up my spine.

Alain Boutin was a corrupt politician. His father, a general, made his name in Algiers before the French got pushed out. I came across the man at a French embassy reception in London where he held a position as military attaché. After the General's death, Alain's father's reputation came useful in acquiring him a posting in the French diplomatic corps. Two years later, an election triumph was a European seat in Brussels. There then followed a couple of scandals involving male prostitutes.

Jessica shuddered. "Wonderful. And he still has a seat in the EU."

"Okay, so he's yours," I said, "I'll take Koskotas."

I turned toward her and kissed her on the cheek. "Please be careful. I'd hate for anything to happen to you."

She returned the kiss. "Stop worrying."

The thought that Ahmet was close by really bothered me. It wouldn't mean anything to him to kill again. It occurred to me that Nico was a sad figure. For all his wealth and power, he had no friends, only enemies. I thought about this for a moment and realised that it might be better to put our inquiries on hold until we had an escape route, just in case we annoyed our host and his associates.

Jessica nodded but said nothing. If she saw through my concerns, she didn't show it.

CHAPTER THIRTY-THREE

A FAINT SMUDGE OF BLACK smoke against a clear blue sky appeared on the horizon. Adonis sat on a deck chair, observing the smoke through binoculars in the aft well. Many ships passed through those waters each day, mainly freighters and tankers. Cruise ships also sailed through during the week, but the freighters interested him.

He left the 'Duchess of Kent,' a small coastal tramp freighter sailing back and forth along the east coast of Britain a year ago. For two years, she had been his floating hulk of home, and despite her appearance, a happy ship crewed by a collection of misfits and a Captain who reeked of whiskey from morning to night. It was a tough life as a deckhand and later as junior coxswain; valuable lessons in seamanship and self-preservation that would help him soon.

He lay the binoculars on the deck, and leaning back, he closed his eyes and thought about Barbara. She would feel betrayed and distraught when she found he had left and her paintings with him.

A whistle disturbed Adonis's thoughts. He sat forward, shielding his eyes. The Turk's launch was anchored some sixty meters away. A couple of the divers climbed out of the water onto the transom while the Turk made his way toward Adonis in a Zodiac.

Adonis drew in a deep breath. He had arrived twenty-four hours before and anchored forty kilometres northeast of Gozo, just outside the Malta Channel. The Turk had arrived that morning after insisting he first put into Valletta for extra stores. The Turk hauled himself onto the deck and waved a folded newspaper under Adonis's nose. He had a present, something of interest from Valletta.

"I don't need presents," snapped Adonis. He snatched the paper held out in front of him and read the headline. 'British Museum Loses Its Marbles.'

"You see," said the Turk, picking his teeth with a little finger and sucking loudly. He tossed a cigar butt over the side of the launch. "The stupid Greek thinks he's going to be something in the European Parliament." He placed a dirty hand on Adonis's shoulder and laughed.

Shrugging him off and gritting his teeth, Adonis turned away and put the paper aside. "I'll read it later," he said coldly.

The Turk wiped a grubby rag over his head. Rivulets of sweat ran down either side of his face as the oppressive heat that hung in the still of the late evening air showed no sign of cooling. He sat on the long bench seat in the well, stabbing a finger at a newspaper page. According to the article, the marbles were in waterproof cases. If they threw them into the sea, he would have to know how to retrieve them. He swallowed a glass of brandy and looked accusingly across the table at Adonis. Even if they got them back, how would they carry them? They had to weigh more than a ton each.

Adonis smiled inwardly. Rescue for the survivors and the marbles would be no more than an hour away. A plausible story took him some time to come up with, but it did sound believable.

Some shouting and laughter carried across the water from the other launch, and Adonis wondered how many of them would be alive in a few days.

He looked at the Turk in the failing light through half-closed eyes and slowly explained how the marbles would float in their unique containers.

The Turk took a mouthful of cognac straight from the bottle and then wiped his mouth with the back of his hand. "And then what?" he said sarcastically.

"You tow them to Gozo and into shallow water in Dwejra Bay behind Fungus Rock and pick them up later."

There was a moment's silence. The Turk looked puzzled. "I can pick them up?"

Adonis stood up and raised both arms as a faint breeze blew across the launch. He would be dead, and so would Hrisacopolis. The marbles were the Turk's problem.

The Turk sniggered. "You are so determined to die, Greek. I understand your hate but at least live to enjoy your revenge." He rose to leave.

"I'll live long enough, and that's good enough for me," replied Adonis.

They climbed out onto the deck, and the Turk departed. Adonis congratulated himself on fooling the man. He watched him climb back over the side of the launch and into the Zodiac. As soon as he heard the outboard splutter into life, Adonis unfolded the newspaper and read the article on the front page. It reported that *Sea Empress* had left the London port of Tilbury with the Elgin Marbles and VIP passengers. A photo of Nico Hrisacopolis accompanied the article. Adonis looked at the face that had haunted him all his life and wondered if the reaction would be when they met.

There was a follow-up story inside. He opened the paper and found the article but did not read it right away. A picture of a group of dignitaries standing on the steps of the British Museum caught his eye. Barbara Fitzgerald smiled out from the middle of the group. He frowned as he recognised a man standing next to her. It was the man he had saved from drowning. They were holding hands. Now, as he looked at the photo of Barbara holding hands with the man, he wondered about them. Out of curiosity, he read through the list of names pictured in the group and found the man's name. A pang of anxiety overcame him as he realised that Barbara was on the liner. The article stated that the head of Trafalgar Art Trust was on the VIP list.

"Ioannis Koskotas," he murmured. He closed his eyes then lay back into the deckchair.

CHAPTER THIRTY-FOUR

THE TEMPERATURE WAS around the mid-seventies, I guessed. The heat from a glaring sun in an empty sky warmed my face and arms. I remembered the lazy summers of my youth. Unfortunately, it was impossible to enjoy the memories for more than a few moments despite the guests' cheery disposition. The Greek nightmare returned as I watched a journalist colleague jump into the pool. Ambling along the deck, I stopped to take in the view and wondered how I would sell the story I was unravelling. Max was going to shout, but then he always shouted.

We were about two hours away from our anchorage in Villefranche, three miles from Nice. Jessica was having her hair done. My train of thought broke as someone stumbled into me from behind.

"Hell, I'm so sorry."

I reached for the handrail and turned unsteadily. I was confronted with a shock of red hair and a pair of RayBans as a distinct Texas drawl owner picked her purse up off the deck.

"Well, thank you. These heels will be the death of me." She reached out and held my forearm while she bent over to adjust her shoes. "Thank you, Pete. It is Pete, isn't it?" She held out a hand as she straightened up.

I guessed her to be in her fifties. She was dressed in a white blouse and slacks and was what I would call a handsome lady but would not have given her a second glance had it not been for the diamonds. They dripped from each ear and sparkled on several fingers of both hands. "You are quite right," I said, "but I'm afraid I don't-"

"Barbara Fitzgerald. I'm representing the Trafalgar Trust. We have done a lot of business with the Hrisacopolis Art Foundation."

The reference got my attention right away. I remembered seeing her name and the Trafalgar Trust on our information sheet. "Well, nice to meet you, Barbara. How did you know my name? Did we meet while I was drunk?" I winked.

Barbara's face creased into a grin. "No, but I'm sure if we had, it would have been one helluva meeting if you're as sassy in private as you are in writing your daily column." She laughed loudly and took a pack of Camels out of her shoulder purse and a copy of The Herald supplement.

Taking a cigarette from the pack, she turned to my photo at the head of the article and said, "I've read the pull-outs on the man, but it's a shame you didn't look a little more closely into his past. When I first heard about the series of articles, I felt pleased, thinking Nico would get his comeuppance with some of your usual verve." With a quick movement of her wrist, there was a sharp metallic click as she flicked open a silver lighter. She bent her head away from the breeze and cupped a hand around the flame. She said, "I was disappointed, Pete, " with one eye on me." She flicked the lighter shut and blew a stream of smoke up into the air through bright red lips.

Alarm bells rang in my head. "I take it you're talking about his business practices and political beliefs?"

She removed the RayBans and looked at me a little sceptically. Shaking her hair, she replaced the glasses and nodded. "People think I'm a rich American dabbling in the arts, a ditz with no grey matter between the ears. Geoffrey, my late husband, who started the Trafalgar Trust, introduced me to Nico. Since then, I've been collecting a lot of art and buying a piece from Nico now and again. Our dealings are purely professional. He still has a couple of art pieces I'm keen to get my hands on."

I leaned against the rail. "So what do you know about him?" I asked.

Somewhat bemused, she turned and adjusted the glasses. As she did, the heavy gold charm bracelet on her wrist rattled and slid along her arm. "I'm not mad at Nico if that's what you're asking," she drawled, "but I did wonder if you were going to have a little dig at some of his past deeds." The corners of her mouth curled in a half-suppressed grin and disappeared as she observed someone over my shoulder and waved. A familiar figure walked toward us. "I guess we'll meet again." She tapped the paper across my chest. "I'll try not to throw you over the side next time."

I winked at her. She raised her glasses enough for me to see her wink back and then stepped forward to greet Koskotas.

"Well, hello Pete, I hope you're enjoying the cruise."

Koskotas held an ornate gold cigarette holder between his teeth. The holder fascinated me. I guessed it to be antique, probably art deco, fashioned in the shape of a short piece of bamboo with an amber mouthpiece. It suited him in his white shirt and the flannels-very Mediterranean. He took Barbara by the arm, flashing white teeth at me.

Koskotas gently placed a tanned hand on Barbara's back and started to steer her away.

"We've got an appointment," he said.

They both waved as they walked away, and I saw something interesting. I watched his hand lightly brush across Barbara's hip.

I decided to take a walk along the deck, acknowledging other passengers along the way with a cheerful nod. On reaching the pool, I was about to turn around and head back when I heard someone call my name. A steward waved a piece of paper as he jogged toward me.

"Excuse me, Mr West," he gasped, "there is an urgent call for you in the purser's office." He handed me the note and indicated a telephone point nearby.

I opened the note and read – Richard Hart – Urgent – Respond Immediately - No Emails. I didn't wait. I pressed for the purser. "You have a call for me," I asked, "the name is West for Mr Richard Hart."

The line buzzed for several seconds, and then Hart spoke. "Pete, how are things?" It was the kind of remark that did not demand an answer. Hart was not interested in how things were going. He was more interested in his issues.

"Fine," I said, "is something wrong?"

He ignored the question. "I have had a conversation with one of your sources yesterday. He told me you discussed a certain Turkish organisation." Hart's voice lowered almost to a whisper.

"Yes, that's correct," I replied.

"When you go ashore in Nice, I want you to call me." His voice had an urgent edge to it.

"Yes, of course. I planned on calling Max because we have-"

He cut me off. "Talk to me as soon as you can and send Jessica home. She's needed here."

Jessica was not going to take the news quietly. She was my assistant on the assignment. Obviously, 'B' had spoken to Hart, but why? 'B' would not have revealed that he was my Whitehall source and ended future meetings without good reason.

"We're docking in two hours, then I'll call."

"I'll be waiting. Make sure we talk in private without Miss Du Rosse present."

The line went dead, and I breathed in deeply. If Hart was involved, then so were a few cronies in Whitehall. I made my way back to my cabin. Jessica had arranged to meet me there, and I decided to tell her everything rather than risk upsetting her.

Thirty minutes later, I was poring over my notes, adding Barbara's information to them, and drinking tea when Jessica arrived. I couldn't tell if her hair were touched at all. I told her she looked good anyway.

"So, did you catch any sun out on the deck?" She walked past me and dropped into a small armchair. Kicking off her heels, she raised her feet onto the bed and leaned back into the chair.

"Not really," I told her of my meeting with Barbara Fitzgerald and the closeness I had observed between her and Koskotas. "I wonder if Koskotas is helping her acquire her collection of paintings, "I said.

"Did she say how she was purchasing them, auction or cash?" Jessica sat up, interested.

We were silent for a moment, and then she said, "How does Barbara Fitzgerald come into this, I wonder?" Jessica's fingers twiddled with an earring, her eyes far off in deep thought. There was something very erotic about that. She caught me watching her.

"Your point being?" I said, coming back to earth.

"Well, if I were Mr Hrisacopolis, I would be concerned if an important member of my Art Foundation board was sleeping with the owner of the Trafalgar Foundation-pillow talk and all that." She raised her eyebrows with a suggestive look and blew me a kiss.

"Ah huh, so why isn't Nico doing something about it?" I suddenly thought of something that had been at the back of my mind since our interview with young Andreas. "Did you notice the pictures on the piano in the old man's cabin?"

"Stateroom," she corrected. "No, why?"

"Koskotas was next to Andronis – Nico's father, then Andreas junior's father Andreas senior and last, Nico Hrisacopolis. They seemed to be in a group all their own. Why?"

"No idea, but as soon as we get to Nice, I shall make a few calls and see if I can find out more about Koskotas."

It was time to break the bad news. "Sorry, my love, but you're going home." I held my breath.

She pulled her feet off the bed and sat bolt upright, her eyes wide, lips tightly pressed together. Her eyes narrowed. Quietly she said, "No, I'm not."

"Hart says you are," I told her about the telephone conversation.

She rose from the chair and folded her arms across her chest. "Why?"

"Jessica, things are pretty dangerous around here." I reached out for her. She stepped back, giving me a look of defiance.

"Did he say I had to go back because things were dangerous?"

"No."

She bent forward, arms still folded, and stared into my eyes. "Then how do you know why he wants me back in London?"

"I don't, but it is pretty obvious."

Jessica shook her head. "Something else is bothering Hart. Since when did he ever care about calling a journalist back from an assignment because things were getting…" she fingered punctuation marks "…a little dangerous?" Her bottom lip was quivering, and I didn't want to annoy her anymore.

"Well, perhaps that's so, but you can't ignore him, Jessica," I reasoned.

"I'm not going to ignore him; I'm going to talk to him." Her hands were on her hips, chest heaving. She turned and walked to the balcony doors and back again.

I tried to calm her down by slowly waving my hands up and down. "Well, just calm down before you do, eh?"

The reaction was sudden and took me completely by surprise. Her eyes widened, and her arms unfolded slowly. "How dare you. How dare you patronise me. Her finger jabbed at my chest as she stepped past me toward the door. "After all the rows, the swearing, the rude remarks I have had to put up with from you and Max – and now Hart – and you stand there and tell me to calm down. How dare you. You and Hart can go to hell, and I'll tell him that too." With that, she reached for the door, tripping over my feet.

"Jessica," I pleaded, sweeping up her high heels.

I was too late. The door slammed, and I was left holding her shoes and wishing I hadn't said a damn word.

CHAPTER THIRTY-FIVE

I WOULDN'T CONSIDER NICE a holiday paradise. It does have a bright side, though. The architecture has remained intact from the turn of the century, including the medieval town centre and the modern Italianate facades. The rest of the modern city is full of concrete and glass junk. Nonetheless, I was looking forward to being there with Jessica, even though I had upset her. She loved France.

Over breakfast, I tried repairing the damage. "Look, I didn't mean I agreed with Hart. I just wanted you to know I was concerned for your safety," I pleaded. "I'm sorry, darling."

That didn't work. As I reached for her hand across the table, she withdrew hers quickly. I walked back to her cabin with her in silence, hoping to cheer her up. She turned on her heel outside her cabin, placed a hand firmly on my chest, and then closed the door in my face.

I stood up against the ship's rail two hours later as we neared our anchorage at Villefranche. The sun had disappeared behind a bank of white cumulus, leaving the distant sky above the horizon a dull light grey, perhaps indicating that rain was coming our way. The stiff eastern breeze whipping across the water created hundreds of small white caps as far as the eye could see. My surroundings reflected my mood.

I followed Jessica later to join a crowd of excited guests disembarking to a big launch tied up against the ship. The launch rose and fell in the swell as crew members helped the women hop from the platform at the bottom of the stairs and into the well of the launch. It wasn't until I was stepping down that I caught a glimpse of Barbara sitting inside the cabin. She caught my eye and waved at me Italian style, her fingers flipping up and down a couple of times from hand held mid-air. I waved back. While the launch took us into shore, I took hold of Jessica's arm.

"Why don't we stretch our legs along the promenade and stay at the Hotel Negresco."

That brought a smile to her face, but I knew she hadn't forgiven me yet. Nonetheless, she did take my arm as we walked along the dock to a cab. We arrived along the Promenade des Anglais not long after and gave ourselves a ten-minute walk to the hotel. Wrapped in a long white woollen coat, Jessica pulled the collar up around her ears and held it in place as we walked. It was getting cold, and I cursed inwardly. With small suitcases rumbling behind us, we crossed the street to the buildings fronting the promenade. There had to be a phone box somewhere.

My short conversation earlier with Hart brought a moment of relief, but that was short lived. I wondered if there was something he and Whitehall knew that I didn't, perhaps to do with terrorists. If that was the case, then I could understand Hart's concerns.

A double telephone kiosk stood at the corner of the next street.

"I have to call Hart," I said. "It won't take a minute."

Jessica nodded. "I'll be having coffee."

She indicated a nearby boulangerie fronted by several little tables covered in crisp white linen. The aroma of fresh bread and dark roasted coffee teased my senses for the last five minutes as we walked.

Walking to the kiosk, I picked up the receiver. Someone had cut the cord. Cursing the vandals, I slipped into the second cubicle only to discover the receiver was gone. I banged the side of the booth and picked up my overnight suitcase.

"I didn't order for you," said Jessica as I joined her.

"The bloody phones were broken." I stopped her from raising a finger for service. "No, I need to get to the hotel. How about we book in, and you go take care of family business while I call Hart?"

Jessica had promised her father she would look up an old family friend, which suited me. I could call Hart while she was out. Call it a sixth sense, but I felt a pang of foreboding. If Hart was talking to Whitehall and, particularly, 'B', I guessed 'B' was worried how far I was digging. In short, Whitehall had seen a looming crisis.

"Okay, but one word of warning." Jessica pointed a long finger at me across the table. "You tell Hart I will call him later, and that's all. Agreed?"

There was too much going on for me to worry about taking sides, as I would have liked to. "Totally," I answered, leaving five euros on the table. Spots of light rain started falling on my head. We hurried along the promenade as the rain peppered the pavement.

Entering the Negresco's huge oval reception area, I felt a little overawed at the surroundings. Chandeliers hung from the tall ceiling, illuminating an inner lining of marble columns that followed the outer wall, creating a cloister passage along which the reception and entrances to restaurant, bar and other facilities served the guests. Built around the turn of the century, it boasted unashamed luxury for those who could afford it.

I would have enjoyed the experience any other time, but I hardly noticed the four-poster bed and magnificent view across the Mediterranean when we reached our room. Jessica dropped her suitcase and, with a little wave, left me to make my call.

I picked up the bedside phone and dialled the front desk. A faint click was accompanied by the noise from a motor scooter tearing along the promenade outside. Stretching the telephone line behind me, I reached out and pushed the window shut.

"Oui, Monsieur? "A firm but polite voice sounded in my ear.

After giving the clerk the number, I waited, not noticing the view. I was too deep in thought.

There was another click, and Hart's voice sounded clear, but guarded. Two people were talking in the background, with one woman arguing. I sat down on the bed.

"Right, now listen to me, Pete, and don't interrupt."

Again he paused, and I could hear his breathing. The conversation behind him stopped, and I heard a door close with a bang.

"Yesterday, I was called to the Foreign Minister's office to meet with his secretary and your confidant, Askew-Broughton. We discussed your conversation a couple of weeks back. Quite frankly, I was annoyed at the time. Max tells me he warned you to back off your unofficial look into Hrisacopolis dealings, but I was glad you continued."

I pulled a small recorder and audio lead out of my computer case and stuck the small rubber receiver cup to the phone. I plugged into the recorder and flicked the switch as Hart filled me in on the meeting.

"Your inquiries worried Askew-Broughton, and he had words with the Foreign Secretary's office. 'B' may be a source, but he is also a loyal servant to Her Majesty's government. He realised how much you knew when you started asking questions and raised the red flag. That's why I attended the meeting. The Minister has been treading a fine line, trying to please the Greek government and at the same time trying to make certain facts known to them about the man they voted into the EU and who, unfortunately, might get the chairmanship of Agriculture and Fisheries."

"Contrary to what you think of Whitehall," Hart added, a disapproving edge to his voice, "the government is aware of the consequences on Cyprus should Hrisacopolis get elected, but no one in the Foreign Office thought he would get as far as he has. The extent of Hrisacopolis corruption, reference French Euro MP Alain Boutin for one, has now come to the attention of MI6. The Prime Minister is hoping the Greek government might deal with the man before his ambitions are realised; the EU, ideally, want to be kept out of things."

I breathed a sigh of relief. At last, the light was beginning to shine.

"This whole situation has suddenly become extremely complicated and very dangerous. Added to what is potentially the biggest embarrassment this government has faced so far, there is a terrorist organisation scheming to kill Hrisacopolis or his grandson or both for all we know."

"KKA?"

"Yes, I understand that came from MI6 too." Hart paused. "Usual bloody mess… None of the security services share or talk to each other. Now here comes the tricky part - and before you say a word, I appreciate you will not like what I have to say."

He wasn't telling me anything I didn't know already. From experience, I was expecting bad news, whatever it was. They could whistle if they conspired to take me off the case. Nothing was going to stop me now.

"Because of our involvement with the Elgin Marbles and our turn at the EU Presidency in two years, we cannot be seen to help the Greek government orchestrate Hrisacopolis' downfall."

My stomach was in knots. I feared the worst.

"It's the PM's wish the man is exposed by a credible source, someone who commands respect in the media. It's the only way, Pete."

I felt a deep sense of foreboding. "I take it you want me to expose him then, do you?" I replied sarcastically. "I'd be delighted to do that."

"It's not as easy as that," he replied, "Hrisacopolis has managed to get the vote brought forward to coincide with the date the marbles reach Athens."

I sank onto the bed, hearing the unspoken 'but' or the exaggerated and regretful 'unfortunately' in his voice. That meant we had a matter of days. He had to let me carry on.

"I can't lose this story now. We are so close, for Christ's sake. There's been a murder, and I suspect an imposter is playing the grandson. This is huge. Surely we can work something out?" I hated myself for pleading, but this was a big story. I banged the bedside table with my fist, sending a small vase with a single stem rose in it, flying across the carpet.

"Pete, listen to me. The important thing is we have to stop Hrisacopolis getting anywhere near that committee."

I listened with a heavy heart as he explained the government's position. It was in their best interests for the man not to die at the hands of the terrorists. If that happened, coupled with a leak of what some ministers had known for some time, it would mean the possible downfall of the government and real tension with Greece and the EU.

"What I want from you is a report on all the dirt you've found so far and anything else you can scrape up on the rest of the voyage."

"Report? Surely you mean story. Surely someone is going to run this story, right?"

"Yes, but unfortunately, I'm afraid we're not, Pete. As I already told you, the British press cannot be the party poopers. We have to give the story to the bloody French."

I tried to remain calm and asked, "How did the Foreign Office know about the threat to Nico's life?"

"You know better than to ask that, Pete. Look, I know this is your story, and I am sorry, but you must see the government's position."

Ignoring the last remark, I said testily, "Okay, the French will get the report by the morning."

"Good, and I take it you've spoken to Jessica?"

Sometimes, some people don't know when to keep quiet when they're ahead. I lost my temper. "She's a big bloody girl, Richard. You want her to go home, then tell her your bloody self."

I slammed the receiver back and threw the phone on the bed.

———◆◇◆———

"Bad day at the office?" enquired Jessica, dripping water on the carpet as she closed the door. Shedding her long woollen coat, she shook her hair, grabbed a towel from the bathroom, and walked over to join me. "It's pouring, and I left my umbrella in the suitcase. Fortunately, I bumped into Barbara, and we shared."

I recounted my conversation with Hart. I could see why we couldn't run the story and, in any case, we didn't have the time to do it justice. Whatever happened, I would carry on until I found out the truth about the grandson and the rest of the family. There was a lot more to it than just the EU issue. Hart could go to hell and keep his bloody job.

Jessica put her arms around my neck and gave me a quick kiss before burying her head in the towel and rubbing her hair. She had visited her father's friends and been caught in a downpour. Taking refuge in a coffee shop, she had met Barbara.

"We chatted for ages. She's quite an interesting person," said Jessica. "It turns out we have a lot of mutual friends in the business." She pulled the towel off her head. "Anyway, we're meeting her for dinner tonight."

CHAPTER THIRTY-SIX

A HMET SHIELDED HIS EYES with a newspaper from the hot sun and glanced at Eren sitting by the private pool on the upper deck. The immediate danger was over, but when the ship docked in Naples, the KKA would be waiting for confirmation that the grandson was dead. Two KKA agents, Assar and Ekrem, contacted him after coming aboard. They were to step in and take over if, for any reason, he was unable to deal with the grandson.

Ahmet regretted killing Ekrem. He later told Assar he suspected the Athens government of being involved in killing and dumping their colleague overboard. Ekrem could have been recognised by Greek agents put aboard to protect Nico Hrisacopolis. Ahmet carefully emphasised that Athens was passing information on to MI6, and Assar had to be very careful.

Since then, Assar, part of the kitchen staff, had spent most of the time in his cabin claiming he was suffering from sea sickness. Ahmet thought he might deal with Assar, too, but the KKA were crucial to his plan. The tightrope he was walking was getting thinner. He had until Naples to find the answer.

Ahmet picked up a hand towel lying across Andreas junior's lounger and wiped his forehead, turning the problem over, trying to find a way to keep them both alive.

"How is he today, Ahmet?"

Ahmet, lost in thought, jerked in the seat. "He's fine, and he's just fine. Today he can rest. There is just the dinner tomorrow night."

Nico placed a wide-brimmed summer hat on his head before stepping through the open French doors leading off the stateroom and slumping into the chair beside Ahmet. He lit a cigar and puffed until the end glowed. Smoke rose slowly, curling in blue strands before disappearing on a breeze. "You look nervous. Is something bothering you? I don't like it when you get nervous. It normally means trouble."

"There is no trouble now," said Ahmet, closing his eyes. The heat was becoming unbearable.

"What do you mean, now?"

Exasperated, Ahmet answered, "You will remember I told you we might have trouble with KKA." He took a sip from a glass of iced lemon water and licked his top lip.

"I hope you're not going to tell me they're on board," said Nico quietly.

"Not anymore," Ahmet lied.

Nico's knuckles turned white as he gripped the arm of the chair.

"He has since left the ship," Ahmet added quickly.

Nico thought for a moment before barking, "He will be found."

"He came on as a kitchen staff," Ahmet parried.

Nico turned to face Ahmet. "How do we know there are not any more agents aboard?"

"If there were, they would have shown themselves by now. The man has been gone two days. It's obvious he was here to kill your grandson or yourself."

Hrisacopolis snatched the cigar from his mouth. "Two days," he thundered. "You never thought to let me know?"

Turning his head, Ahmet coughed as a cloud of cigar smoke blew into his face. He wrinkled his nose and waved the smoke away. "There was no point at the time, and you were about to meet Andreas junior."

Nico bit the cigar between his teeth, removed his sunglasses, and stared into Ahmet's face with large unblinking brown eyes. "Anything else you think I should know?" he growled sarcastically.

Ahmet explained, waving more smoke out of his face, that the captain had been told the day after the agent disappeared that one of the passengers reported a possible 'man overboard.' As the crew only checked the passenger list and the purser had no other reports of a missing person, they reported that all passengers were accounted for. Ahmet made sure the head chef knew that one of his staff lay confined in sick bay and would leave the ship in Nice. No one checked on the man.

Nico eyed Ahmet with suspicion as he listened and then leaned back in the chair. "I hope you did sort things out," he warned, flicking ash from the cigar.

Ahmet dabbed his forehead with the hand towel. "We have to do something about KKA."

"Leave that one to me." Nico wiped his top lip with a finger. "Anything else?"

"There is one other thing." Ahmet took a deep breath and paused. "The passenger who reported hearing the splash was Pete West."

Nico pushed the sunglasses back and took the cigar from his mouth. Rolling it furiously between finger and thumb, he spat on the deck.

"I also saw him having a long conversation with Barbara Fitzgerald before disembarking. She went ashore too." Ahmet sipped his drink, letting the news sink in. He pushed the glass stir stick around the edge of his glass with his index finger. "You know she is seeing Ioannis despite your warning?" he said slowly. "If he should let slip just one word about Andreas's real mother...." He raised his hands and shrugged.

A gull screeched overhead. Nico jerked his head sideways, distracted by a burst of music from the deck below. There was a buzz of conversation, barely audible against the music and an MC announcing an afternoon cocktail party in the main lounge for guests staying on board. As Nico returned to the conversation, Ahmet heard the malicious tone in the man's voice he knew well.

"You know, I think it's about time for our friend and his lady partner to have an accident." He rose from the chair and waved across the pool to Andreas before turning back toward the stateroom.

Stopping behind Ahmet, Nico jabbed a stubby finger at Ahmet's shoulder as he emphasised each word. He said, "You bungled it on Cyprus. Don't let's have a repeat of that."

Ahmet sat looking at Andreas, rubbing lotion on his neck. Biting his lip, he said, "Of course not." His shoulder twitched at the humiliating finger jab.

Nico paused. "I will talk to Ioannis. It is one thing to do business with Barbara, but she has a big mouth. My brother should know better." He jabbed Ahmet's shoulder again. "You just make sure those two journalists go ashore in Naples." Locking his fingers together, he cracked his knuckles. "I'll take care of my lovelorn brother."

Ahmet's hand shook with anger. He turned his head and glared at Nico's back as he stepped through the door. The door slammed. The ice rattled as Ahmet raised the glass to his lips. Throwing his head back, he downed the rest of the drink.

"Well, isn't this nice." Barbara gave me a little wave as she approached us in the restaurant. She wore a light pink silk trouser suit dominated by a dazzling diamond brooch in the shape of a butterfly, pinned to one of the broad lapels. A large silver comb clipped her hair up on top of her head. Her slingback heels clacked on the slate floor as she walked toward us.

After ordering drinks, we pored over the menu while Barbara kept a running commentary on the cruise, her Trafalgar Art Foundation and the weather.

"You know, I would love to invite you to see my yacht," she gushed. "It's moored over in Villefranche Sur Mer. That's about six kilometres down the coast. Unfortunately, we don't have enough time. What a shame." She chattered on about nothing in particular, enjoying Jessica's company rather than mine. They had hit it off.

A muffled ringing tone coming from Jessica's purse interrupted the conversation. Jessica and I exchanged looks, both knowing who was on the other end. Jessica stood and paused to tap the wine list. "I'll have the grilled salmon, and please order the chardonnay too."

Barbara nodded in agreement.

There was a moment's silence as Jessica reached to pick her purse up from the vacant chair. Pushing her chair back, she rose and left us. I took the opportunity to ask Barbara about Nico while we ordered the wine.

"You know," I said, "I wish I had known about you before I wrote those articles on the Hrisacopolis family. You must have seen a lot of what goes on behind the scenes." I paused but saw no immediate reaction. "So, how much do you know about Nico and his political ambitions?"

She knew he wanted into the European Parliament, something we both found disagreeable, exchanging shakes of the head. The long-lost grandson was going to make those ambitions possible.

"Do you have any grandchildren?" I asked.

Barbara's chin jutted out. "No, I don't have any children."

"Neither do I," I said, "but I'm sure if I did, I'd know about it, even if I didn't know the mother. I find it almost unbelievable that Nico would find out he had a grandson after all these years. You'd think Andreas would have told him, or someone else in Cyprus would have. Andreas Jr. was born just after the violence ended."

"I agree. It all seems rather too convenient for Nico," answered Barbara.

"Do you think this grandson is for real then?"

"You are digging then?"

"I'm a newshound; we're good at digging."

She grinned. "I don't know an awful lot." She inclined her head slightly.

We both knew the history, but I wanted anything on the grandson. After giving the waiter our order, I asked, "I take it you were at the news conference?"

"Of course," she said, mocking compliance with a slow inclination. "I was there by Royal command." She raised her eyebrows sarcastically.

"Most people seemed shocked at Nico having a grandson." I watched for her reaction, but there was hardly any, just pursed lips and a slight nod of the head.

"Were you surprised?"

She hesitated. Choosing her words carefully, she leaned forward and, cupping the side of her mouth, lowered her voice and said the news conference was the first she was supposed to hear about a grandson. She had heard about a grandson some years beforehand.

"Which means someone is not entirely telling the truth?" I ventured.

She swallowed hard. "Nico isn't," she said. "I can't think of anyone else, can you?"

I shook my head. "So who told you there was a grandson?"

"Ioannis mentioned Nico's son Andreas in a conversation. He said there were rumours about an illegitimate son in Cyprus." She flapped a hand dismissively. "I didn't take much notice at the time."

She leaned over the table and beckoned me closer. In a light-hearted sarcastic voice, she said, "I'm sure the boy has been dragged out of the family closet now that Nico has found a use for him."

"Figurehead?" I suggested.

Barbara paused and tapped the table with a long red fingernail. "Well, of course, he is. Nico has to ensure continued business from the EU Commissioners."

"Has Ioannis given you any idea who the mother of Nico's grandson is?"

There was a jerk of the head, and I saw the lips tighten; a warning, perhaps. Barbara shook her head but said nothing.

At that moment, Jessica reappeared from reception. She sashayed with ease toward our table, turning heads. Barbara put a hand to the side of her mouth as Jessica sat, whispering, "I wish I could still do that...."

Jessica acknowledged the compliment. I'd have given anything to hear what she said to Hart.

"Everything okay?" I asked.

"Yes, fine." Jessica gave me a quick, sly look before turning to Barbara. "I didn't know Ioannis sang," she said cheerfully. "He's quite good, isn't he? He was up on the stage in the entertainments centre."

Barbara threw her head back and laughed loudly. "Oh, my God," she exclaimed. "It must be the karaoke competition. She placed a hand over Jessica's. "My dear, it's his party piece." Her body shook as she started laughing again, gripping Jessica's hand. "He can only sing one song. I bet he was singing a Nana Mouskouri song, The White Rose of Athens." She shook her head. "He's been singing that for years."

"You must have known Ioannis quite some time," said Jessica. "Did you two hook up on Cyprus?"

Barbara wiped a tear from her eye. "Oh my, yes. Let me think now, when was it?" She snapped her fingers in the air. "I remember... I met Ioannis about twenty years ago at his brother's Art Foundation." She gasped and clapped a hand over her mouth. Her eyes gave the slip away.

My jaw dropped. "His brother?"

There was a sharp intake of breath. Barbara closed her eyes and shook her head.

The idea that Ioannis was Nico's brother had never occurred to me. It would certainly explain the photos on the piano. "I don't understand why there are no records," I said.

Barbara hesitated, her fingers twiddling with the edge of her napkin.

I leaned forward and spoke quietly. "But why?"

Jessica kicked my ankle.

Two waiters arrived with our wine and dinner, breaking our conversation. After they left, Barbara picked up her knife and fork, ignoring the question.

I said nothing, and neither did Jessica.

"We can meet and chat in the ship's salon later," said Jessica, changing the subject as the dinners arrived. "I have to see about my hair." She patted her well-groomed head. The women continued their discussion, all-be-it a little stilted until they warmed to new topics amid the sound of scraping knives and forks and a couple of glasses of wine.

Later, after dinner, we spent time over coffee talking about art, or rather they did.

I was making mental plans to hand my notes over to a Frenchman. I also had another piece of the puzzle. The problem was... where did it fit?

CHAPTER THIRTY-SEVEN

WALL AND CEILING LIGHTS illuminated the ship's main saloon, showcasing an ornate but modern staircase supported by Greco- style columns. A magnificent glass chandelier hung from a ceiling painted with Botticelli's 'The Birth of Venus'. Both gave credence to the illusion of a solid stone structure.

I sank into a green leather armchair as guests, some in dress suits and others dressed more casually, strolled past the casino or restaurant and the deck outside. Brightly lit, there were neatly painted facilities and deck signs everywhere. It was hard to get lost on the ship.

On the other hand, Claude Aurele found it easy. My feet hurt from walking from one bar to another. Eventually, I paged him to meet me in the main saloon, where I rested my feet.

When he did appear, he ambled toward me. I could see he had been enjoying a liquid reunion with some pals.

"Pete, sorry I took so long," he said, shaking hands. He winked and raised an imaginary glass. "Just having a drink with some of the boys and girls, you know how it is."

Claude was in his early sixties and still active and fit. He struck me as a man at peace with himself and on good terms with all those around him as he waved to some colleagues he recognised. I put his contented demeanour down to a long and happy marriage of forty years to Marianne, whom I had met several times in Paris, and seven grandchildren he adored.

He looked comfortable in his dark green corduroy trousers and long-sleeved cardigan with small brown leather buttons up the front.

At just over five feet tall, wearing thick lens glasses and a hearing aid wrapped around one ear, he never struck me as the kind of journalist I associated with war zones. Our friendship went back about ten years, and he was one of the few excellent journalists I got along with.

"Well," I replied, "now you're here; I have to perform something akin to treason."

Claude looked puzzled. "Have I won a prize?"

That sounded about right. I hated giving the story away, and I knew Claude would do it justice. "Yes, you have, and I want you to be very grateful."

"Okay," he said, "how very grateful?"

There are times when giving up titbits can reap a reward further down the road. I wanted information on what would happen in Paris over the Amerigo fiasco, the political aero industry bungle that Whitehall and the White House had got themselves involved in. I kept an eye on developments and planning for my first column when I returned home, although I'd have to ensure I didn't let my feelings run away with me again.

"So, what have you got to give me?" he said.

Sparkling eyes and a heightened colour in his cheeks evidenced a pleasant meeting of friends at the bar. The strong but pleasant smell of whiskey filled my nostrils as I breathed in. I almost wished I'd not taken a pledge to stop drinking. Too many colleagues had ruined their lives and marriages through the bottle. I got the message early on in my career after several no shows at the office and some sloppy work. Max had sat me down and made me see sense. I listened and worked on my career. Two years later, I was given my column.

"Follow me, Claude."

We made our way downstairs to my cabin. Claude gave me some insights into what was happening inside the Palais de Versailles on the way down. The French were stalling over the sale of a contract for military transports, and I didn't blame them. It was still a good story, and I wasn't going to give it up.

While I poured instant coffee from the small brewing pot on the bedside table, I told Claude why Hart wanted me off the story. I explained the politics and the threat Nico was to Cypriot peace and the very seat of power in Brussels.

Claude agreed to dig some more himself and thanked me for the report. I didn't give him any information on the grandson, the attempts on my life, or the relationship between Barbara and Ioannis. For the present, I would keep the promise made to Barbara. Claude needed to bring the political scandal to the public's attention, mainly the corruption and Nico's past.

Those revelations alone would stop his political ambitions while satisfying the EU and the British government. It wouldn't bring justice for Lara, Jamilya or Alexander. That's what I wanted to orchestrate.

We carried on talking for a while, reminiscing. As a young journalist in 1962, Claude covered the end of the revolt led by the FLN – Front De Liberation Nationale – against the French in Algeria and that country's eventual independence. During this time, he began to take an interest in the situation in Cyprus. Although unaware of Lara, he had met Andreas in 1971 and interviewed him at a hideout near the foot of Mount Olympus.

He said, "The photographer with me took some pictures you might be interested in. I can let you have them at dinner tonight."

Thanking him, I handed him the folder and saw him at the door. Claude slid the folder under his arm.

"Just keep it to yourself," I said, tapping the folder. "There are a lot of politicians on board who would love to get their hands on that."

I promised to introduce him to Jessica over dinner as I closed the door behind him. Still feeling bad at having to give Claude my work, I knew the news would break in La Monde before we reached Athens. The Greeks would class the story as pure speculation. The honest power brokers in Brussels would get a warning, and Nico would be dropped.

The ship was due in Naples in forty-eight hours. I decided to figure out a plan of action that would draw out our adversaries.

———————◆◇◆———————

Ahmet studied the small glass notice board at the end of the long hallway without reading a word. His eyes homed in on the reflection of the Frenchman walking towards him.

His instincts had been right. Ioannis had spent most of the morning lounging on his private balcony before heading to the casino at noon. He had spotted West in a huddle with Claude Aurele in a quiet corner. That triggered an alarm, and after the two men's brief conversation, he followed them back to West's cabin.

As Aurele passed him with urgent steps, Ahmet noticed a fawn folder under the Frenchman's arm and realised its significance. Neither Aurele nor West had the folder before they entered West's cabin. Ahmet's heart began to race, and his eyes narrowed. Without moving his head, his eyes followed Aurele until the man turned at the end of the passage.

Nico Hrisacopolis was right. West and Du Rosse had to go, but it would be dangerous killing them now. They were forewarned. He needed to explore all possibilities despite Nico's flippant attitude.

Fighting on two fronts was becoming a headache. West was threatening exposure that would ruin the plans he and Eren had for their future, not to mention upsetting his delicate relationship with the KKA, who now wanted Eren, who was playing grandson, dead.

He walked without haste, not wishing to draw attention to himself, back to the main saloon and into the purser's office. After showing his security pass, he entered the office and searched through the passenger list for Aurele's cabin number. He glanced over a map of the deck B layout looking for Claude's cabin. It was on the same deck as West's but the ship's opposite side.

Before Aurele passed the folder on to his Paris office, the situation had to be dealt with. Ahmet closed his eyes. His mind raced. Reaching for his handkerchief, he dabbed his face and wiped the back of his neck.

He took a sheet of notepaper from the purser's desk and wrote quickly in block letters. His hands shook. He dabbed his forehead again. A minute later, he folded the note and placed it inside an envelope, then hurried away across the main lounge and took the elevator down to deck B. As he waited for the doors to open, he felt a twinge of pain in his right foot. Cursing, he bent over and rubbed his ankle as the doors slid back.

Aurele's cabin was five doors from the elevator to the right. A man's shadowy figure disappeared up the stairway. Ahmet exhaled then breathed deeply. The smell of disinfectant hung in the air. He swallowed hard and coughed.

Striding quickly, he looked back over his shoulder a couple of times. Each white panelled door had a gold number on it. When he reached Aurele's cabin, he took one last look both ways. Without hesitation, he knocked twice on the door. After waiting several seconds, he rapped louder and more urgently.

Ready to pounce, Ahmet stood, feet apart, hands on hips. Sweat glistened on his forehead. He dared not shift his focus from the door for a second. The longer he stood there, the greater the chance he would be discovered. At the sound of a flushing toilet, Ahmet tensed. When nothing happened, he banged on the door with his fist. If someone entered the passage now, he would have to abort.

The Frenchman's voice called out, but the words were too faint for Ahmet to understand. He slowly placed the palm of his left hand on the door, just above his head. The door remained shut. Then he heard Aurele's voice, clearer. He was talking excitedly on the telephone; Nico and Andreas's names were mentioned. Ahmet acted. No panic. He breathed in and out several times and focused on dealing with the

Frenchman. Taking a credit card from his jacket top pocket, he slid it below the lock on the door and jerked upwards. There was a loud click. His left hand pushed, and the door opened a few inches.

Aurele sat on the bed shouting into a small tape recorder with his back to the door. A hearing aid lay on the bed beside him. Ahmet closed the door quietly, surveyed the cabin in a split second, and held his breath. In two strides, he reached the bed.

Aurele neither heard nor saw a thing. Ahmet grabbed him, one hand under the chin and the other at the back of the head and gave a sharp twist. A hollow crack resonated around the cabin, and Aurele slumped to the floor.

Putting his hands under Aurele's armpits, Ahmet pulled him toward the door and stood quite still. He wiped his hands down either side of his jacket before bending over the man. Methodically, he felt inside the man's pockets to check their contents then put everything back, including the hastily written note. He pressed an ear to the door. No sound. Nothing. He wiped his forehead and ran through a checklist.

Aurele's tongue hung from his mouth. Ahmet placed two fingers over the carotid artery to ensure he was dead. He stepped over the body and yanked the telephone flex from the wall. Cutting the other end with a penknife, he knelt beside the body and wrapped the flex around the Frenchman's neck.

Reaching for the folder lying on the bedside table, Ahmet lost his balance, and it slipped from his grasp. A piece of paper with his name on it fluttered to the floor. He picked it up and read the initials KKA. There was no need to read the rest. He knew what that meant. Pete West knew too much.

The papers were loose. Ahmet took them from the folder and stuffed them into his inside jacket pocket. He then checked the penknife and credit card were back in the top pocket. It was time to go. The folder easily creased in half and slid down the inside of his trousers. He wiped the telephone and the top of the bedside table.

Struggling, he set the body upright against the door. With the loose end of the flex in one hand, he wound it around the doorknob. He made sure that the Frenchman's buttocks hung an inch or two off the floor with the flex tight. Last, he wiped the knob then opened the door a crack. The passage was clear in one direction, but he couldn't see the other. He pulled again, keeping his handkerchief around the knob. The door opened slowly as he pulled it against the body's weight. Fortunately, Aurele was very light.

With just enough room to squeeze out into the passage, he transferred the handkerchief to the outer knob and pulled with both hands. The door wouldn't budge. He began to panic, placed a foot against the door frame, and pulled. The door moved inches. He tried again. The pain in his foot was too much, a constant reminder of the torture endured in prison. He winced and let his footrest on the ground. Using all his strength, he gave the door one last pull. It moved and clicked shut.

Ahmet breathed heavily. His shirt felt clammy against his skin. He ran the handkerchief over the upper part of the door panel and then hurried back to the lift. Before pushing the button to summon the elevator, he realised his mistake. If anyone were in the lift, they would remember him. He turned back and walked briskly past Aurele's cabin, mopping his face and neck.

When he reached the end of the passage, he stopped. He banged the wooden handrail, remembering the tape recorder. A wave of panic and nausea coursed through him. It was too late to do anything.

Chapter Thirty-Eight

THE TOP TABLE RESEMBLED a line-up of assorted mannequins, all dressed in evening suits and each with that well practised ear to ear plastic look of happiness. Nico Hrisacopolis, larger than life, played the perfect host with a lot to say, dabbing his forehead with a napkin between mouthfuls of trout, sipping chardonnay, and conducting conversations with those around him by waving his fork in the air.

Just audible above the buzz, a young Greek pianist played Spring Lake, a favourite jazz arrangement. However, the soft melody got lost in the swirling conversation around me and by the constant clink of glasses and clatter of cutlery on china.

As a young waiter served me a prawn cocktail, I leaned sideways, and from the corner of my eye, I caught sight of a white hanky waving at me from two tables away. Barbara sat next to Ioannis, looking at her usual confident self. I waved my fingers at her. Ioannis caught me and raised his glass.

While Jessica schmoozed with a member of the Spanish delegation sitting across our table, I waited for an opportunity to whisper something in her ear. I hadn't had a chance to speak to her since her return from the salon and wanted to get her independently. I needed to know if she'd gleaned anything further from Barbara about Ioannis.

I'd also missed Claude at the pre-dinner reception but put that down to the man being late again. By the time we'd started dinner, I felt a little concerned. It could have been seasickness or many things, but I decided to knock on his door later.

Jessica was still engaged in conversation, and I decided not to waste time but get Barbara on her own instead. I wanted to take her into my confidence and find out why Ioannis changed his name and how much he knew about the grandson, imposter or not. Time was running out. We will be in Athens in a few days. At least Claude had enough to bring the EU Commissioners to their senses.

Catching Barbara's eye as I rose, I tipped my head toward the exit.

I waited outside in the main lobby for a couple of minutes. When she joined me, Barbara was fanning her face with a banquet program. I gently guided her to a sofa after complaining about the cigar smoke.

"Okay, what's up?" she asked. "You're looking very serious."

"I need you to find a way to keep Jessica on board ship while we're in Naples."

Barbara caught my eye and formed an O with her lips. She rose from the sofa and slid an arm through mine, tugging at it and walking me across the lobby to the sliding doors leading to the deck and fresh air. We strolled across to the rail and stood leaning against it, looking out to sea. "Something serious has happened, hasn't it?" said Barbara, brushing hair from her face. She turned toward me. "What's going on? I take it you don't have a secret love you want to visit in Naples?"

I'd already made my mind up to take a big risk. Feeling apprehensive, I asked her to promise me she would keep what she heard from me to herself for the time being. Knowing how close she was to Ioannis, I wondered what reaction I would get when she found out what Jessica and I knew.

As diplomatically as I could, I told her about my suspicions that either Ahmet or a KKA agent were following Jessica and myself, probably keeping an eye on us because we were poking around in the family closet and had rattled some skeletons. Ahmet wanted to keep us from discovering more, or the agent wanted to know what we knew about Nico. I didn't think it would be a good idea to tell her someone planned to kill us. That's when she surprised me.

"You're fibbing, Pete. It's more serious than that. There's a lot to be said for a woman's intuition, and after my conversation with Jessica this morning, I'm sure you are both in some danger. You've got it if you want my help, but please don't allow me a glimpse at the painting. I want to see it all." Her eyes bore into mine while she poked my chest with a long fingernail.

Keeping confidence is part of my stock in trade. I wasn't aware of the conversation between Barbara and Jessica. Still, her understanding of the general situation and the ability to read between the lines convinced me of her genuine concern. I felt a little more confident talking to her.

We walked along the deck and sat in a small alcove opposite one of the lifeboats. So far, I told her our story about the meetings with Jamilya, Captain Stevenson, and about my strange encounter with the businessman Mehmet and an ex-soldier, Murat Kemal, in Istanbul. I left out the bit about the attempts on our lives and what probably happened to Jamilya. I knew Jessica wouldn't have told her, and I didn't want to cause Barbara any unnecessary worry. When I mentioned the soldier's story about the grandson, I noticed a flicker of eyelids as she turned her head away.

There was a moment's silence as we both took in the enormity of my story and the consequences that the situation implied. I studied Barbara's drawn face and saw someone struggling with her conscience. Peering out to sea, I waited, saying nothing.

She rubbed her bare arms and sighed. "Jessica told me about your visit with the British Army Captain. Mind you, that came after she'd grilled me for an hour," she scolded, shooting me a knowing expression. "I didn't object, though." She was breathing heavily and started shivering. "I'm not stupid, Pete. I know Ioannis is no angel and until I spoke to Jessica, I would have dismissed any suggestion that he was involved in anything criminal, but now I'm apprehensive."

She leaned forward as I removed my jacket and placed it around her shoulders. "Thanks," she said. "Jessica and I talked quite a bit this morning. I found the conversation upsetting, to say the least, but as Jessica spoke, there were a couple of moments my conscience troubled me. At first, I was mad at you." Her head jerked sideways as a long red nail poked me in the side again.

I'd promised her not to involve Ioannis in my investigative story unless was necessary, in return for some information on Nico. Of course, we had already seen Stevenson and learned how involved Ioannis was back in the seventies, something she knew nothing about until a few hours earlier. It must have looked as though I'd tricked her, but fortunately, from her demeanour, I assumed Jessica straightened her out.

Barbara's fingers fidgeted with the collar of my jacket as she pulled it closer to her. "I guess it's my turn to come clean, as they say." She rose from the seat. "Let's go inside and wait until the end of the speeches. We could all meet in your cabin if you like… Ioannis too."

I twisted uncomfortably in my seat. "No, let's all meet in the main lounge bar… but no, Ioannis."

If Ahmet followed us to a cabin, he would guess conspiracy. Much better, we appeared to be having a social get together.

Barbara sensed my apprehension. "You think Ioannis is involved in something sinister, don't you?"

"I honestly don't know, but at the very least, he's covering up the sins of his brother, past and present. As you already know, he was heavily involved in terrorist activities years ago. I think it best we keep things between ourselves without putting Ioannis into an awkward position."

Barbara nodded without saying a word and took my arm again until we entered the main stateroom. I hoped she was not too annoyed with me, but she must have seen sense in keeping things to herself for the time being.

The speeches over, guests stood in little groups, chatting and drinking. I spotted Jessica, standing next to Ioannis. She looked relieved to see us. We arranged to meet in an hour for a nightcap. Barbara made an excuse, saying she needed to change into something warmer and left with Ioannis.

While I walked back to my cabin with Jessica, I recounted my conversation with Barbara.

Jessica spent a few moments apologizing for opening up to Barbara. I squeezed her hand and said nothing. There were two questions on my mind, and both concerned Ioannis. I thought it strange that a man within the Hrisacopolis hierarchy would change his name. It bothered me that despite Barbara's assurances that Ioannis loathed his brother, he still danced to his tune. I wondered what Nico might be holding over his brother's head.

After reaching my cabin, we both kicked off our shoes and sat on my bed, comparing notes. Throwing my jacket across a chair, I asked, "Did you find out why Ioannis changed his name?"

Jessica removed her earrings. "Sort of, but I don't believe the story for a minute. Barbara thinks the world of her man, but I think she's letting her feelings cloud her judgment."

I agreed and listened with interest. The story told to Barbara was that Ioannis changed his name after a family argument over their father's will in which he received a yearly income but had no position in the company. Brother Nico got the lot. In protest, Ioannis changed his name and took an editorial newspaper job in Cyprus. Maybe there was some truth to it and maybe not, but I figured the job on Cyprus was part of someone else's plan; something Ioannis, being a good patriot, fell in with and forgot the family squabble while fighting for the Greek cause.

"Was there any hint of some dark secret involving Ioannis?" I asked.

Jessica raised her eyebrows. "Maybe, but there wasn't anything I could put my finger on. We were chatting about the two brothers, and Barbara was firing bullets at Nico about how he treated Ioannis when she caught herself mid-sentence and changed the subject. She told me that Ioannis had made a business trip to Northern Cyprus as the troubles were ending."

Ioannis visiting Northern Cyprus in the seventies meant he had taken a considerable risk regarding his own safety. Northern Cyprus was a Turkish enclave. It must have been important.

Not knowing what the trip was about was frustrating, but I had a fair idea that he went on behalf of his brother to visit... someone. I wondered if he started the trip as Ioannis Hrisacopolis and entered Northern Cyprus as Ioannis Koskotas. My mind was racing. Nico's grandson would not have been born at the time, and Lara may have still been on the island.

I left Jessica so she could change and said I'd be back to pick her up as soon as I'd checked on Claude.

Reaching his cabin, I knocked several times before a steward, followed by two well-dressed men, security I guessed, came striding along the passage. Waving his hands to indicate I stop knocking, the steward reached me, out of breath, and whispered loudly that the French gentleman was now deceased. The two security men escorted me back to the purser's office within seconds.

Ahmet looked into the mirror and ran a brush over his hair. Staging Aurele's death as a suicide gave him a choice. He could either let Nico know that West had passed sensitive information on to the Frenchman and he, Ahmet, needed to silence the man, or he could keep quiet and let the suspicion fall on the KKA.

He brushed strands of grey hair from one shoulder before slipping into his white jacket. He had decided not to do either. Another course of action would buy him time to keep his son safe and rid himself of the journalists and the agent. Nico wouldn't worry about the agent's death, but West and his companion was another matter. Their deaths would have to be at the hands of someone else. Not only that but someone who was an opponent both politically and culturally. The agent was ideal.

Ahmet left his cabin and made straight for the large lower sundeck. The agent was there every morning between six and seven should a meeting be necessary.

The sun was already above the horizon as Ahmet wound his way through the rows of blue and white sunbeds and stood by the ship's rail. Assar, a tall man in shorts and sandals, joined him within seconds.

"You have little time left to deal with the grandson. Our committee will not be pleased if you let us down."

Ahmet looked sideways and replied angrily. "There are other pressing matters. You are supposed to be dealing with West, yet he is still alive, causing trouble for Hrisacopolis and us. That is one reason why I have not completed my task."

He quickly related what happened and handed over the Frenchman's notes. While Assar scanned the papers, Ahmet kept watching across the sundeck. Several guests were sitting at the far end. He turned back to Assar, stepped closer, and spoke quietly.

Their people in the south of the island would be in danger. Ahmet pointed to the report and tapped the page headed Famagusta. The Famagusta container terminal was located just beside the Turkish border and operated by a Greek company that employed Turkish labour. If Hrisacopolis had anything to do with it, they would lose their jobs, giving him a stranglehold over Turkish farm exports. That would lead to unrest and violence. If that happened, Greece would get all the backing it needed from the EU if Turkish troops intervened.

"If UN troops are sent in, our plans to expand the Republic will be ruined, "continued Ahmet. "We have to play a clever game, Assar."

Assar stroked his chin. "Okay, but if we kill Hrisacopolis, we will still have problems."

"True, and think what would happen to our ambitions," said Ahmet, shrugging.

Without the grandson or Hrisacopolis, the EU would have to find alternative shipping and distribution companies from other EU countries. The Greek government could try nationalizing Hrisacopolis' empire to take his place, but the EU would never agree to that. The result would be a political conflict with the Greeks doing exactly what Hrisacopolis would do at Famagusta.

"I can see UN troops being pulled in as our army line up on the border to protect our workers and our exports. The result would be the same, and we would lose everything."

Assar carried on reading.

"Here," said Ahmet, taking the papers and turning them over. "Look at this. West has written that the grandson might be an imposter. If that is the case, surely the KKA could turn him into a useful means of funding as in my original plan."

Assar took the papers back and folded them.

"So how do we get what we want? You say you are going to kill Hrisacopolis."

"Yes... At the right time, after the grandson takes control, that will not be until after we reach Athens," said Ahmet. "We can use the imposter to our advantage, causing political turmoil at our choosing. This will allow us to invade the south before the UN can act. The toothless EU will eventually have to declare neutrality, and the island will be ours."

"And if the grandson turns out to be genuine?"

Ahmet pulled an index finger across his throat. "I doubt he is, or Hrisacopolis would have found a use for him by now."

He was thankful the KKA knew very little about the grandson before joining their organisation and put his plan to them. The imposter had to live.

Assar took a pack of Gauloises and a Zippo from his pocket. Removing a cigarette from the pack, he flipped the lighter. Smoke streamed sideways from his mouth.

"The journalists are going ashore when we dock in Naples," said Ahmet, looking into Assar's eyes. "You can leave Nico Hrisacopolis to me." He turned and walked away.

Chapter Thirty-Nine

A S I ENTERED THE CABIN, Barbara was pacing back and forth, her jaw set tight. Jessica sat on the edge of the bed.

"I cannot believe he could do this to me." Barbara stopped as I quietly closed the door.

"What's up?" I asked.

Jessica smiled wanly. "Barbara had some art stolen from her yacht."

"Two Picassos and a Renoir," interjected Barbara. She was distraught, wringing her hands. "I can't believe it."

I cupped my hands around hers. "Do the police know who took them?"

"She has the paintings back, Pete. The police were tipped off." Jessica rose from the bed and put a comforting arm around Barbara's shoulder.

"They were stolen… He was such a nice young man. I trusted him…." Barbara sniffed loudly. She moved and stood facing the window.

Trying to be as sympathetic as possible, I looked from one to the other and signalled for them to sit. "That is rotten news." I looked at Jessica and frowned. "I'm afraid I have some more."

Jessica looked up at me.

"I'm afraid Claude was found dead in his cabin this morning."

Both women sat up. "What."

Barbara rose again with one hand to her mouth. "This has turned into the worst week of my life."

"It appears he took his own life." I swallowed hard. Claude's death was getting to me. "I was with him yesterday… I know he was fine…."

"How?" asked Barbara.

"They've assumed he hanged himself." I took the small recorder from my pocket. "I am hoping we might get some answers from this. I found it under the bed."

Barbara took a deep breath and brushed the stolen paintings to one side.

I explained I'd been in the purser's office for half an hour, and security insisted on coming with me when I went into Claude's cabin to retrieve my notes. As far as they were concerned, the notes were of no particular importance-just a story Claude and I were working on. Of course, the notes were gone, but I found under the bed while pretending to see if some papers had slid there was a tape recorder and a folder with some old photos.

"Have you played the tape?" asked Jessica.

I flicked the switch on the side of the recorder. Claude's voice filled the cabin. It was just general stuff he was reading, mainly from my notes. The sound of turning pages as Claude's voice echoed eerily added a strange sense of intimacy to the occasion. After reading my notes on Ioannis, he said: "The Greek military originally funded Ioannis newspaper to promote Enosis. I met him in '74 at an interview with Archbishop Makarios in Nicosia. Note… pictures for Pete… this was just before the Greek junta's coup when he fled the island and…" I pointed to the tape. In the background someone knocked on the door – "this was just before the shit hit the fan in Athens. Ioannis was a conduit for his brother, feeding him everything that happened between the Archbishop, Athens, and all interested parties involved in the Cypriot struggle."

Claude's voice stopped abruptly. There was a loud grunt, and then a bang as the recorder hit the floor. Following this was the sound of someone looking around the cabin until the recorder ran out of tape. Shivers ran up my spine, knowing Claude had just died. I glanced at Barbara, who had her eyes fixed on the ground. If she was angry with me over my notes, she kept it inside, but only just. Her chest rose and fell, and her lips began to quiver.

I told her about the hearing aid lying on the bed. "He knew nothing until it was too late."

Barbara remained silent, then placed a hand on my shoulder. "I have a feeling you know an awful lot more about Ioannis than I do." There was a look of desperation in her eyes. She gripped my shoulder. "I guess it's time for you to hurt my feelings."

I sat with Barbara and told her everything, from A to Z, of the attempts on our lives and the details covering Jamilya and Alexander's deaths and my suspicions about Ioannis' involvement in Nico's activities. Ioannis knew what was going on and that Ahmet was a killer.

Then there was a strange trip Ioannis made to Northern Cyprus in late nineteen seventy-four. The Turks were there in the thousands. Why was Ioannis there? It had to be something to do with Nico. Lara was still there then too.

I left nothing out.

As I spoke, the colour drained from her face for several moments, her fingers gripping her knees. Her lips pressed tighter together. She took the glass of brandy from Jessica with shaking hands and sipped. She said nothing. A tear formed at the corner of one eye.

"I'm sorry, Barbara," I said. "There's something else." I paused, knowing I was about to add to her worries. "I believe you may be in danger. We know Nico told Ioannis he should break off his relationship with you on several occasions. He will see you as a threat."

"And the folder with your notes is where? With Nico?" asked Jessica, with a quick mocking roll of the eyes at the ceiling.

I wasn't sure. If Ahmet killed Claude, the folder could be with Nico or the KKA if they killed him. There again, Ahmet could be playing a double game. A fuzzy picture was beginning to form, but I needed time to see if I was getting things right. I tossed photos into Jessica's lap.

"These were with the tape. They're just general shots."

Jessica flipped through them and stopped at one. Barbara shook her head slowly while I took the photo from Jessica. Makarios was sitting at a table with several men in uniform, and some dishevelled men stood against the wall behind him, each carrying a rifle. Alexander stood at one end and next to him, Ioannis. It did at least confirm Ioannis was in the north in '74. Jessica touched my hand as Barbara surveyed the photo. Lowering her eyelids, she deftly slipped another picture into my hand. It showed the meeting between Claude and Andreas in '71. A group of men sat cross-legged while Claude and Andreas shook hands in the foreground. To one side, sitting on a canvas seat next to a tent, was a smiling Ioannis.

I put the photo in my pocket. There wasn't any point in showing it to Barbara. She was upset enough.

"Just stick together and keep visible in public places while docked in Naples," I said. "In the meantime, I have to go ashore, but I won't be too long."

Jessica looked concerned. "Why? What are you going to do?"

"I'm going to meet 'B'," I shrugged. " 'B' will have to deliver my notes to the French himself."

The docks at Naples snugly fronted a five-kilometre bay full of commercial ships and ocean-going liners. A large container complex sat at the far end of the docks while ferries to other ports including Ischia, Sorrento, Stromboli, and Palermo weaved around the liners docked up against the Via Cristoforo Colombo.

'B' assured me the Hotel Romero was a ten-minute walk from the ship. He'd warned me that crossing a busy highway in Italy was an art form. One had to look across the road and step out into the traffic without glancing left or right and walk slowly to the other side. It took me ten minutes to cross the street. Instructions are one thing but hard to follow when a long line of container trucks are streaming along the road at forty plus kilometres an hour.

The Hotel Romero was a modern tinted glass structure that reminded me of London. It raised ten stories into the Neapolitan skyline, a rectangular box looking down on bricks and mortar on either side.

I didn't have to look for 'B'. He waved a hand at me from the reception desk and rushed over to guide me to a circle of plush black leather sofas. One thing about 'B' never changed: his dress. If we were meeting in Saudi Arabia, he would still turn up in a three-piece suit. I smiled inwardly as he lit a cigar. Within a couple of minutes, some ash would drop onto his waistcoat. Coffee and biscuits arrived as we sat.

"Pete, nice to see you, old chap." He indicated the sugar bowl as the waiter poured coffee. "One or two?" He picked at the sugar with silver tongs and waited for the man to leave.

His mood changed as he leaned forward. "Did you bring your notes?" He took the small folder I offered.

It took me into the morning's small hours to rewrite my notes, and I was annoyed to see him stuff them into an attaché case without studying them. He saw the look on my face and raised a finger.

"Pete, I know what's in here. We'll talk about them in a minute."

He looked apologetic. A knot grew in my stomach, my early warning system.

"Sorry, old boy, but I need to tell you a couple of other things. First… Ahmet is a KKA agent and second… Ahmet is working for the Turkish secret service. They pulled him out of prison almost twenty-five years ago, surprising as he's a Kurd."

I nodded. The news confirmed what I had guessed.

"Yes, a couple of weeks ago, MI6 told us that they had a file on him. The PM was furious. The problem is we don't know what he's up to. Hrisacopolis doesn't know, or the little shit would be dead by now." As an afterthought, he added, "In his statement regarding the long-lost grandson, Nico said he found out about the young man through a deathbed confession by the mother. I know that was rubbish. The woman, who came forward with this story, supposedly the mother's friend, is Cynara Takeshi. Ahmet's file lists her as a Kurdish informer. That doesn't mean the grandson is an imposter. He was Turkish, and Nico had to present him as Greek."

"Sorry to disagree with you, 'B', I'm sure we have an imposter, although I'm not sure the real grandson is dead. It's all in my notes. The thing is, where is he if he's alive?"

I should have focused on Ahmet a lot sooner. While I sat thinking about Ahmet, I noticed 'B' looking around the entrance hall.

He said, "Don't worry, they're outside."

I didn't say a word. We both knew. I'd told him of my suspicions about the KKA agent. Sitting back, he crossed his legs and looked uneasy. He threw an arm over the back of the sofa, trying to appear casual.

"Pete, you and Jessica must leave the ship. Richard is concerned for your safety, and I don't blame him. With Claude's death, Nico, or Ahmet, are hell-bent on preventing your story from reaching the public, not that we didn't already know that."

The idea that I leave the ship was out of the question. Barbara was now in the know, and she was never going to leave the ship or Ioannis. The situation wasn't just about Nico and his pipe dream anymore.

I gave him a defiant look. "I'm glad you're for me 'B', but I can't do that. There's another story I'm pursuing. I can imagine Jessica's reaction too."

'B' raised his eyebrows and puffed on the cigar. "I knew you wouldn't, but the powers that be…."

He waved the cigar, and sure enough, flakes of ash settled on the thin pin-striped waistcoat. We sat with our coffee getting cold. I waited as the knot inside got bigger, and he wrestled with what I assumed was a difficult situation. I broke the silence.

"What is it, 'B'?"

His large girth expanded as he exhaled. "Bad news, Pete. The PM has decided that your story will not be read anywhere except at number 10."

I surprised myself by remaining calm for a second time. As I wrote my notes the previous evening, the wider picture raised issues I had given no thought to. As 'B' picked his coffee up, I continued for him.

"Hart told me about Whitehall's concerns over our image; the marbles, the EU presidency in two years, blah, blah. Something has happened, probably planned at a cabinet meeting, to put Britain in good stead with Brussels. Let me guess… knowing the Foreign Office as I do… that something will involve Turkey, so the KKA have the sting taken out of their tails."

There was a moment's silence. "Turkey will enter into negotiations when they join the EU. The Cypriot issue will be high on the agenda. We can't afford failure."

"Good old diplomatic service," I said, throwing my napkin on the table. "Why the hell couldn't they have thought of this before we got into all this crap? People are dying, 'B'. Does anyone in Whitehall even care?"

There was another moment's silence, and 'B' tapped the attaché case. "This is not going to waste. Whitehall will love you again."

"Bollocks, 'B', I'm a journalist for Christ's sake. All I have to show for exposing that bastard are three pull-out supplements on how nice he is."

"That's why the powers that be wanted you out of the way in case the proverbial hits the fan. In the meantime, Nico will be quietly encouraged to retire and sell his empire or let the Greek government nationalise it." He grimaced. "Although we'd rather they didn't."

Ahmet had to be the focus of attention. He had to be orchestrating things. Besides, I had a score to settle on behalf of two women. We finished our coffee and left the Romero, keeping an eye open for furtive figures around every corner. If 'B' was concerned, he didn't show it.

CHAPTER FORTY

THE HIRED CAR WAS PARKED down the side of the hotel, two wheels up on the pavement in typical Italian fashion. After slamming his door, 'B' looked into the driving mirror and announced we had company. Still seething inside at Whitehall, I didn't take much notice. I bent forward and looked casually into the wing mirror on my side. A Mercedes emerged from Romero's underground parking area and sat nose out into the road.

"Hang on." 'B' tapped the steering wheel impatiently with an index finger. We waited for a Vespa scooter to scream by trailing blue smoke. A young girl sat precariously side-saddle as they wobbled, avoiding another car coming the other way. Our windows were down, and the smoke reeked of petrol.

'B' looked sideways at me and nodded. There was a roar as the engine spat into life. The car shot forward off the curb and onto the road with a bone jarring bump. My body went stiff. With his portly frame squashed behind the steering wheel of our little Fiat, I felt fearful and desperate to get out, remembering the near fatal crash on Mount Olympus.

Scared by the way we were rocketing toward the end of the side road and the main drag beyond, I had no time to worry about who or what was following us. I held on for dear life, watching 'B' turn the steering wheel as though he were driving a dodgem at the fairground.

The car lurched violently to one side as we careered around the corner into Via Cristoforo Colombo. 'B's foot stabbed the brake, and we skidded to a halt. My head shot forward, nearly hitting the windscreen. Too late to avoid us, the Mercedes drove into our rear with a horrendous crash. I was flung forward against the seat belt. Winded, I gasped for breath as my head hit the windscreen stanchion. The sound and sight of tearing metal and broken glass and plastic pieces across the road brought the traffic to a standstill. Dazed, I watched B. His hands were working at his door handle. Outside, a crowd of excited motorists and pedestrians were shouting and gesticulating. I could hear a siren in the background.

"Stay here." 'B' shouldered his door open. The door swung back with a loud bang, and he climbed out.

I unbuckled my belt and sat gulping in the air. Police had appeared from everywhere, and I could hear 'B' talking to one of them. My head throbbed. I tried to think straight. A hand came through my window. "Here, take this and dab your cheek. You've got a little cut."

I took the handkerchief from 'B' and held it against my face. "What the hell is going on?"

He climbed back into the car. "One of the men following us was a passenger on the *Sea Empress*. Both he and his colleague are KKA. MI6 again, old chap." He held his hands up in surrender. "I didn't know until yesterday, but I had enough time to chat with our embassy here. They arranged the ambush today with the local police." He pointed out of the window.

Two men were being loaded into the back of a police van. "Some sort of problem with the immigration authorities, I would think," said 'B'. Onlookers were pulling and pushing at our rear fender and, using their feet, smashed it off. After bending out one wing and cleaning windshield glass from the front seats, 'B' waved at the police, and we were off.

"You need a stiff brandy, old chap. Don't worry about this mess. I'll have it all sorted by when you're back in your cabin." 'B' sounded matter-of-fact. I was still shaking and just nodded. Then the irony of the situation made me laugh a little hysterically. "All... of... this," I stuttered. "Three innocent people are... dead, and I'm shot at... and... no bloody story."

'B' said nothing. There wasn't any point. I guessed he was annoyed for me, but his allegiance was with Whitehall.

It was an anti-climax driving back. I was breathing more easily and nursing some bruises when I noticed 'B's hands tremble. He glanced at me out of the corner of his eye, pressed his lips together and smiled as though coming out of a trance. We attracted a lot of stares as we limped along in our wrecked Fiat to the *Sea Empress*. We sat in silence until we reached her.

As I climbed out, 'B' touched one finger to his forehead in mock salute. "The KKA are out of the way as far as the ship is concerned. Be careful, old boy. I'll see you in Athens." With that, he disappeared in a cloud of smoke.

CHAPTER FORTY-ONE

IOANNIS STOOD WITH FEET apart and leaned forward, thrusting his face into Nico, one finger wagging an inch from his brother's nose. "Don't threaten me, Nico. You'll regret it if anything happens to Barbara."

Nico stood impassive as Ioannis shouted insults at him.

Ahmet leant against the piano, fingers tapping the edge of the lid lightly, his eyes darting from one man to the other. The corners of his mouth creased in a masked smile. He was feeling pleased with himself. Jessica du Rosse was still on board, but she would be easy to deal with without West. Turning Nico against his brother over Barbara was a bonus, causing just the right amount of tension. Barbara could cause problems, especially if Ioannis' tongue started wagging. That situation alone would end Nico's dream.

Red-faced and breathing heavily, Ioannis pointed an accusing finger at Nico. "I'm warning you; you stay out of my business…."

"And what are you going to do?" Nico spoke with quiet menace. "Let slip a few family secrets or have a word in Brussels' ear?" Hot flakes of ash flew through thick swirling smoke as Nico angrily crushed a cigar butt into a glass ashtray. "All you're going to do is draw attention to yourself." Jabbing a finger in Ioannis' chest, he warned, "You just remember Lara Akchote." He stared into Ioannis' face. "I don't think you want that…," he growled. Ioannis took half a step back as he was jabbed hard in the chest again with a clenched fist. "…so do as you're told. Our whole future-"

"Your damn future, not mine."

"Our future." thundered Nico. "Your woman is a walking time bomb. I used to worry about you and her. Now I worry about West, you and her…." He rose to his full height and narrowed his eyes for a second, breathing deeply. When he opened them, he glared at Ioannis and spoke through clenched teeth. "You're so damned stupid. You think she'll shrug off what he says?" He snapped his fingers through the air as he spoke.

Ioannis' face became a mask of calm. There was a tremor in his voice. "I know she won't say anything."

"Oh, shut up." Nico's face contorted into a vicious sneer. Ioannis blinked several times as Nico's finger jabbed the air in front of his face. "You'll stay away from her while I deal with West." He took a deep breath and wheezed. "Who's going to listen to a washed-up art dealer anyway? I'll arrange for the press to crucify her."

Ioannis' mouth sagged, his face wide-eyed and taut. "You bastard, West would-"

"West won't be around. Now sort Barbara out." Nico glanced toward Ahmet as he reached for the cigar box on the table.

Ioannis marched out of the room and slammed the door behind him.

Nico turned to Ahmet. "When we get to Athens..."

CHAPTER FORTY-TWO

THE SUN HUNG LOW IN the sky, setting the far horizon afire with a golden glow tinged with a shade of purple blue. Two seagulls kept pace with us, darting back and forth on the breeze, their wings performing a delicate balancing act. We were two hours out of Naples, and I had just finished telling Jessica and Barbara about my ride with 'B'. We were quiet. I was trying to come to terms with the fact there would be no story. An urgent knock on the door ended the silence. Barbara opened it, and Ioannis stepped into the cabin, red-faced and out of breath. His shirt was stained under the arms, and his hair dishevelled. The polished Mediterranean look of a well-heeled socialite had disappeared. I exchanged looks with Jessica but said nothing.

Ioannis' eyes flickered everywhere without settling on any of us.

"Barbara, I need to speak to you," he said, his voice shaking. His hands were shaking too. He pushed one inside a trouser pocket and used the other to straighten his hair.

Barbara grabbed hold of a lapel and yanked him into the cabin. Reaching behind him, she pulled the door shut with a loud click. "We all need to talk to you," she said sharply. "Sit down."

Ioannis was still catching his breath as he sat. "Look, I need to speak to you." He hesitated and started to rise again.

Barbara placed a firm hand on his shoulder to stop him from getting up. "Stop right there," she said angrily. Taking a deep breath, her tone became more conciliatory as she added, "Now sit and listen." I had visions of a mother chastising a naughty boy. She nodded in my direction. "Pete, tell him what happened today."

Ioannis sat but couldn't stay still.

"Ioannis, we need to sort things out." Barbara went tight-lipped.

"Today, someone tried to kill Pete." Barbara held a hand and waved it to stop him from speaking. "And it's not the first time."

I watched Ioannis closely. He looked down at the floor. He was an angry man. He sat upright, eyes and mouth wide open like some pantomime dame. The act was not good enough. I'd caught the transformation. The boyish face that quickly replaced the impatient and angry glare was too contrived. He sprang up from the bed and moved to the window, his arms outstretched as he turned to face Barbara. "I have never hurt anyone," he blurted. "Of course, I know about some of the things that happened in the past, but I swear I had nothing to do with them."

His hands danced in and out of his pockets and eventually found a pack of cigarettes. All the time, he avoided eye contact with Jessica and me. Despite the sagging shoulders and shaking head, his sincerity was not genuine. He'd lied about Captain Stevenson's photograph, which meant he knew who Lara was. Being on Cyprus, north and south, during and after the troubles, he was the news conduit, feeding his brother all types of intelligence, probably keeping track of Jessica and myself on our visit too.

Ignoring his protests, I retold the day's events and told him that his brother's political ambitions would not be realised.

"I hope not," he replied. He pulled a Du Maurier from the pack and sifted through his pockets again, presumably for his holder. He gave up, put the cigarette between his lips, and sat back on the bed. A little more mystique had vanished from his social veneer without the gold and amber holder. "He's threatened to deal with us all. I hadn't realised how far he was prepared to go…" He held out his hands, "…but this… I've never known him like this."

Jessica angrily rounded on him.

Ioannis' whole life was a lie, and because of his weakness, people had suffered, including Barbara. He was asking us to believe he knew nothing about the imposter upstairs or the imposter posing as Andreas's mother.

Ioannis raised a hand as though trying to push the questions away. "Andreas is not an imposter. Nico and Ahmet invented the story about the mother because Nico didn't want anyone to know Andreas, or Baki as he was, has been in the Turkish army. Surely you can understand that."

I was sure they were convinced Andreas was real while listening to Ioannis and remembering how Nico was enthused about his grandson when we first met. We were all missing a piece of the puzzle, although only I was aware of that. "I suggest that since he was on the island during the troubles, he must have known the lad's mother, Lara."

"No, stop." He snatched a handkerchief from his top pocket and wiped his forehead. "All I know is that Andreas is not an imposter. Ahmet visited him regularly and eventually won him over to join Nico."

Jessica slapped her thigh. "For God's sake, Ioannis, wake up."

It occurred to me that as weak as he was, Ioannis had one secret he would rather die with than tell us. I was still curious why he changed his name, especially from one that translated into industrial power and prestige. "Was that because you visited Northern Cyprus in seventy-four. I watched his eyes darting between the three of us, mainly at Barbara.

"You told Barbara it all stemmed from your father's will, but it didn't?" Jessica asked.

Ioannis jumped up, his face contorted with anger. "Enough. I don't have to sit here and take this."

A knock at the door interrupted us. I opened it to find Nico's steward standing there. "Excuse me, sir, but Mr Hrisacopolis requests Mr West join him to drink in his stateroom."

I'd been expecting the invitation since I re-joined the ship. If Nico knew what had happened, he'd want to distance himself from any involvement. If he didn't know, maybe he was aware I was talking to his brother. Whether he or Ahmet knew about my notes, I had no idea. I just wanted to stay focused on spoiling Nico's plans and somehow deal with Ahmet.

I closed the door and turned to Jessica. "Whatever else happens, please stay together. I'll be back shortly."

Jessica lipped 'Take care' as Ioannis sat next to Barbara.

"You need to explain things to me," said Barbara, pointing a long finger in his face. "I want answers, not excuses."

"There's nothing to tell." Ioannis wrung his hands and rose again, his body shaking. "I'm going back up there. I'll sort this out. I promise I will."

Jessica and Barbara pulled him down onto a chair as I left. I had a good idea why Ioannis went to Northern Cyprus and what happened to Baki. Nico was finished. My real problem was staying alive to enjoy the satisfaction of seeing justice done for Lara and Jamilya.

.

CHAPTER FORTY-THREE

T
HE CRUISER ALTERED COURSE and came about into the wake of the *Sea Empress*, a mile distant. Her stern was well lit. She was easy to pick up. Adonis shivered as cold air came through the cockpit shutters and hit him sideways. Through filtered night glasses, he picked out the coast lights of Gozo to the south. In an hour, they would be past the harbour of Valletta and through the Malta Channel into the Ionian Sea.

Adonis gripped the glasses and pressed them against his chest with both hands. He stood with feet apart on the vibrating wheelhouse deck, keeping a close watch on the stern of *Sea Empress* as he remembered a day he had lived with all his life; a day he lived as a Turk named Baki.

After a meagre simit bread breakfast, that day had started like any other day at the workshop. It took twenty minutes to reach the Kazlicesme district, but the pungent smell from the tanneries hung thick in the air long before the workshops came into view. Hussein, his stepfather, had spoken of plans for some new workshops in Pentik, away from the slums, but they were still an idea for the future.

Every day he arrived before dawn, turning on the dust-covered light hanging over the worktable. Then he would sort the lambskins by quality and price, ready for working into bags and purses. The old workshop opened to the street as soon as Hussein arrived half an hour later.

With the sound of the sewing machine working nonstop throughout the day, he sat on a chair outside in the street, hoping to snare traders and introduce them to his father. Each new order helped his mother run the house and feed them on the meagre pittance Hussein gave her after drinking raki with friends.

It turned out to be a bad day with very little business. He left Hussein outside the tea house and went home to help his mother. Help meant sweeping the small apartment while his mother prepared their evening meal, a chopped salad with mackerel stuffed with pilaf or sardines rolled in grape leaves.

That night, after finishing his work, he sat with his mother, waiting. On many other occasions, he listened as she told him about his real father, a strong and wonderful man, a secret they shared. They looked at a photo of him she took from a small tin box hidden behind a brick at the back of the fireplace. She took a letter from the box and told him it contained a big secret that would change his life once he was of age. He would have to contact his grandfather, who had sent the letter to his father, Andreas. Later, one of Andreas's friends delivered the letter to her. Baki remembered looking at it, but neither of them could read it. Excited, he looked forward to meeting the man who wrote it.

After an hour, they had their dinner, and he went to bed. He had no idea how long he had been asleep, but he awoke to angry shouts and screams. There was a terrible fight between Hussein and his mother. He crept to the partially open kitchen door and peered through the crack. He was frightened but felt overwhelming anger as he watched Hussein punch his mother in the face. She fell back awkwardly against the table before collapsing to the floor, writhing. The letter fell from her hand and lay next to the tin box on the table. Hatred and anger welled up inside Baki as he burst through the door and flew at Hussein, punching him. Hussein grabbed hold of him by one arm and threw him across the kitchen. He turned on Lara again in his drunken state, pulling her from the floor by her hair.

He couldn't stop Hussein's brutality and grabbed the first thing that came to hand, a kitchen knife. Unable to get free from her husband's grip on her hair, Lara watched in horror as he came at them with a knife raised. She screamed and pleaded with him to put the knife down, but it was too late. He lunged at Hussein and buried the knife into his stomach. The man collapsed, bleeding profusely, and died almost immediately.

Baki remembered his mother kneeling on the floor with arms locked around him, sobbing. He told her how much he loved her and didn't want to see her hurt anymore. They hugged for several minutes until finally, she pulled away from him, telling him to go and tell Mehmet what had happened as he would know what to do. Baki remembered refusing at first, saying he wanted to make sure the city Jandarma knew why he had killed his father, but she insisted he go while she dealt with the body.

Mehmet was a businessman who loaned money to traders like Baki's father. He had become a wise friend who taught him many things about Turkish culture.

Making sure his mother was all right, he ran from the house to Mehmet's home. When they returned, Mehmet entered, telling him to wait. Baki became anxious after a short while and ran into the house, too late for Mehmet to stop him. Lara lay on the floor with the knife embedded through her heart.

He was inconsolable. Mehmet led him away after neighbours called the Jandarma. Within two weeks, he was in the army while newspapers spread lies about his mother. Mehmet advised him to say nothing. Lara had died for him, and her ordeal was over. He received a photo of his mother and a letter that Mehmet read to him. It laid bare the truth about his mother's past and the reason for her squalid existence since, signed by the hand that sentenced her. From that moment on, Baki vowed justice for his mother.

The stern of *Sea Empress* loomed large before the launch veered across the frothing wake to starboard, yawing violently. Steadying himself, Adonis peered through the darkness and waited for a flashing torch from the lower store's hatchway. It came immediately.

"Take over."

One of Turk's men took the wheel and closed in on the ship, allowing the narrowing gap of the rising sea to draw them alongside and under the open store's hatchway. From the darkened interior of the vessel, two shadowy figures threw ropes down to secure the cruiser as Adonis, standing in the bow, threw up a rope attached to a scrambling net. Within seconds the net was secure, and men carrying backpacks and light automatic weapons scrambled silently up into the store.

Adonis waved the first cruiser away from the ship and flashed the Turk's cruiser. Within a few minutes, all men were aboard and the cruisers in line astern by a quarter-mile.

"I'll take six men. We must hold the bridge," whispered Adonis hoarsely. "I'll make for Hrisacopolis' stateroom after. Give me ten minutes."

The Turk nodded. "Ten minutes…"

The men were split into two groups, each taking one side of the ship, taking control and herding passengers to the lifeboat stations while Joseph took the third team and lay all the charges below the waterline.

"Whatever happens," said Adonis, checking his automatic, "you must get the lifeboats into the water. Get the passengers off." Adonis motioned for some men to follow him while recalling the ship's layout from memory. A steel ladder at the far end of the equipment store, just in front of the entrance leading into the galley pantry, led up to an emergency hatch on the port side promenade deck. Four steps led up to a 'crew only' entrance a few feet from the hatch. Beyond that, four flights of stairs through crew's quarters and radio room led to the bridge.

Moving fast, Adonis led the men to the end of the store and climbed the ladder. At the top, he carefully raised the hatch cover. The promenade was deserted. It took less than a minute for the men to enter the 'crew only' door. Three men raced along the passage to the other side of the ship before both teams were in position to search the duty crew's quarters on both levels below the bridge. With six crew locked in one cabin minutes later, Adonis entered the bridge and took the captain and bridge crew by surprise.

"Do as you are instructed, Captain," commanded Adonis. "Tell the crew and passengers to co-operate. Everyone must assemble at his lifeboat stations. You will then slow the ship within a mile and, if necessary, reverse engines and drag her to a stop. You will then lower the crew and guests safely into the water."

The captain looked at the pistol in Adonis's hand and gave a curt nod.

<hr />

Jessica slipped her shoes on and stepped out into the passage. Ioannis had raced out of the cabin in a fit of temper, threatening to face his brother again. Barbara followed him before Jessica could stop her.

Looking in both directions, she found the way clear. She walked quickly to the stairs at the end of the passage but stopped, startled at the sight of a pair of black combat boots and the barrel end of a machine gun coming into view as someone descended the stairs. Her heart began to pound. Without thinking, she looked around for an escape route.

Opposite her was a door marked 'laundry.' She reached for the handle and pushed. Once through, she closed the door behind her, careful not to make a noise. There were rows of laundry skips and a line of huge washing machines that led to metal steps leading downward on the other side of some racks. Jessica kicked her shoes off at the top of the stairs and skipped down the steps. At the bottom, there was a short passage at the end of which two large rubber doors led into a food store. She stopped for a moment, breathing heavily, confused and frightened.

A door opened above her. Putting a hand over her mouth to suppress the noise of her heavy breathing, she padded across the floor and pushed through the rubber doors into the food store. Another door to one side was ajar. There were rows of racks inside, each loaded with tinned and boxed food and other cooking supplies. She could hear several booted feet on the steps and started to shake despite a conscious effort to remain calm. She crouched behind a rack and breathed deeply, exhaling quietly. The footsteps had stopped. She relaxed, and almost immediately, the door swung back with a crash. Clamping a hand over her mouth, she froze, trembling.

"Se deplacer," barked a deep voice.

The two men left the store, and she could hear them going back up the stairs. Waiting until she was sure they were gone, she grabbed the corner of a rack and pulled until it fell, blocking the door with a loud crash,

'Terrorists,' thought Jessica. 'KKA. But why are they speaking French?'

There was a muffled bang. The ship shuddered, and Jessica fell. A large box fell from a rack behind her as she got to her feet. Unable to get out of the way in time, the box struck her head, and her surroundings vanished into the darkness.

CHAPTER FORTY-FOUR

I WALKED INTO HRISACOPOLIS' STATEROOM with one hand hooked in my trouser pocket and my summer jacket draped over the other arm. Layers of cigar smoke hung in the air and caught the back of my throat. I started coughing. A small length of white tape flapped below a gently rattling metal grill in the ceiling above me, suggesting the air conditioning was on but ineffective against Nico's chain smoking.

Nico stood with his back to me in white flannels and open neck white shirt, his hands locked together behind his back. Despite the steward announcing my arrival, he ignored me by looking through the French doors and across the private swimming pool. His fingers twitched as I stood just behind him and to one side, following his gaze. I wondered what he was thinking about, if his argument with Ioannis still played on his mind or if he was thinking about Andreas.

Andreas, the man I was certain, was an imposter, lay sprawled on a lounger by the edge of the lit-up pool area with a drink in his hand, earphones plugged into an MP3 clipped to his shirt. One of his feet jigged up and down to whatever he was listening to. I hadn't realised it on the first visit, but Nico's private pool was empty. At the far end of the pool were tarps covering some cylindrical shapes. At that moment, I remembered Jessica telling me where the marbles were stored.

A slight movement to my right distracted me. Standing behind the piano in the corner, Ahmet stared directly at me from behind half-closed eyes. I hadn't noticed him, half-hidden in the shadows. He appeared angry and reminded me of a snake ready to strike. Nico had hired him as the Istanbul agent in his shipping business, but he was also a hired thug. An uneasy relationship existed between them, given Greeks and Turks had been fighting each other for hundreds of years.

Nico controlled him, but I wondered to what extent he trusted him? The man worked and moved around in areas and met people Nico would never visit or talk to. There had to be a trust of sorts, but my guess was Ahmet could make his boss feel uneasy. My heart started thumping. Despite that, I wanted to grab his scrawny little neck and throttle him. I saw Jamilya's face when our eyes locked. Nico had no qualms trusting Ahmet to carry out his brutal orders. I took one more step closer to Ahmet's boss, and anger tightened my insides.

I knew I was there to hear that Ioannis was upset over a family quarrel, and I wasn't to take too much notice of what he said. I thought I'd get one over on Nico before he started giving me some well-rehearsed lines; let him know I knew about his threat. Despite the feeling that I was inviting an angry reaction, I knew it was time to test my intuition. How much these two men learned about each other's little secrets didn't matter.

"Ioannis is pretty upset," I said. "He's telling Barbara you'll deal with her unless he gives her up. I didn't realise you had absolute power over your family – or is it over life and death?"

Nico spun around, his face contorted in a snarl, while Ahmet took a quick step forward.

I rocked back on my heels. At last, I could see the real Hrisacopolis.

"Perhaps," snapped Nico, "you've been listening to a blind man besotted with an art thief."

"Stealing? Barbara?" I looked appropriately shocked.

"You don't know everything." Nico's jaw was firm, and the veins stood out from his neck as he spoke with a deliberate emphasis on each word.

Ahmet shuffled two little side-steps into the light. His right hand eased into a jacket pocket in one slow suggestive movement, the threat pretty obvious.

Nico waved me to an armchair. A trail of smoke wafted over his shoulder from a cigar clamped between his teeth while he hurried to the small bar. "Her husband was a drunk and a womaniser. Did you know that?" he said over his shoulder.

He turned. His mouth was half-open on one side, snarl-like, still biting on the cigar. He handed me a generous glass of Scotch and sat opposite. Ahmet still hovered in the background with his hand in his pocket, which worried me – maybe that was the idea.

Crossing my legs and sipping the Scotch, I tried to look serious. "Surely," I answered in mock surprise, "you're not telling me Barbara is a fraud? I can't believe that, particularly as Miss Du Rosse has interviewed her at great length." I stopped sipping and lowered my glass to emphasise my point. I had a sudden dangerous thought but knew it was one way to rock Nico's confidence and asked, "Talking of Miss Du Rosse, her father knew one of your son's colleagues from the seventies. I hear you did business with him." I gestured my glass in Ahmet's direction. "I thought Ahmet might know something about Alexander Gravari."

The effect was immediate, and Ahmet snapped to attention. His hand came out of his pocket, holding a small pistol. Nico held a hand up, and the gun disappeared again as a shiver ran through me.

"Of course, we heard about the man's death, but I'm not surprised. He was a villain who tried to blackmail me over some art." Nico swallowed the Scotch and waved a hand at Ahmet. "Ahmet sees danger everywhere." He snapped his fingers and glared at Ahmet. "Take no notice."

I did think about taking things further and confronting him with my visit to Jamilya's but put it out of my mind. At that precise moment, Ioannis broke up our conversation. An ear-splitting crash jolted us out of our seats as the door swung into the room and smashed into a glass cabinet, sending ornaments and glasses across the floor.

"You bastard."

Ioannis stepped inside the room. He shook with rage. I stepped away from the chair and held a hand out to him, worrying that he would do something stupid. Nico glared at him. At the same time, I tried to get out of the firing line. Ahmet had moved forward and was pointing his pistol at Ioannis. At that moment, Ahmet had not said a word, and I wondered if he was enjoying the drama. It was hard to fathom him out.

Nico looked from Ioannis to me and back again. His demeanour calmed. Ignoring Ahmet, he pointed at both his brother and me.

"You Idiot," he snarled at Ioannis. "You're screwing up my plans, and you can't see it." He snatched the cigar from his mouth and threw it at the glass ashtray. It bounced out and fell onto the floor. "And you," he said, rounding on me. "Mr West, you have tried to sabotage my plans. Your government told you to stop." His top lip and forehead glistened as he glared at me. He fidgeted with a handkerchief. "You didn't."

I nodded. The pistol was still in Ahmet's hand but back in his pocket. "That's because I could smell corruption seeping out of your generous offer."

Nico picked up a copy of The Herald and grinned sarcastically at me with pursed lips. "Enough of the sarcasm, Mr West, I hear from my sources in London that the lies and innuendos you have tried to print will be – how do you say it – binned?"

The paper hurtled across the room and fluttered to the deck. I said nothing.

Nico picked his cigar case up from the bar, thumbing off the lid, took out a cigar, and pointed it at the broken door. "You are free to go. With no story, I'm sure anything you stir up will come to nothing." He shrugged and lit the cigar. "That goes for the lovely Miss Du Rosse too."

My thoughts turned to Jessica. She was safe for the time being. Now that things had come to a head, I wanted to be where I could keep an eye on her and Barbara, but I stood my ground and glanced at Ioannis. Something was going to break. I felt it.

Ioannis read my mind. "Well, I'll have to tell West the rest of the story then, won't I?"

Nico smirked. "Don't worry, Mr West, nothing is going to happen to my brother or Mrs Fitzgerald despite my brother's vivid imagination."

"You're damn right it's not."

We all turned to see Barbara standing with hands on hips just outside the door. The look in her half-closed eyes was murderous. Ahmet's hand was once again in his pocket.

Nico wiped the back of his neck. Both hands held out in a gesture of friendship shook.

"Barbara, we have to talk about the situation."

"You're damn right we do, mister."

She stepped inside the room, pushed past Ahmet and stepped on his foot. Surprised, he stumbled back against the wall with a thump. I admired Barbara for that. Ignoring Ahmet, she pulled Ioannis back by one arm and bypassed Nico's hands, poking him in the chest.

"Who the hell do you think you are? If you…" Her voice drifted away.

The following few seconds were surreal and frightening.

I wasn't taking notice of Barbara. As Ahmet put the pistol back into his pocket, my gaze shifted to his face. A gradual transformation from lounge lizard to the open-mouthed shock of a frightened man spread across his face. That's when I realised something was wrong. Barbara had stopped talking, and an eerie silence surrounded us.

I felt a sudden moment of panic, the kind that's accompanied by a pang of fear and I froze. I didn't know why. My mind raced, and all I could think of was Jessica. I hoped she decided to stay put.

I looked away from Ahmet's face. Barbara had moved forward and was standing in front of Nico. She was mesmerised. Nico turned. His Adam's apple danced up and down, and smoke curled up from the cigar gripped in his right hand - but he wasn't smoking it. He was scared.

Engrossed in everything around me, it took seconds before I looked in the same direction as the others.

Framed by the French doors, a man dressed in combat gear stood with a machine gun pointing directly into the room.

The tannoy clicked loudly in the background. With that, we all jerked back into reality. "Ladies and gentlemen, this is the captain speaking. We have an emergency, nothing for you to be alarmed at but as a precaution, would you all please assemble at your lifeboat stations – crew to evacuation points, please."

Nico turned slowly, first one way and then the other, unable to determine what was happening. His face creased into anger once again. I noticed the slight nod he gave Ahmet, who was moving toward the French doors.

Ioannis stared, open-mouthed, at the figure. "What the hell is he doing here, Barbara? What is going on?"

Barbara didn't answer. The colour had drained from her face.

My eyes focused on the automatic weapon, and my throat dried up. Behind the intruder, I caught a glimpse of 'imposter' Andreas outside, running as fast as he could down the steps at the side of the pool to the first-class deck. Two other menacing figures joined the first, and a foot crashed through the door. Glass sprayed across the deck and crunched under their boots as they entered. I knew intuitively who the first guy was but never imagined this was how I would meet him. What did surprise me was that Ioannis and Barbara also knew him – or did they?

Ahmet had moved swiftly away from our little group and positioned himself to one side of the doors, his hands in plain sight.

"What's going on?" Nico stepped back, his face a mask of terror. "Who are you?"

Before anyone could answer, there was a loud explosion from the ship's bowels. The deck beneath our feet vibrated.

"Dear Christ." Ioannis, wide-eyed, clutched at Barbara while I grabbed the back of the nearest armchair. The whole room shuddered. From outside, there were distant cries and screams from many frightened voices. Someone was barking orders.

Trying to remain calm, I said, "Nico, meet your grandson."

The gasp from Barbara and Ioannis confirmed my suspicions.

"Adonis, what..?" was all Barbara could say.

"Quiet." Baki stared around the room before nodding at Barbara. With a little shake of the head, his voice became conciliatory. "My name is Baki, Barbara. I'm sorry, but I did what I had to do." His expression changed. He turned and jerked his gun toward Ahmet while the other two gunmen threatened the rest of us with their automatics.

"You'll suffer for this." Baki swung the automatic back toward Nico. "I have longed for this moment."

Ahmet's face reminded me of kids' plasticine. He could model his rubbery face to suit every occasion. He took a step forward with hands outstretched and palms up. He was a good actor.

"Baki, we are on the same side. I am a member of KKA, and we have been working on the downfall of Hrisacopolis. I only did as I was told." He gave a little shrug. "You understand I only did as I was told? I thought you were dead."

Nico's face turned deep red, and his eyes narrowed. "You lying swine," he spat.

If there hadn't been guns involved, I'd have gladly sat down and listened with interest, but I was scared. Barbara sent me a sly wink. Nico stood shaking and probably for the first time in his life, unable to do anything about the enemies surrounding him. All of a sudden, he was very old and vulnerable. We all stood still except Ahmet.

Baki clenched his teeth and sneered at Ahmet. "You are on no one's side but your own."

Nico repeated himself. "What is going on, Ahmet? Who is Andreas?" He faced each of us in turn, waiting for someone to explain. Ahmet remained silent. I decided to do the honours, but Baki interrupted me.

"You will pay for my mother's death," he said, poking Nico in the chest.

He was getting emotional. Something clicked as I remembered my conversation with the businessman Mehmet. I learned a lot about Lara and her husband but very little about their son. Mehmet had loaned the father money, so he was protective of the boy. Mehmet let anyone who asked about Baki know he died in the explosion even though he could not have been sure.

Baki took a paper from his top pocket and unfolded it. He waved it in Nico's face. "Let's see if you remember this letter." He held the letter out and began to read, his lip trembling and his voice full of emotion.

"Andreas, if you wish to use a prostitute, that is one thing. Using her and then marrying her because she is carrying your bastard is another. There are bastards all over Cyprus. The sooner they die, the better. This whore you claim to love would stick a knife in you sooner than give up what she believes. Best to silence her tongue rather than have the world know the Hrisacopolis name is stained with a Turkish whore's blood. You will see this is for the best. Let this woman go, and I will deal with her. May God bless your fight for Greece."

Tears were running down Baki's cheeks as he replaced the letter in his pocket. Nico was stubbing his cigar out, his eyes on Ioannis. I felt a pang of sympathy for Baki.

While Baki was confronting Nico and Ahmet, I noticed Ioannis. His face was white, and he was trembling. Barbara, on the other hand, stood firm with hands clenched by her sides.

Chattering gunfire filled the air outside. Tracers were shooting skywards. We all ducked like a choreographed dance group except Baki and his men. There was a moment's silence in the room. A large figure dressed in combat fatigues entered through the broken doors and stood between the two silent guards standing behind Baki.

Distantly barked orders, and screams echoed from the decks below in that brief silence. I knew the lifeboats were being deployed. There was another explosion, and the floor shook violently. My feet almost left the floor, and I slipped forward, bumping into Nico. Near hysterical screaming was getting louder outside. All I could think of at that moment was Jessica. My body thumped inside. I wanted was to escape. I hated Barbara for being there and wished she'd stayed with Jessica.

"Everything has been taken care of," said the big man.

Baki kept his eyes on Nico as he spoke. "Okay, make sure all the passengers and crew are off safely. You know what to do later."

"Oui." The man left with the other two gunmen.

Baki turned his attention to Barbara. "You must leave and get into a lifeboat, Barbara." As an afterthought, he nodded at Ioannis. "And take that idiot with you. I don't wish to kill a man I've already saved."

Ioannis gave Barbara's hand a gentle tug and, without looking at me, said. "He's right. Let's go."

She pulled back from him. "My paintings."

Baki looked at her. "You will get them back."

Barbara stepped forward. "Baki, you don't have to do this."

"Go."

Ahmet looked confused. He drew closer to Baki. "That would be a mistake," he said softly. "This is the man who tried to kill your mother while you were still in her womb." He pointed toward Ioannis and added. "Your uncle has no conscience."

Baki glared at Barbara, then Ioannis. "Uncle?"

Ioannis grabbed Barbara but too late.

Violence and emotion erupted in the next few seconds, unravelling and tying loose ends of a tragic story together in my mind with clarity.

A face full of hate and an ear-shattering bang made us duck again as Ioannis fell backwards and hit the floor like a rag doll. Barbara collapsed on top of him. A frightening, endless scream stilled us all for a moment. Her blouse was covered in blood. As the screams stopped, her mouth remained open as she tried to breathe in. I felt sick to the stomach. Her face was contorted in shock and grief.

I didn't think. My instinct took over. I bent forward and slapped her hard on the back before pulling her up and putting my arms around her. We hugged each other tightly as tears clouded my eyes. Lara had told Jamilya about someone shooting at a friend while she worked. I'd thought of Ahmet, not Ioannis. So now we knew.

"Leave her alone."

I turned on Baki, angry and defiant. There had not been time to appeal to him to rethink what he was doing. Ahmet had seen to that. Holding on to Barbara, I turned my back on him.

Nico was on his knees, his shoulders shaking. His glasses lay on the deck. He was bewildered, staring at a gaping wound in his brother's chest.

Baki's eyes were on fire. Thirty years of carrying that letter had burned a little more hatred into his heart every day.

I was feeling unsteady on my feet. The chair I had a hand on moved. We were starting to list. The stern of a launch came into view in the half-light of dawn as it left the ship's side. I could see a light in the cockpit but no navigation lights. That meant the other terrorists and the lifeboats were getting away. Once again, I thought of Jessica, hoping she was in one of the lifeboats.

"Barbara, go," I whispered, looking at Baki.

"Not so fast. Not you," Baki waved the automatic at me.

Barbara turned back, but I waved her on. She stepped out into the corridor, and I heard her sobbing as she left.

"Now, who are you? You are not the imposter. Where is this, Andreas?" He slapped the loaded ammunition clip fixed to the automatic.

I was looking down the barrel and wasn't feeling brave. "I'm a journalist, and I have no idea where he is. Perhaps he's in a lifeboat."

Nico stood up in the middle of the room, glaring at Ahmet. He clenched his fists. Tight-lipped, his cheeks rippled as he gnashed his teeth.

"We can work together, Baki. You and I are Turks. This man is threatening the Republic of Cyprus." Wringing his hands, Ahmet advanced a step toward Baki.

"Damn your Republic. You will never live to see it."

Baki pushed Ahmet away with the automatic, and in that instant, Nico decided to run. Unsure if Baki was going to shoot Ahmet, I stood unsteadily against the dining table that had slewed across the floor.

Another explosion ripped through the ship, and all three of us fell to the listing floor.

I rolled over as Baki got to his feet. Nico was on the other side of the shattered French doors, slipping and sliding across the listing deck to the ship's side. Baki raised the automatic and aimed.

"Die, you bastard!" Ahmet was on his feet in an instant, pistol in hand.

I lunged forward and pulled him to the floor as he fired. "Damn you, you swine!

Too far away to do anything, I watched helplessly as Baki followed Nico over the side into the grey sea. Whether Nico or both he and Baki were dead or wounded, I couldn't say.

Then I smelled smoke. I panicked. My nightmare was becoming a reality. Ahmet was crawling under the piano to retrieve his pistol from the deck. I cursed inwardly that I had left 'B's gun in my cabin. If I stayed, Ahmet would shoot me.

Scared and worried about Jessica, I scrambled outside the broken doors and ran and slid toward the steps leading down to the first-class deck.

CHAPTER FORTY-FIVE

I HAD TWO THINGS ON my mind: Not getting shot and Jessica. I started going down the stairs. Trying to scramble down steps that leaned several degrees from the horizontal was like walking through the 'Crooked House' at the fairground. I reached the bottom and pushed through the swinging door to the outside.

Above me, Ahmet's feet crunched on broken glass as he chased me. There was a loud crack. A wood chip flew off the ship's handrail, and I yelped as it stung my forehead. I ducked from his sight, rubbing the spot.

I ran to the next steps and slid down to the lower deck on the handrail and the promenade deck. Gasping for air, I looked back over my shoulder.

There was a loud ping as the next shot ricocheted off the railing. I ducked too late. A hot stinging sensation coursed through my left forearm. The bullet had creased through my jacket and skin. Blood covered the palm of my hand. I grabbed hold of the ship's railing and stumbled sideways along the side of the pool. Ahmet was at the other end, trying to keep his balance. Water leaked over the side of the main pool making the deck slippery. It was becoming difficult to remain upright as the listing ship rose and fell slowly. Jessica's whereabouts consumed me. I was desperate to find her.

I pushed one of the stacks of chairs at the end of the pool sideways and guessed I had about a minute before Ahmet reached me. In the gathering dawn and out of sight, I clambered behind the stack and crouched as still as possible. There was only going to be one chance to save me. I could have dived overboard, but I wasn't going anywhere until I knew Jessica was safe. I stayed still, straining to hear the slightest sound.

What seemed like minutes rather than seconds went by. The sky lit up, and a tremendous explosion boomed seconds later on the horizon. I paid it little thought. In that brief moment, the sky turned a brighter shade of blue. I saw Ahmet, or rather he saw me. Half of his face appeared, his dark little eyes staring at me around the edge of the chairs. I kicked out and pushed a chair at him. He fell out of sight and something; I guessed his gun, clattered across the deck. I rolled out from behind the chairs and jumped on top of him.

Neither of us spoke. I was out of breath, and so was he. I held him against the stack of chairs with one hand holding his neck and an arm wrapped around his body. He managed to break free despite this, and an elbow crashed into my ribcage. Winded, I bent double, and he fell back into the space. As I gasped for air, he crawled across the sloping deck to where I assumed his pistol had landed. Grabbing an ankle, I pulled him back on his stomach and stepped over him. The gun lay next to the railings, and I kicked it over the side.

I turned to face him, throwing a right as I did. It landed to the side of his jaw. I felt his jaw give. "Remember, Jamilya, you swine?" I gasped. "Remember Claude, remember?"

Ahmet slipped and fell without saying a word.

I had all but forgotten the wound in my left arm. Ahmet grabbed it.

"Argh!" Crying out in agony, I dropped to my knees and fell forward, punching out at him. We rolled to the edge of the deck. Sitting astride me, Ahmet gripped my neck with both hands.

Ahmet snarled, "You will not remember for much longer."

I couldn't breathe and knew I only had seconds to live. My leg was free. I knead Ahmet in the back, unbalancing him, and he fell back onto his side. I pushed him sideways and spun out from beneath him with what strength I had left.

Before I could recover, I felt his hands around my ankles. Fear and blind panic took hold of me. I found myself slipping towards the edge of the deck. Ahmet was pulling, and I had nothing to hold onto. Fear shook me.

"No, you bastard. No." I tried kicking, but he had my ankles firmly held.

My body slewed in an arc, a sure sign he intended to swing me under the rails and overboard. I saw the gap between the bottom rail and the deck and reached out for a post as my nose brushed the underside of the rail. Ahmet's hands let go simultaneously, and a sharp pain shot through my side as he kicked me. My only thought was to get up and away from the edge. I saw the sea coming up to meet me, and fear took over.

Ahmet's foot crashed into my ribs again. I grabbed the foot and pulled. There was a grunt as he fell, and then everything was still. I could hear people calling from far off. I picked myself up in a daze, alert and expecting to see Ahmet ready to pounce. Instead, Ahmet's head and shoulders were poking through the gap between deck and rails. He hung onto a post.

"Hold on," I screamed. I stumbled, dropped to my knees, and then took hold of his arm. "Let go the post, and I'll pull you up." There was a strange look in his eyes, and it wasn't fright. It was almost one of resignation, of giving up. I gripped him tightly. "Let go the post. I'll pull you up," I repeated. The pain in my left arm was becoming unbearable.

"Look after Eren," he gasped. I gripped harder and pulled, trying to wrench his hands from the post. "Look after my son... He did as he was told." With that, he let go of the post and punched my face. I fell sideways, and he was gone.

I sobbed with exhaustion and gathered my breath with mixed feelings flowing through my mind. Ahmet's son, Eren – was Andreas. The final piece of the puzzle was in place.

"Pete. Pete!"

On hearing my name, I stood unsteadily. I could not see the owner of the voice. Dawn was breaking. A pale blue sky hid behind billowing black smoke from the stern of *Sea Empress*. Huge flames shot skywards from the superstructure. I looked out to sea and could make out bobbing lights and the white shapes of the lifeboats some way off.

"Pete, Pete!"

I recognised Barbara's voice. She could see me. Choking, I peered through the smoke.

"Pete, I can't find Jessica," she screamed.

I turned as fast as I could and made for the port stairs leading down into the ship. Unfortunately, *Sea Empress* was listing away from the port side, and the cabin was to the starboard, closer to the water. It proved much easier to negotiate the passages and stairs if I stepped foot over foot and kept both hands on the walls.

The smell of smoke was thick in the air. This dangerous combination made my efforts to reach the cabin more urgent. When I reached the level our cabins were on and moved across to the starboard side, the smell grew stronger. I began sloshing through water and started to shake.

"Jessica, are you there?" I shouted hoarsely.

My dry throat made it hard to shout. For a moment, I closed my eyes. Flames and smoke surrounded me. I opened my eyes, and the flames and smoke were still there. This nightmare that had lived inside me was now set to devour me. My whole body shook, and my head spun with fear. Now, frantic with worry, I could see the same thing happening to Jessica behind a door, screaming for help and no one there for her. I put the crook of my uninjured arm over my mouth and took a deep breath despite the smoke.

My arm hurt but had stopped bleeding, and my moist eyes stung from the smoke. Focus. I had to focus. I swallowed several times and shouted again, dreading the thought of going further unless it was necessary. Our cabin was three doors down the passage. The smoke was dense, and I saw flames coming from beneath a door just visible through it. There was a crackling sound from burning wood and a rumbling beneath my feet. I pushed the terrible vision out of my mind and shouted again. Above the noise, I heard a distinct knocking sound. Again, I shouted.

"Jessica, keep banging. I'm coming!"

Almost immediately, I heard several faint metallic bangs in the direction of the fire.

I tore my jacket off and threw it over my head. Stinging eyes made it difficult to see. I inched forward into the smoke, and I kept tapping on the wall as I progressed. The smoke was thicker, and I started choking. In front of me was a wall of flames curling across the ceiling. The thumping was louder, banging against a pipe. I jumped forward and landed awkwardly on the sloping floor, ankle-deep in water.

My lungs burned. I coughed and leaned against the wall gasping. "Jessica, where are you?"

Again, I heard metallic thumping. The response was faint. A short distance away at the end of the passage was a large door marked 'Laundry.' I pushed it open with my feet, and the banging got louder. By now, the ship's list had increased. I shouted again.

"Keep banging. I'm here. I'm here!"

This time the answer was more urgent. Black choking smoke drifted across washing machines and baskets that had rolled across the floor and crashed into the wall. In one corner, some metal steps led down, and it was from there the banging was coming.

Sitting on my rear, I pulled myself across the floor by gripping the wastewater pipe until I reached the top of the stairs and climbed down on the railing.

"Jessica, where are you?"

"Pete! Peeet-er!" Her frightening scream sent shivers across my spine. I slid down across the sloping floor and through two rubber doors. To my right was another door. I tried opening it, but it would only move an inch or so.

"Pete! Please help me! Help meee!"

"I'm coming," I cried hoarsely, "I'll get you out."

It was impossible to stand where she lay trapped. I grunted with pain as I tried shouldering the door. My injured arm throbbed. I turned, used my right shoulder and hip, and moved the door enough to squeeze through. Jessica jerked her head several times to stop the water from entering her mouth. I pulled a rack off her enough for her to crawl out. Exhausted, I slumped down beside her. She flung her arms around me and sobbed.

I pushed her away. "We can't hang about. Do as I do, and we should be all right." I could hardly talk.

She followed me, pulling herself up across the floor to the metal steps and then climbing the step rails to the passage. Smoke blocked out all light save orange flames that licked around us as we stepped into the passage.

I realised she had no jacket and gave her mine. "Put this over your head. We'll soon be off this tub."

She tried laughing, but it was hysterical. the wild look in her eyes betrayed her feelings. At the top of the stairs, we took a deep breath and crawled through the door into the passage. The roar of the flames and the loud splintering of burning wood indicated how quickly the fire spread. I could feel the heat singeing the hairs on my arms and hoped my jacket kept Jessica safe. It felt like an eternity, but it was only a few minutes before we climbed the last stairs leading up to the deck. Exhausted, I fell out onto the deck and sucked in a lungful of air. Jessica pulled me away from the edge as we choked and coughed.

Daylight now illuminated the dreadful scene, and I was able to see the lifeboats standing off. Barbara stood in one of them, waving her sun hat furiously at us. Jessica waved back. I looked at Jessica, both hands steadying her progress as she slid carefully down to the railing trailing a torn dress. My jacket fell from her bare shoulders as she lifted one leg after the other over the railing and waited for me.

Following suit, I sat on the top rail with her and coughed. "You're not going to jump in, are you? Can't we wait for a lifeboat? I haven't got a bloody life jacket, remember?"

Her hand grabbed the scruff of my neck and pushed.

CHAPTER FORTY-SIX

DESPITE ITS REPUTATION FOR being a warm sea, the Mediterranean can be extremely cold. I came to the surface beside Jessica and immediately heard Barbara screaming at us. I couldn't answer; my teeth chattered while I floundered with Jessica's arm around my neck. The sun glared into my eyes as one of the many drop-type inflatable life rafts appeared. A rope snaked across my head and splashed in front of Jessica. Within seconds Barbara hauled us unceremoniously over the top of an inflated double wall.

"Here, wrap yourselves in these…" She tossed us two thermal foil blankets.

I threw the blanket over my shoulders and realised we had company under another that wasn't moving. Barbara did the honours.

"Baki." She shrugged. "Ironic, isn't it? Such a waste of life."

Jessica put her arm around Barbara.

"Nico is alive, you know. I saw him on another boat," said Barbara.

I felt sorry for Barbara, but Claude, Lara, Jamilya and Alexander had helped end the Hrisacopolis nightmare, and I was pleased there was justice for them.

Fifteen minutes later, as the sun rose and warmed us, the Royal Navy arrived. None of us had noticed that *Sea Empress* was gone. With its sinking, all of Hrisacopolis's dreams for power dissolved.

———◆———

A week later, my phone rang while I was having breakfast. It was Jessica. Hart had asked her to see him in Seattle. He had a photo assignment for her, and I hoped she would be back by the weekend. I was missing her and was waiting impatiently for her.

Before I could say a word, she spoke.

"You won't believe this, but I have had a fantastic offer from Hart. He wants me to head the art section in our New York office."

My heart sank. I knew what was happening. Hart had stolen her, and the position offered meant working from New York.

"That's wonderful," I replied. "I'm sure you will be a great success. Congratulations."

Jessica was silent for a moment. "There is an official statement from Whitehall, of course. Have you read it?"

"Yes." I knew 'B' had drafted the statement when I read 'A Whitehall source was quoted yesterday, saying…' He hadn't done a bad job either. The story was well wrapped in plausible half-fiction and explained that the terrorists who blew up *Sea Empress* were killed when security forces destroyed their cruisers as they escaped. It was speculated that they were members of the radical Turkish KKA group, financed by a shady section of the Turkish secret service. It added that the EU was calling for new talks on the future of Cyprus that would result in proper unification. A postscript reported that a Royal Navy frigate visiting Malta had retrieved the marbles, and they were on the way to Athens.

"So, you will be in New York while I trot around London," I said.

"I am sorry, Pete. You'll appreciate that our close relationship would be quite out of the question with what we are doing."

I felt a knot in my stomach and nodded. "Yes, of course."

"I'll never be able to repay you, Pete, for saving my life. It seems cruel to leave without seeing you again, but I am off to Florida tomorrow."

We chatted for five minutes before saying goodbye, promising we would bump into each other on purpose, but people always say that. I was devastated. After coming through the nightmare, I had looked forward to a happy ending.

The only nightmare I had to face was a small man called Max who left one message after another asking why I was not back at work and threatening to get another journalist to write my column. Life was back to normal… well, almost. His last message was urgent.

"Pete, get your arse here as quick as possible. The Greek government is taking over the Hrisacopolis empire. That makes this a public affair. Claude didn't write anything, so it's back on your desk."

Seconds later, I was on my way.

Have you got a book in you? Want to get published?

DreamEngine provides extraordinary support for aspiring authors who want education, expert marketing, and an author mythology that actually sells books. Talk to us today!

publishing@dreamengine.co.uk

dreamengine.co.uk

ABOUT THE AUTHOR

Journalism is an art form as is writing fiction. Both take many years to attain an appreciative audience and a lot of work to keep that audience. One of my earliest recollections as a cub reporter was my editor telling me that every story must be factual and truthful and backed by good research to prove authenticity. It was a hard life that I chose. One that made me realise after a couple of years how important it is to reveal what is important in the world around us. In my case as a new boy, local news. It's a well-worn phrase, sometimes used in ridiculous situations, but the public do have a right to know about anything that costs taxpayers money – and that's most things.

By the time I was twenty-two I worked for another local paper and started reporting on more important news such as local politics and crime stories. It was during this time that I received my first pat on the head from my editor. I exposed a local fraud within the local council chambers involving the misuse of waste disposal funds by two councillors. Further political reports and a blossoming association with a local member of parliament earned me the attention of a London broadsheet.

It was like starting all over again when I successfully applied and was offered a post there as a reporter. I wanted to get my teeth into politics but to my dismay I got the mundane assignments no-one else wanted. It took a further three years before I got what I wanted. A colleague went sick as a general election was announced and I was put on the team. I interviewed the likes of cabinet ministers and prospective candidates. Asking the right questions that sometimes trip politicians up or embarrass them is something I learned from an old experienced reporter I was teamed up with.

During the following years, I graduated as a foreign correspondent and spent plenty of time in Westminster and Whitehall. It was Brussels, though, where I gained quite a reputation, lifting the lid on a lot of corruption in the early days of the European Union. Those were the roughest years of my career. You can't expose crime in the upper reaches of government without making a few enemies. Many of them tried using the law to gag me but due to strong backing from my boss and public outrage when my articles appeared, I stayed ahead of the pack. This was the sharp end of politics and the dirtiest. I got knocked around a few times but that made me dig the dirt more to uncover the bad side that damages the integrity of the corridors of power and the public's trust.

After living from one hotel to another, never knowing when I was going to get a break, I retired later than I could have. With a wealth of experience behind me, I decided to write fiction about a political columnist. My experience in politics and a long relationship (not friendly) with the security services involved heavily in government shenanigans, helped a lot in making my stories believable.

Today I write political and contemporary spy thrillers that expose how it really is behind the plastic smiles and limp handshakes in Westminster.

I have added again the barcode laras-secret-back-cover-barcode.jpg to the folder. It should display now.

URLs
https://twitter.com/rayraycdoyle
https://www.facebook.com/RAYCDOYLE
https://raycdoyle.com/.

ALSO BY DREAMENGINE

Ocean Boulevard
by David Baboulene

An epic and exhilarating journey all the way...from a boy to a man. If PG Wodehouse had gone to sea...

Jumping Ships
by David Baboulene

What more do you need to know than what other people think? If PG Wodehouse had joined the Merchant Navy...

Fires of Brigantia
by Tina Zee

The Roman army. One Yorkshire woman. They never stood a chance.

Surface
by Violet neill

Book 1 of the Hollow Trilogy. Lucas Spencer loves his wife Adele. She is beautiful, intellegent... And dead.

Life's a Peach
by Steve Askham

Extraordinary fruity business you didn't know that you NEED to know... The secret life of an international fruit trader.

The Magical World of Lilly Lemoncello
by Carolyn Goodyear

Fate decides Lilly's start in life. So she chooses to let Fate decide the rest of it too. A heartwarming and remarkable work of human goodness.

The Shock Tube
by Paul Curtis
Anybody reading this book will learn something uncomfortable.
About themselves...

Nonfiction:

The Story Series
by David Baboulene

Learn how stories work.

Printed in Great Britain
by Amazon

80448453R00153